The Demo
from him with
separate us, th
glared at me.

My fingertips tingled as I started to shift.

Not fast enough.

The Demon lunged. His long nimble fingers closed around my neck as I shot my hands out, inside his arms, and dug my claws into his face. My elbows pushed against the insides of his arms. His hold should've weakened, but this Demon possessed uncanny strength. His frame stretched, growing to almost eight feet in height and giving his body an emaciated appearance. He pulled me close, his nose touching mine. I wrenched to the side, but my toes dangled above the floor.

"Bola sends his regards," he said, his breath hitting my face.

My gums stung as fangs protruded, and I hissed at him, ready to make the full change and get my fight on. I yanked on the mountain lion and spurred her into action.

"By all means, little nugget, shift into one of your animals." He gnashed his sharp teeth together. "I love to rend the flesh of livestock, to mutilate the bodies of creatures, and to smash the bones of beasts."

Praise for J. C. McKenzie's Carus Series

"*SHIFT HAPPENS* is a fast-paced, humorous, sexy paranormal. If you like your heroine to be butt kicking and brave…then you will love Andrea."

~*Annetta Sweetko, Fresh Fiction*
~*~

"There was action, sexual tension galore, alpha males, a stubborn heroine that you don't want to tick off, a smidgen of romance, some suspense, loads of danger, and a uniqueness that will have you deeply hooked."

~*Brenda Demko, Crazy Four Books*
~*~

"…wonderful cast of supporting characters…Blond Norse-god-like werewolf Wick, sinfully handsome (or is that sinful and handsome?) human servant Clint, chiseled-featured Asian vampire Allan, and the citrus & sunshine wereleopard Tristan (meow!)"

~*Charlotte Copper, Author of Heart Shifter*
~*~

"Sassy, snarky action, packed with wonderful one-liners and irreverent laughs, J. C. McKenzie delivers a wonderful paranormal romance in *BEAST COAST*."

~*Katie O'Sullivan, Author of My Kind of Crazy*
~*~

"Non-stop action, kick-ass heroine, two tempting love interests, and a whole lot of supernatural excitement. Five ++ stars!"

~*C.J. Burright, Author of Wonderfully Wicked*
~*~

"Ms. McKenzie has a fun style of writing, part humor, part sass that rounds out a good plot."

~*Karilyn Bentley, Author of Demon Lore*

Carpe Demon

by

J. C. McKenzie

A Carus Novel, Book 3

This is a work of fiction. Names, characters, places, and incidents are either the product of the author's imagination or are used fictitiously, and any resemblance to actual persons living or dead, business establishments, events, or locales, is entirely coincidental.

Carpe Demon

COPYRIGHT © 2015 by J. C. McKenzie

All rights reserved. No part of this book may be used or reproduced in any manner whatsoever without written permission of the author or The Wild Rose Press, Inc. except in the case of brief quotations embodied in critical articles or reviews.
Contact Information: info@thewildrosepress.com

Cover Art by *Debbie Taylor*

The Wild Rose Press, Inc.
PO Box 708
Adams Basin, NY 14410-0708
Visit us at www.thewildrosepress.com

Publishing History
First Black Rose Edition, 2015
Print ISBN 978-1-5092-0146-4
Digital ISBN 978-1-5092-0147-1

A Carus Novel, Book 3
Published in the United States of America

Dedication

To my son, with love.
Your cackling laughter and wide smile
always warm my heart, even on the coldest days.

~*~

Acknowledgments

I'd like to thank my incredible critique partners and beta readers: Jo-Ann Carson, Charlotte Copper, Shelly Chalmers, Katie O'Sullivan, and Karilyn Bentley. You guys rock!

~*~

I'd also like to thank my publisher, the Wild Rose Press, for the support and for believing in this series.

~*~

A big hearty thank you to the cover designer, Debbie Taylor of DCA Graphics, for another outstanding cover. It's gorgeous and I love it.

~*~

Thank you to my editor, Lara Parker, who wrote me an email to tell me she hadn't finished it yet, but she loved it and, "Girl, you better resolve this right! Ha, ha!" Thank you, Lara, for the laughs, and all your support and help. This book truly shines (at least in my eyes) because of your input.

~*~

To my family, friends and readers: thank you for your continued support. I really appreciate it.

~*~

Finally, last but not least, and always on my mind and in my heart, to my husband and son, thank you. I love you both.

"Ever notice 'Demon' in the word Pandemonium? Coincidence? I think not."

~Andrea "Andy" McNeilly

Chapter One

"We're more interesting if we are dysfunctional."
~*Rupert Everett*

When I thought of all the things I'd rather be doing right now, most ideas that came to mind involved large quantities of chocolate and alcohol. None included hanging out with blood-sucking fiends stuffed in designer suits. They pretended to be civil, but their dead odours and cold expressions gave them away for the monsters they really were.

Two steps behind Lucien, the Master Vampire of British Columbia's Lower Mainland, I bent my head in false supplication, and envisioned punching him in the back of the neck. Andy McNeilly, the all-mighty Carus, reduced to basic security detail.

Subtle night fragrances of summer, lilac and jasmine, drifted through streams of decay, and the lingering heat of the day clung to my skin. Sandwiched between Lucien's Werewolf Alpha and his Vampire second-in-command, I itched to run free into the summer's warm night, to rip off this tight black pencil skirt and cream satin blouse that made me look like a cream puff, and sink my claws into sun-warmed soil to race through the moon-lit forest.

But I couldn't.

Blood bonded to the Master Vampire, I had to do

his bidding. As much as I detested waiting on Lucien like a glorified body guard, it beat the alternative—a blood bag to quench his thirst. Thankfully, I wasn't his type.

Hah!

Expensive artwork hung in heavy ornate frames and a super-sized, bright red Persian rug with intricate patterns decorated the black marble flooring. The air in the large boardroom ran stale as the Vampires of the North American Vampire Association (NAVA) debated an alliance with the Demons. The underworld had grown increasingly volatile in the last few months, and the Vampires of NAVA wanted to subdue the unrest, and at the same time, increase their own power.

I'd almost punched a fellow agent in the junk fifteen years ago when he told me about NAVA at the Supernatural Regulatory Division's training camp. I thought he'd made it up to help me fail the SRD's boot camp, but I passed, and sadly, the association was very real.

NAVA probably existed before the Purge, but under a more archaic, less norm-friendly name, like the New World Berserkers or the Nosferatu Kings. Lucien had pursed his lips and refused to answer when I'd asked.

They didn't have a webpage. I checked.

Currently, NAVA debated some obscure point, and the argument flip-flopped between various languages. I had many skills as a Carus, but multilingualism was not one of them.

When will this be over? I asked, using mind speech. *Is it wrong to wish someone goes into a blood rage and rips into some of these suckheads?*

Steve warned me about this, Wick, the Alpha Werewolf standing beside me, replied in my head. As a Were, he could mind speak with members of his pack...and me. His voice rubbed against my brain cells and sent my focus to a screeching halt as my heart took a swan dive in my chest. The wolf familiar inside my mind paced back and forth, urging me to rip off my clothes for a different reason. My wolf fera wanted to mate with Wick, and the feeling was mutual. Most of the time.

The wolf wasn't the only voice inside my head.

Wick leaned in, bringing his delicious scent closer to me. A present day Norse god. Tall, muscular and blond, with chiseled features, but instead of Viking blue, his eyes were melted dark chocolate.

I had a sweet tooth.

His sugar and rosemary aroma wrapped around me in a silent hug and warded off the otherwise unpleasant stench of the room.

What did Steve say about me? I asked, trying to distract my raging hormones. Wick's enforcer, Steve, had accompanied me and Clint the last time I'd been forced to a NAVA event.

He said you have an inherent disregard for your own well-being. A berserk Vampire on a rampage is the last thing we need right now. It's not good for anyone's health. Including yours.

I huffed. *This is boring. Half the time I have no clue what they're saying, and the rest of the time, I want to poke their eyes out. Look at them! Fifty Vampires and fifty human servants, and no decisions. Certainly no shades of gray. They should revise the "too many cooks in the kitchen" saying to something more applicable to…whatever this is.*

I would rather be bored at a Vampire summit than any of the alternatives, Wick said.

You're no fun.

I'm plenty fun. Just say the word, Andy, and I'll show you.

My body flooded with warmth. I swallowed, and glanced over at Wick. He stood, soldier straight, watching the Vampires. He acted like the perfect Werewolf minion. The slight tug at the corner of his lips his only giveaway.

Lick, my wolf rumbled with approval.

Things were complicated between me and the Werewolf Alpha of the Vancouver pack. I'd spent most of the trip here trying to act indifferent toward him, but my libido and wolf had other ideas.

Allan leaned in from the other side and whispered into my ear, "Unless the two of you are planning to let me watch, shut the fuck up."

Wick's head snapped to glare at the Vampire, but Allan ignored the Werewolf's death stare and returned to diligent guard mode.

I clamped my mouth shut, and studied Allan. As Lucien's second in command, he was probably the largest Asian Vampire I'd ever seen. Without a pinch of fat, he stretched the seams of his designer suit, and his angular features made him way more handsome than he deserved. We mutually tolerated each other. He liked to feed off fear and push my buttons; I liked a Vampire who didn't want to drink, beat or bed me, but no trust existed between us. With reading minds as his special Vampire skill, not mind speech, I constantly found myself on edge around him. He could pluck thoughts out of my head.

How much longer? I asked no one in particular.

Wick answered. *We should hear the closing remarks from those opposed, then break, then vote. Pay attention.*

He was right, of course. I should pay closer attention. As much as I hated Lucien for blood bonding me against my will and dragging me to this cursed event, his continued good health was imperative to mine. At least until I found a way out of this blood bond.

"Think of me as another fera in your head, dear *Carus*," Lucien had said after the forced bonding. "A blood sucking one."

My mountain lion sprang up in my mind and hissed at the memory. *Not prey.*

I needed to slip this bond in a way that would keep Wick safe. Lucien liked to use the Werewolf Alpha against me. Another reason I attempted to keep Wick at tail's length.

"Objections?" a Vampire barked out. My thoughts faded, and I focused on the present.

A Vampire stood up, and a hush fell over the others. Long slender neck, elongated face with high cheekbones and a sharp chin, almond-shaped eyes, full lips, delicate arms and fingers on a tall, willowy frame; despite looking almost delicate, the Vampire radiated strength so powerful it hung heavy in the air. His scent carried across the room. Ancient, the regular Vampire cloy of death and blood faint to nonexistent. He smelled instead of old dried leaves, like the ones at the end of summer before the autumn rains started.

His gaze travelled over the crowd, but he remained

silent.

My newest animal familiar pressed against my legs and trembled. The ghost-like fox fera had slept soundly at my feet, and I'd forgotten she'd come with me. While my other feras remained in my head like sentient thoughts, I'd expelled Red from my mind a couple of months ago. I couldn't shift into a fox anymore, but my mind was no longer a chaotic battleground for fera dominance games either. Now Red accompanied me everywhere like a ghost pet, but only I could see, feel and speak to her.

I looked up from my quivering fera in time to observe the strange Vampire sit down. Fabric rustled as other Vampires fidgeted and shuffled in their seats. Everyone else remained frozen like the veggies in my freezer.

Anticlimactic, much?
Who's that? I asked Wick.
The Pharaoh, he replied.

Instantly, the classic 80s song about walking like Egyptians popped into my head. Good song for karaoke with my next door neighbours. Those Witches loved hits from the past. I mentally sang along with the chorus. *Way-oh-way-oh-way-ooo-aaa-ooo...*

Allan grumbled and pinched his nose. I flashed him a smile. *Mental note: more singing in my head. Allan loves it.*

Said Vampire clenched his jaw, but kept his gaze forward.

After a few minutes of uncomfortable silence, the host of events stood up. Ian cleared his throat and spoke. "We will reconvene in half an hour for the vote."

Lucien rose out of his seat with fluid grace and

tugged at his shirt cuffs, looking the ever-perfect Italian runway model. He nodded at his human servant, who rose to stand with him.

Tall and built like a brick house, Clint's broad shoulders made a girl want to learn how to leap tall buildings in a single bound. Except me. I wanted to take a wrecking ball to him and sing about it.

Peck his face, my falcon demanded.

Later, I told her.

Lucien and Clint turned and looked at the rest of our group with expressionless faces. Without words, we followed as they moved out of the boardroom with the rest of the Vampires and their entourages. The exits opened into a grand ballroom with exquisite furnishings, and tapestries.

"Lucien!" a deep voice called. The mass of observers parted like the Red Sea to allow Ian through. Attractive like the rest of his kind, Ian resembled a young Rob Lowe and carried himself with enough swagger to put a pimp to shame. A lean, mean, blood-drinking machine clung to his arm. One of the rare female Master Vampires in the boardroom, she appraised, then dismissed me as they approached.

"Ian," Lucien greeted the other Vampire. I could never tell with these guys whether they were happy or annoyed to see each other. Guess I'd have to wait until they started snapping at each other's necks. When I'd met Ian at the last Vampire get-together, Clint described him as both friend and foe, which in fitting with all-things-Clint, told me nothing.

"Lucien," Ian repeated as he closed the distance and stood beside us. His slow, calculated smile spread. "I hoped you'd be here and share a drink with me."

Ian's gaze fell on me, and my spine snapped ramrod straight. My knees locked. His attention gave little doubt as to what, or whom, he wanted to drink.

Gross!

Ian's gaze held no heat, only hunger as he studied me. Just another Vampire after his next meal. He spoke again, "I believe we met once, my dear, but Clint was negligent with introductions."

The woman on Ian's arm sneered, but she assessed me again, and her expression turned thoughtful.

"This is Ambassador Andrea McNeilly, of the SRD." Lucien flipped a noncommittal hand my way. He didn't mention the blood bond.

Despite my fancy title as "Ambassador McNeilly," the acting liaison between Lucien Delgatto's Vampire horde and the Supernatural Regulatory Division, I essentially played the role of a slave—to both the SRD and the Master Vampire. Sometimes I wished I'd stayed in the forest as a mountain lion. Life was simpler.

"She smells delicious," Ian said.

The female Vampire licked her lips and nodded.

Not prey, my mountain lion hissed again, repeating her earlier statement.

Lucien's hand snaked up and curled around my neck, squeezing a little. My muscles vibrated as all my feras screeched in my head.

Bite! my wolf demanded.

Red leapt forward and latched onto Lucien's ankle, snarling. Lucien's eyes narrowed and he looked down. Could he feel her sharp little teeth digging in? I hoped so.

Cut it out, I told Red. *He's protecting me.*

It still took every ounce of control not to punch him in the face.

Red released Lucien, and sat by my side. The little ball of ghost-orange fur leaned against my calf, and I shuffled to keep my balance while Lucien gripped my neck in a show of ownership. At least he didn't plan to pee on me.

"This one," Lucien shook my neck a little, "is not for sharing."

My feras settled, and I relaxed my muscles. *I'm not for biting, period.*

Allan coughed into his sleeve, while Ian's eyes sought mine, but I dodged whatever visual message Ian wanted to convey by looking at my shoes. *Hah! Take that.*

"A shame. Find me later, Lucien. We have much to discuss," Ian said, and once Lucien nodded, Ian turned gracefully and slipped away with his lady friend into the vibrating crowd of mingling Vampires and humans. The low murmur of voices raised to a steady thrum, punctuated by clinking glass and barks of laughter.

"Mingle," Lucien murmured, not looking at any of his entourage in particular, but we all heard him, snapping to attention and careening forward to catch his next words. "Disperse."

Everyone scattered like a herd of students after a stink bomb, but when I attempted to step away, Lucien's cold fingers dug into my neck. My gaze flicked to his.

"Stay close," Lucien said before releasing me.

I rubbed the back of my neck, still tingling from the Vampire's contact. His words might be for my protection, but I needed a way out of this bond, fast.

"As you wish."

Lucien smirked and lifted his chin at Clint. The human servant hadn't gone far, and he sauntered up to his master, gaze raking my body before his full attention turned to Lucien. Whatever drama they concocted, they wanted it private. Bending their heads close together, they spoke in hushed tones, too quiet for even my Shifter hearing to pick up in the steady chatter that filled the room.

Whatever. I needed a drink. Unease churned in my stomach.

You should heed the Vampire's words. This is not a place to be alone, Red warned. When she discovered I'd named her after a colour, she pitched a fit and refused to speak to me for a few days. Her fault. She should've given me a name. Besides, Red was better than Fire Crotch.

When I didn't respond, Red nipped my ankle. What was with feras and ankle biting? I kept my eyes forward and scanned the room to find the bar, trying to ignore the fox circling my feet. Since no one else could see her, it would appear odd if I kept looking down.

I know. I know. I'll be careful, I told her. *Besides, Wick's following me.* He stayed a few steps behind me, but his presence raised my body temperature to an unhealthy level, and warmth thrummed through my veins.

Red snorted and trotted ahead of me, weaving through the throng of Vampires.

"Mmmm. Little Carus. I hoped you'd be here." A voice that could only be described as verbal rough sex broke through my thoughts and set my teeth on edge. My body tensed, but I didn't need to turn around to

discover who stood behind me.
    Sid the Seducer.

Chapter Two

"War does not determine who is right, only who is left."
~*Bertrand Russell*

This whole evening sprouted one nasty surprise after the other. I turned to find a naked Demon appraising me from a not-so-safe distance. With dark brows framing dark eyes, ink-black hair and olive skin, seven feet of sexual energy bore down on me. His almond scent curled around my body, alluring and seductive, enticing me to take one step closer, and then another. Fucking Demons. "Sid."

How do you know this creature? Wick demanded, stepping up to stand beside me on the Italian slab tiles.

I'd used this Demon for information on my last case, and had no desire to tell Wick about the deal I'd made with Sid the Seducer. Even now, his energy tried to coil around me. I had no interest in this vile creature whatsoever, and despite his powerful sex mojo, his interest in me only extended to his next meal, much like the Vampires.

"Have you forgotten our time together so soon?" Sid's eyelids drooped into half slits. "I think about it often. Keeps me warm on cold nights in hell."

My wolf growled.

See what his insides look like. My mountain lion pawed the inside of my skull.

Great. My inner kitty wanted to learn Demon anatomy.

What the heck did Sid mean with his cold night reference, anyway? The underworld wasn't cold. Before I could tell the Demon where to stick his nether bits, Wick straightened his shoulders, and inserted himself between Sid and me. Sweet. But unnecessary.

Red stepped forward and growled at Sid. Also sweet. And also extremely unnecessary.

The Demon held his hands up. "Fine, fine. But you might want to play nice."

"And what makes you think I play nice?" I asked. My skin prickled as the urge to shift rippled through my body.

"Oh, I don't think you play nice. I know," Sid purred. "Besides, you can't afford to piss me off."

My hands flew to my hips. "What the hell does that mean? Why are you so cryptic? And why are you here?"

"I'm not being cryptic. As Satan's assistant, I'm here as the representative of the Demon Court, charged with providing information and returning with NAVA's decision. And it means, dear Carus, I'll see you later." And then the Demon gave me his back. The nerve. The view from behind showed his chiseled muscles tapering down to a nicely corded ass. I wanted to plant the pointy end of my heel into his right butt cheek.

What's he talking about? Wick asked, his voice heavy with a hot searing weight that shattered any calm resolve I had left.

Later, I shot back. I needed a drink. Sid the Seducer could get lost, but seeing him tonight brought reality crashing back. The early unease swirled in my stomach again. I hadn't told Wick or Tristan about Sid's payment.

Wick hesitated, and then his attention snapped to something behind me. *Here comes Lucien.*

Wick's hand gently pressed on my lower back. Warmth radiated from his body through the thin material of my blouse. My wolf rumbled and nudged me to turn into the heat of Wick, to nuzzle his neck and press against his hard muscles.

Time to go, Wick whispered.

I nodded, swallowed and willed my body to move forward. We fell in line with Lucien and the rest of his entourage as the Master Vampire wandered around the room, nodding at people and exchanging the occasional dialogue.

I never did get a drink.

I would like to know what you are thinking about. I can hear the wheels turning from here, Wick said. His chocolate brown eyes sought mine.

Heat flared in my cheeks, and I looked away. Thoughts of another man surfaced in my mind, a man absent from tonight, a man who'd wrestled his way into my heart alongside Wick. With the Werewolf Alpha so close, how could I not contemplate my complicated love life? Like some pathetic female in a tragic love story, I wanted two men. The thought of the absent Wereleopard resurfaced, and images of Tristan flashed through my mind, dunking my libido into the gutter. I squeezed my thighs against the flow of blood travelling rapidly to my crotch.

I'd managed to keep my raging hormones fairly locked down on this trip. Had Sid and his sexual energy broken down my resolve?

"You're giving me a headache," Lucien hissed at me. He pinched the bridge of his nose with his forefinger and thumb, and shook his head in little minute movements as if to clear his imaginary headache.

Dammit! I liked to forget the Master Vampire could sense my emotions through our bond. At least he couldn't read my mind.

"But I can," Allan said. The large Japanese Vampire reminded me of his special Vampire skill. "And you're giving me a headache, too."

Before I could open my mouth to say something I'm sure would be considered either extremely witty or completely childish, Clint stepped up from behind and leaned in over my shoulder to whisper in my ear. "You make me ache elsewhere."

"Ugh!" I drove my elbow back into Clint's hard abs.

The human servant grunted and took a step back. I glared at him without fully turning around, and he had the audacity to grin at me.

Like to tell me what is going on? Wick asked. He rubbed a large hand through his short blond hair.

Not a chance. It was impossible to tell him something I didn't know myself. *Nothing,* I told him.

Wick looked unconvinced, but his mouth snapped shut when Lucien turned to face the group.

"I'm hungry," the Master Vampire stated.

None of us moved. Apparently, he'd been plotting devious plans with his human servant this whole time, and not sipping on a snack.

Clint folded his arms, his lips compressed into a thin line. "Wick and Allan, follow Lucien. Andy, accompany me."

Lucien spun on his heel and strolled toward the section of the mansion that provided private rooms for feeding—his pace leisurely, his shoulders relaxed. Allan followed close on his heels, but Wick hesitated, casting me a wary glance.

"Don't worry, puppy," Clint said. "I'll keep her from meeting another Were to mate with in your absence."

Wick snarled and stalked off, presumably to attend Lucien.

I crossed my arms and turned my best death stare on the human servant. My blood heated as it raced through my veins. Trust Clint The Jerk to bring up painful shit during an already tense situation. "Why are you such an asshole?"

"You ripped my throat out," Clint said, ignoring the glances some of the surrounding Vampires and humans sent our way.

"You requested me as a sex slave for all eternity."

The human servant shrugged. "The position's still open."

"Keep dreaming."

Clint leaned in with a predatory gleam in his eyes. "I will have you."

My falcon squawked and sent me images of pecking out fish eyes.

I snorted and looked away. Like acclimatizing to the smelly gym bag in the backseat of a car, I'd somehow become impervious to Clint's perversions. It didn't mean I liked them or him. It certainly didn't mean I trusted him. But the fear I once held for the "Clint Threat" had evaporated over the last few months.

Sometimes, I got the impression his lewd remarks were made with half-ass effort, like he merely acted to fulfill his role as resident douchebag. Whenever I relaxed though, he'd say something truly deplorable, and I'd go back to despising him.

We walked in silence to one of the mansion's many bars, weaving around the groups of guests as they mingled. I wished Lucien's meticulous planning hadn't involved my attire. I had to shorten my stride to avoid ripping the material of my skirt. The high heels pinched my toes, but at least they weren't the four-inch hooker pumps with straps Lucien had bought me. Wick had tried to make me feel better by suggesting the skirt might be easier to shift in, but one look at my ass packed into the tight material and he'd stopped talking.

When we approached the bar, the bartender dropped his cleaning rag and hustled over to us. Before he could open his mouth, Clint held a fifty dollar bill out. "Glenfiddich, neat." His gaze flicked to me, and I nodded. "Make two." He placed the bill on the counter and pushed it toward the bartender with one finger. The bartender didn't touch it until the drinks were in our hands.

Turning back to the crowded room behind us, Clint took a long sip from the single malt whiskey before letting out a long breath. "So what's the deal with you, Wick and the Wereleopard king?"

My lip curled up in a snarl. He meant Tristan. Not sure how to answer, and pretty sure I didn't want to say anything nice, I took a sip of my drink instead. I hated that Clint and I shared a love for good whiskey. I preferred mine on ice, though. Enthusiasts everywhere would cringe at this confession—whiskey should be served at room temperature, and maybe, if anything, with a little water added to numb the punch of alcohol and let the whiskey flavour come through—but this knowledge didn't take the truth away. Regardless of quality, I liked whiskey *chilled.*

"Are you fucking them both?" Clint asked.

"None of your business," I said.

"I disagree, Andrea. You belong to Lucien, Wick belongs to Lucien, and Tristan is a powerful leader living within Lucien's domain, and should belong to Lucien. It is precisely *our* business."

I slammed back the rest of my drink, letting the amber liquid slide down my throat and burn. Squeezing my eyes shut, I focused on the warmth heating my stomach, and thumped my empty glass on the counter. Tristan had just escaped the service of another Master Vampire, one I had a hand in killing. He deserved to be free, not shackled to Lucien. "I'm not fucking anyone."

"No wonder you're so bitchy."

My eyes pinged open. Clint wore a smarmy, half smile that I wanted to slash off his face. He ignored my death stare and casually checked his watch.

Bite him, Red urged.

I think he'd take that as encouragement, I replied. Still, punching him in the kidneys would make me feel better.

Several pale women, and a few men, staggered from the private rooms with fang marks on their necks, wrists and thighs. They wore minimal clothing and house servants waited with fluffy white robes to cover them up and escort them somewhere else.

"It's time," Clint said, and held out his arm. I ignored it and stalked back to the group who'd already made their way to the oversized boardroom. Lucien stood by his chair, cheeks unnaturally flushed and eyes half lidded.

I quickly surveyed Wick for marks, but his skin appeared flawless as ever. He could've healed the bite marks by now, but knowing Lucien's preferences, he probably sucked back a curvy blonde.

"You have something…" I pointed to the corner of Lucien's lip. When he wiped at it with his thousand dollar suit sleeve, I bit back a triumphant smile. There hadn't been any blood there. The other bloodsuckers flowed in, and Lucien took his seat at the same time as if they were all synchronized swimmers.

Guards, including myself, moved to protect their masters' backs. We formed a rectangular ring around the enormous boardroom table. Where'd they find this piece of furniture? And how'd they get it into the room?

I nodded at the other guards sandwiching us in. The two female Vampires returned the gesture, but no other expression crossed their faces, either to reflect my own insignificance or because they were incapable of moving the muscles in their faces—like any Hollywood actress over forty who experimented with Botox.

Well, holding hands and singing "Kumbaya" must be out then.

Mentally shrugging, I tried to focus on the Vampires in front of me without nodding off. Finally, the time had come for them to vote on their relationship with the big bad Demons from the nether realm.

After everyone settled, a rotund man with a red sash across his black suit thumped the floor with a long golden staff to get everyone's attention. He smelled funny, like dandelions and celery.

Bite, my wolf demanded.

My mountain lion hissed. *See what his flesh tastes like.*

I ignored both of them, but when the announcer took his place by the entrance to the board room and another waft hit my face, I reconsidered. Maybe I should take a chunk out. My skin itched, and my mountain lion pawed at my brain to shift. Unease skittered across my arms and legs.

Many gazes flicked in our direction as we waited for Ian to take his place and commence with the vote.

What the hell were they looking at?

Ian strode in and deposited his intimidating female companion at the table. The host of events waited for the lingering conversations to hush before projecting his voice to carry over the table. "Fellow esteemed members of NAVA—"

An enormous boom fractured Ian's speech, followed by the thunderous sound of cracking wood. I staggered back a step as the ground moved beneath my feet. Something large and dark rose out of the floor, splintering the broad, solid oak table in front of the Vampires in two. Collective gasps rebounded off the walls, and the room flooded with the scent of something cruel and demonic. A roar vibrated the air, sucking it out of my lungs and jostling it back again before I could inhale.

A Demon with the head of a feral dog, and the body of a nine-foot professional weight lifter, stretched his insanely large black feathered wings out and landed in the centre of the Vampires with one foot on each half of the table, straddling the hole he emerged from. An absurdly large penis dangled between his legs. He rested his hands on his hips, and his eyes scanned the room.

The brutal scent of steel and blood seeped from his every pore, replacing the normal demonic almond scent. His canine jaws gaped open, showing fangs dripping with thick saliva. His breath reeked of grass, but not the nice summer kind; the kind that had gone bad and stagnant for weeks. The scent, oddly tinged with the pungent odour of money, meant one thing—cruelty. For once, my feras remained silent, no demands for attack. They wanted to flee. So did I. The flight response so strong, I had to will my feet to remain planted. Sweat trickled down the curve of my back. My nails dug into the palm of my hand. *I will not run. I am not prey.*

I needed to protect Lucien.

The Demon turned his head in my direction, and our eyes locked. Dead and black, with no discernible pupil or iris, his gaze revealed no living soul lurked within. Instead, raw, unbound malice glared back at me.

And then he smiled.

Chapter Three

"Do not take life too seriously. You will never get out of it alive."
~*Elbert Hubbard*

My clothes constricted against my skin as my body began to expand and started to shift. The response, instinctual. Without breaking the dark hypnotic gaze of the Demon, I kicked off my heels, thankful I'd refused to wear the strappy contraptions Lucien originally suggested. The synthetic material chafed against my skin. I moved my hand slowly to the neckline of my top, ready to rip it away to make the transition easier.

Wick grabbed my hand.

He hasn't attacked yet, he reasoned in my head.

The Demon shifted his gaze to take in the Vampires surrounding him as he continued to straddle the broken super-sized table. The normally unshakable bloodsuckers remained frozen in their seats doing their best mannequin impersonations. Released from his disturbing gaze and the inherent power behind it, I let out the deep breath that had been stuck in my lungs.

So we wait until he draws blood? I asked.

We wait for someone to act. He might be a representative from the demonic realm. He certainly likes a showy entrance. He squeezed my hand before releasing it. *I won't let anything happen to you.*

As macho as he sounded, a gentle wave of calm flowed through my veins at his words. I could take care of myself, but hearing Wick would protect me sent a warm girly flush through my body.

Run, Red yipped at my feet, running circles around them. *Now!*

The Demon dropped his head back and opened his jaws. Sharp fangs and pointed teeth littered his giant, gaping maw, ripe with dripping saliva. A roar ripped from his throat, low, pulsating, like the deep thundering of an earthquake or waterfall. Malice and hunger called out from the unnatural sound. One of the oversized gold-framed paintings fell to the floor with a bang. A few others followed, adding a clattering beat to the Demon's roar.

No one moved.

Except the Demon.

Cutting off the cry with a strangled sound, he launched from the table remains to the end of the room and clamped his giant dog-shape mouth over a Vampire's head. His jaw snapped shut and bones snapped as the Vampire's body shook. Ian, standing beside the victim, fell back, landing hard on the floor, sliding back enough for us to see him from across the table. His face turned up in an expression of…fear? On a Vampire? Cold prickled along my skin, raising the tiny hairs before settling at the back of my skull. *Never seen that look on a Vampire's face before.*

I stepped forward and clutched Lucien by his thousand dollar suit and hauled him out of the chair, shoving him behind me, Wick and Allan.

Twisting, the Demon ripped the Vampire's head off, and his throat bulged as he swallowed it whole.

Blood sprayed across the room and painted Ian's face, among others. The rest of the Vampire's body crumpled to the Demon's feet and turned to dust.

Must've been young.

Move! Red hissed at my feet.

The Demon's actions spurred the Vampires into action. Chaos erupted throughout the room. The Vampires surged from their seats and dispersed like a frantic marmot herd, funneling out of the boardroom through the four different exits. Allan gripped Lucien's arm, and they ran for the main exit to the left.

With Vampires zooming away in every direction, I turned and ran into the giant hall, my back just one of many. My skirt ripped to the waistband, and I lengthened my stride. Wick's hand pressed into the curve of my spine, prodding me forward and reassuring me with his presence. I needed him safe, too.

To hell with this place, I planned to get out of the building, and gauging from the pressure on my back, Wick agreed. We needed to grab Lucien and get him to safety.

Following the mass of Vampires converging with speed on the main entrance, I put my chin down and charged faster. The expensive interior design blurred as I ran by. Wick kept pace, refusing to leave me behind. As a Were, he could easily outrun me in our human forms, but he didn't. My quads burned and my lungs dried out, each shallow breath rasping against the raw tissue. How big was this stupid building, anyway?

Where was Lucien?

The Vampires ahead of us funnelled toward the main entrance. The giant wood panels loomed in the distance above the bobbing heads of hustling men and women. The doors crashed open, and the Demon exploded into the main hall from outside, dominating the large area. His hand swiped at the closest Vampires, knocking them over and throwing them to the side like bowling pins. I staggered and threw all my weight back to stop my forward momentum. Sharp pain lanced up my back as I landed on my tailbone. "Gah!"

"Get up!" Wick grabbed my arms and hauled me to my feet. "Go. Hide!" He shoved me toward the bar, and then ripped off his shirt.

"We need to find Lucien." I glanced at the Demon. He picked off the Vampires closest to the door. Pounce. Bite. Snap.

He had a number of Vampires to go through before he reached us.

"Your safety, first." Wick gave me another push.

I stumbled forward, but halted after a few steps to turn back to Wick. "Come with me."

"I'll get Lucien," Wick hissed. He kept his gaze on the Demon and tugged off his jeans, showing me and anyone else looking he went commando. The sight of his toned butt stirred a warmth in my belly, entirely wrong for the current situation. Wick rolled his head back, stretching, and peered at me. "Lucien's calling me. Can you feel the tug?"

I checked on the Demon—still munching on Vampires—and then closed my eyes to focus inward. His Vampire taint ran through my blood, coursing with each pump of my heart and concentrating around my liver. Unfortunately, my body couldn't filter Lucien out like other toxins.

"No," I said. "Nothing."

"Then hide." Wick gripped my shoulders and

pulled me to him, planting his lips firmly on mine. Slanting his head, he delved his tongue roughly into my mouth. It was a raw, needy kiss and I loved it, melting into him despite the inherent danger. He bit my lower lip before pushing me away, nodding again at the bar. "Be safe."

"You, too." I turned and sprinted for cover, Red close on my heels.

Two human bartenders, one male, one female, both norms, huddled in the corner. I ignored them and took cover behind the bar, peeking around the side. Red bumped up against my leg, huddling close to it.

I don't like this, she said.

Me neither.

Wick completed his messy change; blood, plasma and tissue splattered the tiles around him. His Werewolf was one of the largest I'd ever seen—black with a white tipped snout, white boots and mitts. The wolf turned to me, his bright yellow eyes meeting mine, before turning away and running to wherever Lucien hid.

I could end this. One shift to my beast. I peered around the side of the bar to see three Vampires launch themselves at the massive, dog-headed Demon. He stood over nine feet tall, more than double the size of Wick as a Werewolf and at least half a foot on me in beast form.

The Demon spun and caught a Vampire before the bloodsucker landed a strike. The Demon ripped him in half, dust exploding into the air like confetti.

Could I take him? *Maybe.*

My beast might lay the beat down on the Demon, but at what cost? I'd successfully shifted into the destructive form three times. It took me over thirty years to recuperate from the first shift, and while I'd had more control during the other times, I didn't trust my beast form. I couldn't risk losing my humanity when I'd just reclaimed it.

Last resort, I decided.

"Interesting turn of events, wouldn't you say?" Sid's voice sprung up behind me.

I yelped and spun around. Fixing Sid with a death stare, I asked, "What the hell are you doing here?"

Sid's smile broadened, and he sat down in front of me. All seven feet of naked, olive-toned skin plunked down on the bare ground. He smiled as he crossed his legs, exposing more of his boy bits. "Watching the show, same as you."

To prove his point, he conjured up a bowl of…I sniffed the air. Popcorn?

My gaze snapped from his crotch. My shoulders tensed. Stupid Seducer Demons. I moved forward to threaten him with bodily harm, but halted.

Screams erupted from the adjacent room. The Demon must've moved to a new location. Maybe the entrance was clear now. Still in a crouch position, I leaned around the bar to look at the exit surrounded by decaying vamp bodies and piles of dust. The two massive solid oak doors hung half off their hinges, and the outside beyond beckoned.

"Wouldn't risk it," Sid said, as if reading my thoughts. "He'll sense it."

I turned to Sid. "Aren't you going to do something?"

The Demon had the nerve to shrug. "I will if you want me to." He popped a kernel of popcorn into his mouth and then set the bowl aside. His gaze drifted down to my ripped skirt and exposed leg. "Will you pay my price?"

"At a time like this?" I tugged at the ripped skirt and covered enough of my upper thigh to block Sid's view of my panty choice.

"With absolute pandemonium and the scent of blood and fear?" Sid took a deep breath in and closed his eyes. "As a backdrop to your sensual hip swivels and bouncing full breasts, I couldn't think of a better time."

"You're a pig."

"Demon," he reminded me. His eyes popped open and settled on my chest, thankfully still covered.

Another roar ripped through the room, rumbling the air and shaking the glasses hanging above the bar. The clinking a spastic harmony to the noise erupting from the Demon.

Wick was out there somewhere.

"Will you take a rain check?" I asked.

Sid shook his head and popped another kernel into his mouth.

I'd rather embrace the beast than go through the humiliation of dancing naked for Sid to feed off my sexual energy.

Sid chuckled, probably reading the thoughts on my face. "Relax. Looks like you're saved from having to make a decision. They finally got their shit together." Sid nodded over the counter. "Took them long enough."

I scowled at Sid before turning to peek over the counter top. Sure enough, the Vampires and their minions, including Wick, surrounded the Demon who towered over them, nearly double in size. Knifes, swords and teeth jutted forth, attacking in a controlled unified front. The Demon dropped his head back and placed a palm on his belly as he shook with laughter.

"Fools," the dog Demon bellowed.

Wick leapt to attack. The Demon's backhand impacted Wick hard in the abdomen. A sickening thud. Wick flew across the room. He hit the floor, limp.

"Wick!" A strangled cry expelled from my throat. I shot up, ready to run to him when two dark, Demon eyes locked on mine. I halted in my tracks.

The dog Demon licked his chops. "Mmm, Carus. I've missed you."

Huh?

Before I could yell profanities at him, the Demon let out another ear-shattering bellow and launched himself out of the room, bursting through the large skylight and into the night.

Sharp shards of glass hailed down in his wake. I flung my arms up. Tiny slivers sliced by me and clattered on the ground. The room filled with the sound of glass hitting tile, almost like a colossal wind-chime concert. It lasted seconds.

When the room turned silent in the glass-hail aftermath, I let my arms fall to my sides. Small trails of blood ran down my skin. Mere flesh wounds. Barely worse than a bunch of paper cuts. Others were worse off.

Wick!

A groan rippled across the room from his crumpled form. I left the bar and ran to him, sliding along the floor for the last few steps. The Vampires turned to me with questioning expressions. Screw them. My mind focused on one thing only.

Wick had shifted back to human. Turning him

over, his head face up and on my lap, I checked his body for injuries. Gashes closed up as I watched, and a large bruise on his midsection faded away. I stroked the blood away from his cheek.

"Andy..." Wick's usual whiskey and cream voice softened into something tender. With his eyes opened to slits, he smiled at me.

The tension in my muscles eased with my next breath, and my eyes stung with the sudden welling of unshed tears. I blinked rapidly. *Don't cry. Pull yourself together. He's going to be okay.* Thank god for Were healing.

"How do you know that Demon?" Lucien's demanding voice from behind straightened my spine.

"I don't." I stroked Wick's short blond hair. He'd closed his eyes again, but I smiled down at him anyway.

"Then what was he talking about?" Lucien asked.

"No clue." My eyebrows pinched the middle of my forehead. I'd never met this Demon before. A dog with wings was hard to forget. The only Demons I'd come across were Sid, and that repulsive creature who'd...

Little black spots danced in my blurry vision as my heartbeat thrashed in my ears. I stilled my hand on Wick's head. The room filled with the sickly sweet smell of my fear. My feras growled in my mind.

Dylan's Demon.

Chapter Four

"If two wrongs don't make a right, try three."
~*Laurence J. Peter*

I held back my urge to throttle the Seducer Demon and counted to ten. My nerve endings tingled from the denied shift, burning as if I'd spent too much time in the sun instead of starting and stopping a transformation. It took multiple deep breaths and a silent mantra regarding a dead ex to calm down. By then, the Vampires had collected themselves and cornered the remaining Demon for interrogation. They looked ready to break out the gimp, and I didn't blame them. Sid pissed me off, too.

Ever notice the word "Demon" in the word pandemonium? Coincidence? I think not.

Sid placed his half-eaten bowl of popcorn down on the bar counter and straightened to his full seven feet, unperturbed by the congregation of pissed-off Vampires surrounding him. "I could give you the information you seek. But no one here seems willing to pay my price...yet." His gaze scanned the room and settled on me for a moment before continuing. "There's always later."

Ian cleared his throat, and the bloodsucking heads swiveled in unison in his direction. "Should we go through with the vote?" he asked. "Since we're all here?"

I looked around, taking in the scattered piles of Vampire remains that decorated the Italian marble flooring of Ian's grand entrance and ballroom. My heart still raced from lingering adrenaline. The air smelled dank and dirty with the cloy of ash and death.

As if following the same line of thought, Ian spoke again. "Well, most of us, anyway. The seconds will stand in for any fallen masters, of course."

I turned to Lucien, still hale and hearty, and unaffected by the Demon attack. For some reason, relief washed through me. If I somehow survived his death, I doubted I would've escaped alive from a Vampire summit without a master to protect me. It would turn this whole event from bad to horrific. Looking relaxed and at ease as if he recently fed instead of faced down a Demon, Lucien shrugged. "May as well."

Some of the Vampires murmured agreement, while others remained silent, but they all must've agreed, because they filed back into the boardroom and sat down in their original spots around the broken table. Some seconds stepped up to vote now that the leader of their horde had blown away with the breeze.

What the heck? These suckheads treated the Demon consuming their brethren like another tactical break. Sure Vampires lacked a beating heart, but geez...

Then again, I wasn't exactly shaking in my boots either. At least, not anymore. My recuperation time from traumatic or scary events seemed to constantly improve. Must be all the recent "practice" I'd received.

I followed Lucien and kept one hand clamped on the ripped edges of my skirt. Not that anyone besides

Wick was interested, but these guys didn't need a show. I took my place at Lucien's back and surveyed the area.

Wick hobbled in after us and took his place at my side. By the time the vote finished, he'd be fully recovered. His warmth radiated against my skin and sent a soothing balm along my nerves.

Clint turned in his seat to face me. "You might need these."

Oh look! My shoes. Completely unscathed and dangling from Clint's forefinger. Would nothing go right tonight?

"Your butt looks better with them on." Clint winked.

I snatched them from his hand. "Funny, you would look better with them stuck up your ass."

"Children," Lucien hissed.

Clint smirked before turning back to the damaged table, leaving me to waste my death stares on the back of his head with his perfectly slicked hair. I stuffed my already sore feet back into the shoes, my feet so traumatized and swollen, I could've gone a size up.

"All those in favour of creating an alliance?" Ian called out. He raised his hand, along with Lucien. The female vamp who'd been with Ian earlier, sitting at the far end of the table, also raised her hand. Everyone else looked away.

Hmmm...What did this mean? Obviously the dog Demon had rattled a few Vampires, but they shouldn't be so easily manipulated.

Ian's gaze cast back and forth before he lowered his arm awkwardly to his side. "All those opposed?"

Vampire arms shot up in unison, crinkling the air with the sound of their clothing.

"Forty-seven to three…" Ian glanced at Lucien before averting his eyes. "NAVA has spoken. There will be no alliance."

A deep chuckle filled the room, and fifty Vampire heads along with their minions swiveled to the doorway. Sid leaned against the frame, legs crossed and one hand on his naked hip. Someone needed to get this guy some tighty-whities. I, personally, was over looking at his junk.

"I will pass along your decision," Sid announced. He straightened, gave the room a shallow bow and disappeared, presumably swallowed up by the demonic realm. No one had to expel him. And no circle had contained him. He must've struck a deal for a limited time outside the circle with the promise to do no harm.

Lucien stood and straightened his suit, somehow still immaculate despite the recent events.

"Come." Allan nudged me. Lucien, Clint and Wick moved beside him, looking at me expectantly. Guess we were on the move.

"Dawn arrives soon, and I'm hungry," Lucien said before nodding at the door. Hungry? His flushed cheeks and rosy red lips contradicted his statement. Lucien wanted out of here, and I didn't blame him. I did, too.

We walked in silence toward the exit. I hobbled along with my pinched toes, and Red trotting alongside me. The feras in my head grumbled and prodded me to move faster.

The Pharaoh stepped into our path, right in front of Lucien. Allan and I both moved to insert ourselves between them, but Lucien waved us off. We returned to our previous positions.

If the Pharaoh gave a smug smile, would Lucien

punch him in the nose? Did the Pharaoh plan to challenge Lucien to a fight after school by the monkey bars? I leaned forward to peer around Clint's massive shoulders and watch the scene unfold. The Pharaoh wore no expression, the Vampire blank slate I so despised. Lucien faced away from me, but his must've been the same.

The other Vampires milled around as these two remained frozen.

I shifted my weight from foot to foot, trying to regain feeling in my toes. The pads of my feet had swelled even more and my arches ached.

The Pharaoh and Lucien didn't move.

They stood three feet apart staring at each other.

Awkward.

Maybe they spoke telepathically to each other, slinging insults back and forth. I'd pay to listen to that conversation. Imagine the repertoire of slurs these two had collected over the years. Should I be worried about more mayhem and bloodshed? My muscles tensed, and I instinctively moved my weight to my numb toes. If shit went down, I'd be prepared.

Then Lucien ruined my dreams of watching two ancient Vampires duke it out like high school girls. He chuckled.

The Pharaoh inclined his head and stepped aside. No words uttered. Nothing. And as abruptly as we stopped, we marched to the exit and the limo parked outside.

When we climbed in, Red leapt onto my lap, curled up and closed her eyes. Must be exhausted. I knew the feeling. I stroked her hair, and kicked off my heels. Both feet throbbed in response and started to swell.

Wick took the seat beside me. His long thigh brushed against mine, and my wolf sent images of our naked bodies entwined together.

Not fair, I told her and crossed my legs.

She snorted.

The door shut, and the silence in the limo drew my attention away from Red's soft ears. Everyone watched me with furrowed brows and looks of disgust. They couldn't see Red, so I got how weird it must look to them. I clenched my hand and dropped it to my side.

Clint turned to Lucien. "Well, that fucked things up a bit."

It took me a moment to realize he meant the vote, not me petting my invisible fera.

Lucien nodded, but chose not to comment. The limo rolled forward as a nameless minion drove us away from the gong-show of a summit.

"The Pharaoh got his wish," Allan said after we had been driving for a while.

Lucien hissed, and punched the seat beside him with such force his hand punctured the leather and penetrated through the seat. Nobody moved, but everyone tensed. The air smelled wary. Lucien's lips curled back, revealing fangs, as he wiggled his hand free from the upholstery. When he glanced up, I made sure I looked elsewhere.

"Fucking idiots played right into his hand." Clint reached into the limo's bar and grabbed a glass and the scotch. "That Demon achieved his goal."

"The question is," Allan said. "Why would a Demon sabotage a vote that would build an alliance? They want it just as much as we do."

"And why wouldn't the other Vampires see the

intent of the attack?" Clint asked.

"That's easy," Allan said.

We all turned to him.

"They're idiots," he said. "We need to determine whether the Demon is working with or for the Pharaoh."

Red let out a deep sigh in her sleep and rolled onto her back, splayed out. A little rumble vibrated against my legs. *She's snoring!* I bit back a smile, and kept my hand clenched by my side.

"Why is the Pharaoh against the alliance?" I asked and flinched as everyone's attention swivelled to me like bobble heads. I pushed my luck with questions.

"We don't know," Allan answered.

"You can't pluck it out of his head?" I tapped my temple with my forefinger for added theatrical effect.

Allan's shoulders straightened. "Most of the older Vampires can shield me. And the Pharaoh is very old, the oldest I've met."

Huh. Mental note. Allan's skills had limits. The limo hit a pothole, bumping us off our seats. I readjusted my skirt and turned to Lucien. I'd glean as much information as possible before he went all "master" on me. "Why do you think he's against it?"

Lucien's face slowly lost the freshly fed flush as he studied me. "The most obvious answer is the Pharaoh doesn't wish to risk his power base. The Demon alliance could do exactly that—enable other Vampires to grow enough in strength to challenge him."

"But?"

The Master Vampire tilted his head. "What makes you think there's a but?"

"Doesn't sound like you believe the *most obvious*

answer."

"The Pharaoh usually operates at a more subtle level," Lucien said.

"Nothing subtle about him standing up in the middle of a Vampire summit."

"Precisely," he said, as if that explained everything. Maybe it did. I sank back in my chair and ruminated on what Lucien said. I wanted to ask more, but I had already pressed my luck. Lucien was being uncharacteristically chatty with me, and I found it unnerving, to the point where I suspected he operated at his own *subtle level*, giving me select information as if manipulating me somehow. Dang these Vampires and their stupid Vampire politics.

"What went on between you two? Back there. The staring contest between you and the Pharaoh, I mean," I asked.

Allan drummed his fingers on his armrest. "Vampire posturing. Nothing more."

I looked around the limo's cab, but no one seemed inclined to enlighten me further, including Lucien. Fine. The limo drove over uneven pavement and jostled everyone in the car. Lucien remained immobile the entire time.

"We need to know more about the Demon." Clint took a deep drink of amber fluid, carefully avoiding Lucien's vamped out gaze. Guess he didn't want to be food tonight. Should've thought about that before signing up for the human servant deal.

Do you know what's going on? I asked Wick. The heat of his thigh radiated through his clothes and warmed my skin.

No idea. Lucien keeps me out of the loop regarding

all the Demon stuff, and anything to do with the Pharaoh. I'm always ordered out of the room. Wick kept his eyes forward, trained on Lucien.

"Andrea," Lucien's voice whispered across the limo cabin.

My muscles tightened, and I pursed my lips. My mountain lion paced, but I shushed her before she could hiss at me.

"I'm not food," I said.

Lucien's lip quirked up at the corner. "You will be if I say so." He held a hand up as my mouth gaped open to make some sound. "But that is not what I planned to say."

"Oh."

"This Demon knew you."

"But I didn't know him." At least, I didn't think I did. I'd only met two. Sid and Dylan's Demon—Bola. He always possessed a Werewolf body, so I never saw his true form, nor scented it. Could this Demon be Bola? A shudder racked my body. Maybe. I hoped not. That was one messed up Demon, even by demonic standards. But all Demons liked to mess with people. Maybe Bola had talked about me to his brethren, so other sadists could learn of my past. Stomach acid bubbled up my throat. I swallowed.

"You have a Demon contact you can ask," Lucien said, interrupting my thoughts.

I clenched my teeth, my lips flattening into a straight line.

Wick snarled a warning, but it annoyed me. He didn't own me, and he couldn't act against his master. That had been made quite clear to me when he held me down for Lucien to drink my blood, Wick's prickly warning as empty as Lucien's heart. My own heart pained with the regret of a spoiled relationship. Things had been going well until that night. Now, things were weird, and Wick's attempts to defend me didn't always cause rainbows to dance through my mind.

Besides, I could take care of myself.

"You will contact your Demon, pay his price, and find out about this one," Lucien stated.

"You forgot something," I said.

"I am the Master Vampire of the Lower Mainland. I will not say *please*."

I shook my head. "You forgot to add the 'or else' part. You know, where you threaten me with something."

Lucien's eyes crinkled, then his gaze slid to where Wick sat. "I'd think by now you'd know what's on the line."

And I did. Ice flowed through my veins, and my back straightened. Last time I'd refused to pay Sid's price, Lucien had threatened to gut Wick over and over again between healings, and force me to watch. Despite my complicated feelings for the Werewolf Alpha, I cared. Deeply. The thought of him hurt…well, I already went through that once tonight. Lucien didn't fight fair. He got down and dirty.

"What price?" Wick asked.

No one answered, and an awkward heavy silence consumed the limo.

"Lucien," Wick started. "I don't think Andy—"

Lucien's teeth elongated, and Wick stopped talking.

"I don't ask you to think," Lucien hissed. "Be quiet and assist Andy."

Wick sat back in his seat. This time, along with silence, burnt cinnamon flowed off Wick in angry waves and swamped the limo.

Going to be a long night.

Chapter Five

"They say marriages are made in Heaven. But so is thunder and lightning."
~*Clint Eastwood*

Wick treaded close behind me with my luggage as I walked the concrete path to my building's front entrance. So close, his angry huffing brushed the hairs on the back of my neck. So close, he might clip my heels or trip over Red. Was it possible to stumble over an invisible fera? I said nothing as I unlocked first the building door and then once inside, my apartment's. I pushed the door open and stepped aside to let Wick in. He passed me, the scent of anger mixed with the sour tang of anxiety trailed behind him like the wake of a large shipping vessel.

My, my, my. Someone's pissy.

I'd met Wick a few months ago when I'd attempted to take Clint's life on what I thought were orders from the SRD. After I botched the "Kill Clint" assignment, Lucien had Wick imprison me in his house for weeks, and we'd become close, our wolves closer. Under any other circumstances, I'd have jumped his bones by now, but he belonged to Lucien even more than I did. The Master Vampire commanded wolves—Were, Shifter or otherwise—as one of his special parlour tricks.

Dropping my luggage in the middle of the living

room on the wood flooring, Wick turned and crossed his arms. I kicked off my stupid extra-high heels and wiggled my numb toes, trying to force some feeling back into them. *Ugh.* I got my wish, and pain trickled up my big toes and the small ones ached. *Forget this! Numb feet were better.*

I shifted my weight and clasped my hands behind my back to avoid wringing them. *What was up with Wick?* He looked like a berserk bull staring down a red flag. "Ah…thanks for bringing my luggage in," I said.

"Andy." Wick's husky voice vibrated the air as I sucked it in.

"Wick."

"I'm not leaving until you tell me about the Demon."

"I already told you, and everyone else for that matter. I don't know who the dog Demon is." I eyed the bedroom door as a possible route of escape.

Wick's nose flared. "Maybe so, but why do I smell your fear?"

"Um…maybe because he ripped powerful Vampires in half and popped their heads into his mouth like candy? Kinda scary." My hands flopped uselessly to my sides. My thoughts flittered around in my head: Could the dog Demon have a connection to Bola? What would that mean? And where did Wick get off demanding answers from me?

Take a deep breath. Control your environment.
Then go to bed.
Sleep, Red agreed.

My luggage sat behind Wick. He probably wouldn't let me unpack until he finished with his demands for answers. Fucking Alphas.

Wick shook his head. "It's more than that." He held his hand up when I opened my mouth to argue. "But he's not the one I asked about."

"Oh." I glanced away, Wick's yellow gaze too intense. I'd ask what he meant, but I couldn't play dumb that well.

"Andy."

"Yes?"

"Who is your Demon contact?" he demanded, though he probably already knew given my interaction with Sid at the summit.

My teeth clenched, and I pursed my lips. Would he believe a lie? No, he'd smell it. I could refuse to answer, but he'd never let it rest. I pushed my shoulders down from my ears.

If Wick seriously wanted to be my mate, and if I could forgive him for the blood bonding thing and forget Tristan, he needed to know more of my past, the good and the bad. And I had a whole barrel of bad. Sucking a deep breath in like a pharmaceutical-grade pipette, I spoke on my exhale. "You've met him."

Wick frowned. "But I've only met one…" His back straightened, and every muscle in his body stiffened. "Sid? Sid the Seducer? That's your Demon?"

"That's the guy."

A long pause. "What price did you pay, Andy?"

I didn't answer, didn't want to. This was the question I feared, so I puttered around the room "tidying" as if I cared about a clean home. I had little in way of possessions. This place had basic furniture and dish requirements and that was about it. No agent kept items they couldn't leave at the drop of a body.

"What did you pay?" Wick kicked one of my hard

luggage cases, sending it flying against the wall with a thud.

I glanced over at the dented plaster. Crap. I just had that wall fixed. When a horde of humans had swarmed my apartment during a Kappa incident, my living room looked like a demo site. Maybe I could get a frequent customer discount?

Waves of acrid anger emanated off Wick and pried my attention back to him. He continued to wait for his answer. Squeezing my eyes shut, I spoke. "I danced for him."

"That's it?"

"Naked."

After a drawn out pause, Wick threw his fist into the closest wall, crashing through the drywall. Flakes of paint and splinters of wood flew through the air. He stood facing the wall, his right arm embedded to the elbow, panting. If I went to the other side of the wall to my bedroom, I'd see his fist.

What do I say? One wrong word or move would make him explode. *Stay absolutely still.* Like prey caught in a predator's sights, I waited to see what he'd do.

Wick's body shook and heaved with each breath. His forehead rested against the wall as he slowly pried his arm out of the hole he'd made. More flakes of paint and plaster flittered to the floor. His breathing slowed to a more normal rate, and he turned to face me.

His eyes! Yellow and piercing, their intensity made me stagger back. His face…Wick had partially shifted to a wolf. As I watched, his snout reduced to his normal slender nose, and his fur receded to smooth northern European skin. Claws retracted to fingernails, and dense fuzz shed away to reveal normal arm hair. To stop and reverse a shift already underway showed immense power and skill. He probably pulled energy from his pack to prevent a full shift.

Warmth spread across my cheeks. His pack would know. They'd feel the pull and the anger, and they'd know I was the cause. Perfect. As if they needed more reasons to hate me.

"Your answering machine is blinking," Wick said.

Oh, shit. "I'll check it later."

"Check it now."

Well now, someone's asserting their dominance. Bad timing. Normally, I'd placate him, do anything to calm his nerves, but only a few people had my home number, and half of them were out of town in Lucien's entourage with me. That left three possibilities— Tristan, Booth or Donny.

Given Booth recently revealed her Egyptian goddess status as Renenutet and took off with her long lost lover, Sobek, she most likely had more important things to do than ring up her former employee, or act in any capacity for the SRD. Agent Donny O'Donnell, my former handler, not current, had no foreseeable reason to contact me now that I represented the SRD as an ambassador, doing my liaison thing. Plus, I normally contacted Donny for information, not the other way around. Only one option remained.

Tristan.

The tiny muscles under my eyes twitched, and my mouth dried out. Maybe I should get some water. I glanced over at the kitchen, where temporary escape awaited. No way could I let Wick listen to a message left by Tristan, his competition. Not when he'd lost his cool already.

"I'll check later," I said.

Wick kept his yellow eyes trained on my face for three ticks of the second hand on my grandfather clock, and then stalked over to the machine. He turned to face me, his furious gaze meeting mine once more before he extended one finger down to press the button in slow motion.

"Don't," I said. Tackle him? Pounce?

I remained frozen in place.

Wick shook his head, and hit the button. A loud beep sounded, followed with a voice I hadn't expected.

"Andy, it's Stan. Huge massacre down at the Steveston docks. Need to borrow your nose. It's Friday, twenty-one hundred. Call me when you get this."

The breath I'd held escaped my lungs with a big whoosh of air. Stan Stevens was the officer I'd hijacked from the local Vancouver Police Department to help out with hunting down the Kappa. In return, I'd offered my supe skills to help him get ahead and, hopefully, a promotion. Wick knew all about him, and knew he posed no threat.

In the old days, Steveston would've been outside VPD jurisdiction, but after the Purge, most law enforcement agencies merged. The VPD took care of anything west of Coquitlam River, and north of the Fraser River. The Surrey Police Department oversaw the rest of the municipalities within the Lower Mainland. Their boundaries and zones might've changed, but their names hadn't.

The answering machine beeped again, signalling a second message. I sucked in stale apartment air and dug my toes into the rug.

"Andy," Tristan's voice purred. "I found a nude subject for you to paint. Call me."

A bark of laughter ripped from my throat. *Oh Feradea! Where's the help?*

Wick's head swiveled to me. "You paint?"

Oh boy. "Not really. No." Inside joke.

Wick's eyes narrowed and the stench of old cat piss wound around my body and punched me in the nose. My nose hairs curled at the jealous scent. "I see," he said.

"Wick..." My voice trailed off, because what could I say? What would take his pain away? And remove the ache of helplessness in the pit of my stomach?

Angry vibrations of energy rolled off his body in cinnamon waves. Part of me wanted to reach out and soothe his anger and pain away, the other part thought he deserved it. Hadn't he hurt me? If he hadn't allowed Christine to throw her scantily-clad body all over him, if he'd fought Lucien's compulsion harder, if he hadn't been used against me again and again by Lucien, my decision might've been made already. Not all his fault, but still painful.

We could've been bonded before Tristan ever had a shot. Even now, when my decision appeared obvious due to the obstacles, I hesitated to commit to Tristan because my wolf and a part of my heart still yearned for Wick.

Wick's yellow gaze softened, and the muscles in his face relaxed, but his back remained ramrod straight. "It's okay. I get it."

He walked up to me and smoothed his hands up my arms before cupping my face. Leaning down, he placed a soft kiss upon my lips. No heat, just...sweetness.

"I hope you make the right decision," he said, pulling away.

So do I.

Chapter Six

"One scent can be unexpected, momentary and fleeting, yet conjure up a childhood summer beside a lake in the mountains; another, a moonlit beach; a third, a family dinner of pot roast and sweet potatoes during a myrtle-mad August in a Midwestern town."
~*Diane Ackerman*

I let the door slam as I exited my car, an older-model canary yellow Honda Prelude I bought to replace the rusty red Ford Contour as my A to B car. I couldn't decide whether to call it "The Poo-lude" or "Lemon," both names fit. It needed a paint job to make it less conspicuous. Or maybe I should go the other direction with the car's appearance—tint some windows and put on a pimped-out spoiler. Then I'd fit right in with some of the sketchy areas I frequented for work. Good thing about owning such a crap car? No one wanted to steal it. Bad thing? No way would I take the officers by surprise with the sounds my car made.

Red bounded out after me and wove around my feet, her warm fur caressing my skin. Despite being almost midnight, the summer air licked my skin, warm and heavy with humidity. I wore shorts, an old black T-shirt with a faded AC/DC logo and black flip flops—items easy to rip through or pull off in emergencies. Shifter fashion would never make the covers of any magazines.

"This better be good," I warned Stan as I stepped forward and shook his hand. Middle-aged and balding, Officer Stevens smelled of soap and leather. I liked his uneven teeth the most. They pointed in different directions like individuals with multiple personalities, adding character to his otherwise stern face.

"Got someplace better to be?" he asked with a grin.

Summoning Sid for Lucien so I could dance the naked hokey pokey? No, not really. I shook my head.

Stan lifted his chin, nodding at the officer beside him. "This is my supervisor, Sergeant Tony Lafleur. He's filling me in on witness accounts."

Lafleur stepped forward and offered his hand. If I looked up "cop" in the dictionary, Lafleur's unsmiling face would be smack dab in the middle of the definition. With steely blue eyes, shaved head, smushed-in nose and slightly rotund, but solid belly, Lafleur screamed career cop, and smelled of gun oil and paper.

"Okay." I shook Lafleur's hand and met his cop stare-down, his grip strong and sure, but not bone-crushing. I glanced around the parking lot. Did Stan expect me to strip down and shift in front of another norm? Not happening.

"He knows," Stan said. "About you."

My eyes narrowed at Lafleur, who had the intelligence to look away.

"How?" I asked.

"Not me, if that's what you're asking," Stan grumbled.

"How then?" I demanded, glaring at Lafleur.

"Your agency contacted me," the sergeant said, his

voice a crisp even tone. "They wanted to know how the liaison agreement was working out for us. Imagine my surprise. I was not aware we had such a relationship."

I opened my mouth to argue. A liaison? With the VPD, I had acted on my own, not as an SRD pimp.

Stan cleared his throat and shook his head in a slight movement. Lafleur caught the action and squinted at us.

"They named me as the liaison?" I asked instead. "And Stan as my contact?"

"Yes."

How'd they figure that out? I'd contacted Stan to fish for a connection between recent thefts and the objects my retrieval target had pawned. Had I told Agent Booth? I couldn't remember, but she handled that entire case off the books anyway. She wouldn't have blabbed to anyone. Gauging from Stan's current expression, he hadn't filled anyone in either.

Stan had only called on my services once—to sniff out a mass murder body dump site compliments of a turtle-shaped supe, called a Kappa, hell-bent on making supe-smoothies for breakfast, lunch and dinner. The Kappa had a formidable appetite.

Sergeant Lafleur was absent at the time. At least, I don't remember seeing or smelling him there. He had a countenance that would plaster itself to my memory. So many people milled around the crime scene—experts, contractors, technicians. The other officers hadn't taken any special interest in me, and if a supe had been present from the SRD, I would've scented them. So how'd the SRD catch on? Those were the only times that I'd been in contact...

My place!

I'd called Stan in to help clean up a Kappa-induced mess in my apartment. The Kappa had sent a team of possessed norms to my place. Lucky for me, he'd underestimated my skills in badass-ery. The SRD must've run surveillance on my house and put it together.

"Who did you speak with?" I asked. Sweat trickled down my back.

Lafleur pursed his lips and looked toward the building doors, illuminated with police lights. "Seems like I should be the one asking the questions."

I bit my tongue and rocked back on my heels on the asphalt.

"Is it true?" Lafleur asked.

"What?"

"You can change into an animal?"

"Yes."

"Where's your—"

I growled a warning. He almost asked the whereabouts of my fera. A no-no question for Shifters. Red howled and launched herself at Lafleur's calves. Not that she'd do any damage, but it made her feel better. And me.

Settle, I told her.

Red huffed, released the sergeant's pant leg and slunk back to my side.

Lafleur glanced down as if sensing some of Red's attacks and cleared his throat. "My apologies, Agent. I forgot how touchy your kind finds that question."

"Touchy? *Your kind* used the information to eradicate countless lives of innocent Shifters." I dug my nails into my palm.

Kill, my feras screamed in my head. They preferred

to strike first and ask questions later.

Red surged forward and batted his leg one last time, snarling her frustration, before darting behind my legs again. What a wuss. The sergeant couldn't see or touch her, much less harm her in any way.

My wolf growled. The falcon squawked.

"Forgive me for not pointing you to the nearest and easiest way to kill me," I said.

Lafleur tucked his thumbs into his belt and pushed his belly out, reminding me of a bad television actor playing the quintessential cop cliché. "Not fair to judge me for past actions made by other people. Not like any of us here were around during the Fork, anyway."

A lot of norms used the "Fork" instead of saying the "Purge." They found the latter more derogatory. It did insinuate the events exterminated norms like unwanted pests. Regardless of the name, it was a horrific time for both norms and supes. Natural disasters and viruses rampaged across the globe, and the fragile humans dropped like hot potatoes to reveal the existence of death-defying supernatural beings.

Norms reacted by reaching out and killing all things "weird," and unfortunately, Shifters were one of the easiest to spot, constantly accompanied by animals. Every redneck with a gun took out their anger, frustration and fear on the animal familiars, decimating enough Shifters to give the first couple of years during the Purge the label Shifter Shankings.

A lot of house pets were innocently slain as well.

The Shankings occurred almost eighty years ago. But Sergeant Lafleur was wrong. Born in the first year of the Purge, I was there. I'd always assumed my birth parents died during the volatile time, shot down by a

Billy Joe or Betsy Loo. A small part of me hoped they still lived, giving me up for my safety, but I've never confirmed or debunked any of my theories. I might have family—a mother, father, sister, brother. Or I might have absolutely nothing.

Realizing Lafleur and Stan awaited a response, I mumbled. "Whatever. Do you want my help or not?"

"Yes," Stan said.

"After I'm done, you'll tell me who you spoke to on the phone?" I asked Lafleur. He inclined his chin with the slightest of movement.

"Where can I shift?" I asked.

Lafleur pointed to the public outhouses, available year round for the hordes of tourists flocking to the area.

I blinked.

My wolf huffed.

"For you to undress," Lafleur explained.

Ewww. "Gross. No. I'm not placing my clothes on an outhouse floor, no matter how upscale the area."

Lafleur grunted and shared a look with Stan.

"Told you she'd say no." Stan shrugged.

"Show her the van, then."

Stan nodded like a bobblehead. He waved low with his hand for me to follow, a little too much like an owner beckoning their pet dog for my liking.

"I'm not fucking Fido, you dolt. Just point out the van and when I paw at the door, let me out."

Stan's cheeks flamed red, and he pointed to one of the nearby vans. I stalked over to it without further commentary, Red close on my heels. When I threw the van doors open, two techs, both incredibly nerdy-looking, gasped and looked at me with round eyes.

"Out," I said.

They scrambled to their feet and scurried out of the van to stand by Stan and Lafleur. After they brushed by, I climbed into the back, waited for Red to hop up and slammed the doors shut. The van reeked of perspiration and many hours of too many people crammed in a confined space. A divider separated the front seats from the back portion I crouched in. No windows to reveal my naked form. *Good.*

I glanced around at the various switches and buttons and mini screens. The surveillance van looked exactly like those ones in the movies. Go figure. Hollywood got something right. Movement on one of the screens caught my eye. A man in a white plastic body suit moved around with a camera taking pictures. The bright flash distorted the images on the monitor every few seconds, blanketing the screen with fuzzy white. The camera man moved around an object and kneeled down to take another picture. Flash! What was that? Flash! Was that a…Flash! An arm?

My stomach rolled. I leaned forward. Between the flashes, I made out more of the objects. Five arms, three legs, one head, or at least half of one.

My wolf growled, *Death.*

What is it? Red stood on her hind legs, hopping up and down, and strained to look at the screen.

Nothing good, I replied.

A knock on the back door made me jump.

"You ready?" Stan called out.

"Give me a sec," I said. With one last glance at the screens, I shucked off my clothes and folded them into a neat pile on top of my shoes. Rolling my neck back and forth, I stretched before willing the change. Bones crunched and extended, muscles condensed and skin folded in upon skin before fur erupted from every hair follicle. The familiar sting and strain lanced across my body before my shift completed.

Hunt? My wolf asked.

Track, I answered. *Hunt later.*

Now a wolf, my senses heightened. The body odour of the techs flashed into my nose. One had a substance abuse problem; the other had a girlfriend who liked to drown herself in rose-scented perfume, and they'd had sex recently. Outside, Stan shuffled his feet back and forth, and the sour tang of his anxiety leaked through the doors. I huffed and raked my claws against the metal.

Stan grunted before opening the doors. "I hate that sound." His body shook as a shudder racked his body. "You did that on purpose, didn't you?"

I jumped out and opened my mouth wide, the closest to a smile I could achieve in this form.

"Look, I'm sorry I called you like a dog." Stan's lips twisted into a grimace, and he looked away, stealing a moment before he spoke again. "The crime scene begins a block that way. I figured you'd want to work your way in."

Stan pointed toward the docks on the other side of the van, and I bobbed my head up and down to show him I got the message.

Red hopped out of the van and jumped up to bump her small body against mine.

Not play time, I told her.

She leaned against my front leg. *I know,* she said.

Let's go see what all this fuss is about. I loped around the van in the direction Stan indicated, and knew after my fourth step my life had become more complicated. The faint scent of almond wafted with the breeze and grew stronger with each step I took toward the crime scene and flood lights. Demon.

My jowls curled up into a snarl.

Hunt now, my wolf demanded. *Not later.*

With short successive breaths, followed by a few long ones, I filtered through the olfactory messages to read the events as if they unfolded in the present instead of the past. The Demon's trademark stench stamped each horrid image after another.

And not just any Demon, the same one that had attacked the Vampire summit.

Times like this made me wish I could shut off my sense of smell. I rounded the corner store building, and the full force of the massacre hit my nose like a wrecking ball. I halted and recoiled from the power. Red screeched to a halt, and cowered behind my front legs.

Along with the overpowering demonic almond smell, old and new blood, flesh, bone, burnt skin and hair assailed my nasal passages—the stench so strong, my wolf eyes stung.

Taking a moment to acclimatize, I rubbed my snout under my front leg, trying to clear my eyes. Then I set out, skirting various charred body parts and pools of blood. The trail led to the docks and concentrated. Most likely the landing point. I turned around and tracked it back through the massacre site. The trail wafted up from the pavement and led to a short alleyway between the store fronts before it disappeared. I had what I wanted. Sprinting back to the van, I leapt into the back, Red close on my heels.

Stan closed the door, and I shifted as fast as I could, bone stretching, skin ripping. Fast equalled painful, but I didn't care. I needed the stench of the bodies out of my nose.

Red sneezed. *Awful.*

I agree.

After pulling my clothes back on with shaky hands, I opened the doors and scrambled out of the van to a waiting Stan and Sergeant Lafleur. The wind gusted off the ocean and carried the stench of the massacre to me like a tidal wave. I shuddered. My pulse raced. After the gust passed, I took short breaths to clear my senses.

"So?" Lafleur demanded.

"Awful," I said, parroting Red's previous word.

"Yes, and?" Lafleur said.

And if I punched him in the balls, could I get away with it? *Hmm. Doubt it.* But the instant gratification would be awesome.

Lafleur cleared his throat when I didn't respond immediately.

My eyes tingled as I let the cat partially shift. They'd glow yellow and gauging from Lafleur's widened eyes and the sickly sweet tang of fear rolling off of him, they had the exact impact I intended.

"It was awful," I restarted. "One Demon. Landed on the dock, moved to the storefronts, went on a rampage and then slipped around the Sweet Little Things gourmet cupcake store and took off."

"Landed?" Stan wrote down in his notepad. "Took off? This thing flies?"

"That's the only thing that would make sense. Plus, I smelled feathers," I said.

"How are you sure there's only one?" Lafleur

asked. He probably didn't mean to be a dick this time, it just came naturally.

"Everyone has a unique scent. All Demons smell like almonds, but each one has something different infused with it. In this case, the Demon smelled like burnt almonds, steel, blood, stagnant grass, and money."

"And money?" Lafleur's lips puckered up, and one of his eyebrows twitched. "Is that all? And you're *sure* there was only one Demon, with all those smellies floating around?" He waved his hand around in the air like a flamboyant fairy, presumably representing the errant "smellies."

"Yes, there was only one. The scents are fused together. It's hard to explain. That's the best I can do."

"Looks like another case for the SRD."

"Maybe not."

"Explain."

"A number of the norms weren't killed by the Demon, but by each other."

"Say what now?" Lafleur looked up from his notepad.

"The ones not burnt. The Demon didn't kill them." The VPD handled all norm on norm cases, which meant they'd have to work with the SRD on this one.

Lafleur swore.

"Andy?" Stan shuffled his feet. "How do you know?"

Now Stan doubted me? Super. Maybe he had to ask, to do his job, due diligence and all, but his question still rankled my skin. "The Demon's scent wasn't on them. At all. He never touched them."

"He?" Lafleur's eyes narrowed.

I swallowed. "I've smelled this Demon before." Should I share what I knew? It wasn't much, anyway. "He's got the head of a dog, wings of a griffin and body of a man. Stands about nine feet excluding wings."

Lafleur scribbled something down and then peered up at me. "That's consistent with eyewitness reports. The SRD will probably take over this investigation."

If they had eyewitnesses, why bother me? To confirm it? Didn't feel like they trusted my judgement as an "expert." My focus narrowed on Stan. He flipped his notepad closed, and looked at his feet. Coward.

Lafleur pasted a fake, half-smile on his face that didn't reach his cold cop gaze. "Thank you for your time, Agent Mc—"

"It's ambassador, actually," I snapped.

"My apologies. Thank you for your time, Ambassador McNeilly. If you think of anything else or find out anything pertinent to our investigation, please contact us." He held his hand out.

I stared at his hulk hand and the vice-like grip it represented and then back to his steely gaze. "The contact?"

"Pardon?"

"You promised to tell me who you spoke to from the SRD."

The wind changed direction and carried the putrid smell of dead bodies our way. I flinched.

Lafleur's hand dropped, and his face paled. He swallowed before answering my question. "So I did. It was an Agent Tucker. Know him?"

I did. And boy how I wish I didn't.

Chapter Seven

"Demons are like obedient dogs; they come when they are called."
~*Remy de Gourmont*

As much as I'd wanted to run to the SRD headquarters downtown and curb-stomp Agent Tucker's face, something else kept tugging at my dendrites. I *needed* to find out more about the Demon of Mass Destruction. Who was he? And how did he know me?

Wick's continued good health depended on me not only getting answers, but getting them quickly. Lucien had little patience.

I knew one fast, yet degrading way to find out.

And I needed the help of my karaoke-belting Witch neighbours.

When their apartment door swung open, the vanilla and honey scent of Witches overwhelmed my nose. One of my favourite scents, even if I associated it with tomfoolery and hijinks. These Witches had a penchant for retribution via pranks. And good ones at that. I'd sent them a threatening letter regarding their nocturnal karaoke singing, and they'd responded by tampering with my computer's autocorrect feature and packing my apartment with small cups full of water.

"Andy." Ben greeted me with a half-smile that

illuminated his plain face. He took a step back to let me in his apartment. "To what do I owe the honour? More karaoke? We could've used your shrieking last night."

"No doubt. I liked your Michael tribute." I snorted. They'd sung the greatest hits of Michael Jackson into the wee hours of the night, but this time instead of getting angry, I smiled and went back to sleep, comforted by their close proximity.

I walked into the living room where two of Ben's other denmates lounged on the well-loved sofas. Matt's green eyes sparkled behind shaggy, dirty-blond hair as he waved back, and Patty's lips quirked, my presence somehow amusing him. Everything amused him. He saluted me.

I nodded at the Witches before flopping down on the couch. Red jumped up on my lap. "I wish I was here for social reasons. Where's Christopher?"

The Witch in question, magically spelled into a mute, hated my guts, because, well, I'd called him a mute. I hadn't known his past or his vocal predicament at the time I made the comment.

Matt and Patty glanced at each other before Matt spoke up. "Haven't seen him since last night. Had a hot date."

Christopher? Hot date? Never expected to hear those two things in the same sentence. Not that he wasn't attractive in a gruff, logger-caveman kind of way, but Christopher could be a bit uptight, and surly.

My doubt must've read clearly on my face because Ben laughed. "Believe it or not, he's a hit with the female Witches."

"It's always the quiet ones," I muttered.

"They all want to try to 'fix' him," Patty said.

Eww. A scene of horny Witches in pointy hats trying to cure Christopher with sexual healing seeped into my brain. Doing the horizontal mambo on a blood-wrought pentagram surrounded by candles. Gross! More images flickered across my imagination.

Make it stop. I squeezed my eyes shut. Not working. Still there. "Thanks for that mental image."

"Anytime." Patty chuckled.

Ben opened the small bar fridge beside the sofa, and pulled out a bottle of beer. He held it out to me, but I shook my head. Shrugging, he popped the beer cap off with the edge of the fridge door, before kicking it closed. "So tonight's visit isn't social..." he prompted.

"No." I coughed into my fist. How should I start? "I need to summon Sid again."

Matt and Patty perked up from their spots on the couch. Ben took a long swig of beer before placing it on the fridge. At least he didn't spray the beer across my face like the last time I'd asked for a summoning. "Are you sure? He may ask for more this time."

"I'm not paying more." I picked up Red and placed her on the floor before getting up. The Witches studied me as if I'd grown three heads.

"When do you want to do this?" Ben asked, folding his arms in front of his lean frame.

"Tonight?"

Ben pursed his lips and looked over at his fledglings. "Doesn't give us a lot of time to bang out the agreement details."

"I'd prefer not to *bang* out anything, thank you very much," I said, placing my hands on my hips.

"Not getting any?" Patty quipped.

A growl ripped out of my throat before I could stop

it. The stare I cast at Patty must've conveyed the wrath and destruction I intended because he looked away and mumbled something of an apology. Slim and short, I could take him easily and the Witch-fledgling couldn't stop me, not even if he threw on that cute Irish accent he sometimes did when he was drunk.

"Stop dominating my roommates." Ben punched me in the shoulder. "That's my job."

My mountain lion hissed.

"Fine." I settled back into the couch and shushed my mountain lion. "Can you do it tonight? I know it's still a few days until the new moon."

Witches drew their strength from the new moon. The same night Wereleopards had to shift, and Werewolves and Vampires were at their weakest. Supernatural nature preordaining the terms.

Ben shrugged. "It will require more concentration on my part, but the summoning is manageable."

"Let's do this, then."

"Your place or mine?" Ben asked.

Usually I heard a more slurred version of that question after a heavy night of drinking. "Mine."

"Can we come?" Patty and Matt asked.

Ben shrugged and looked my way.

"Only for the summoning. Then you have to leave." No way would I let them witness my payment to Sid. "Same goes for you," I said to Ben.

Ben nodded, and turned to his brethren. "Get the stuff."

I really appreciated Ben not making me repeat my threats of pain and suffering. Made everything more efficient. The Witches squealed with delight and jumped off the couch, rampaging through the apartment gathering supplies. The smell of new crayons filled the room.

"Let's meet them over there," Ben said, taking my arm. I let him lead me out of his apartment, down the hall and into my place. Red followed, trotting along behind my heels.

"Why are you doing this?" Ben asked.

Ah. So he wanted me alone to interrogate me. "I need answers, and Sid has them."

Ben huffed a little, and his bottom lip squished under his top one.

"His price isn't that bad," I said.

"Is your dignity worth so little?"

My arms hung to my sides, and my throat grew suddenly thick. I cleared it, along with the emotions flashing through my brain. Did he think that poorly of me? I counted him as a friend. My heart stung. I took a deep breath and tried to wipe away some of the pain from Ben's comment.

The best defense was a good offense. *I have nothing to be ashamed of.* I repeated the mantra silently a couple of times before I cracked my knuckles and shoved a stiff finger in Ben's face. "Don't you dare judge me. You don't know what I've done, or where I've been. Trust me. This payment is chump change, and I'm willing to pay it compared to the alternative."

Ben's chin dipped to his chest as his posture slumped. He took a couple of deep breaths before speaking. "Sorry, Andy. I forget sometimes you've got all this baggage to deal with, and alliances pulling you in different directions. I just…worry sometimes."

That I'll lose myself.

He didn't need to say it, but the realistic danger

churned my stomach. I'd lost myself to the beast before, and I never wanted to repeat the experience.

Matt and Patty barged into my apartment, stinking of clean lavender, crayons and sweat. Matt carried a ceremonial knife, point facing down, and Patty clutched two boxes of salt. They vibrated with excitement.

Ben stepped away from me, and drew his shoulders back and straightened his spine. "Draw the circle," he ordered, taking the knife from Matt. The words he'd uttered hung between us, but Ben stalked around, all business.

Patty handed one of the boxes to Matt, and together they poured the salt out to form a large circle in the middle of my living room. When completed, they stood and looked at Ben. He nodded, moved toward the circle and drew the ceremonial knife across his palm.

Ben clenched his fist and walked around the summoning circle, letting the thick red liquid splatter at even intervals against my beige rug and along the salted line. The cleaning company I hired must love me by now. The bitter scent of his blood filled my nose.

When finished, Ben stood between Matt and Patty and they chanted: "*Hekate. Si placet, ancora nobis ad orbis terrarium. Gratias tibi ago.*"

I'd heard this chant before. *Hecate. Please anchor me to the world. Thank you.*

White Witches started a summoning by calling upon the goddess Hekate and asking her to anchor them to Earth. The more powerful Witches didn't have to vocalize the incantations, and I knew from experience that included Ben. But he chanted along with the others because he was their teacher, setting a good example. And he thought it looked more badass.

The importance behind the words hummed through the air. If Witches didn't properly anchor their spirit to the living world during a Demon summoning, a powerful Demon could rip the Witches from their roots, and pull them through the portal. Witches, apparently, were the cat's meow in the demonic realm, the ultimate play toy. That's if the Witch survived being torn every which way from the streams of demonic power in the portal. Anchoring was serious business. Given the alternatives, including an eternity as a Demon's bitch or shredding of the body, mind and soul, I got it.

The Witches continued chanting: *"Hekate. Si placet, advoco Daemonium Sidragasum ad nobis. Gratias tibi ago."*

Hecate. Please summon the Demon Sidragasum to us. Thank you.

Red ran around the circle growling. A shiver of anticipation ran through my veins as the air in the room rose with a familiar stir, rushing around and flinging my hair about, before a portal snapped into place in the midst of a powerful maelstrom. A dark figure crouched in the middle of the circle. The Demon straightened and turned to us, the last dregs of wind flowing through his hair.

"Oh, little Carus. I knew you'd call."

Chapter Eight

"I used to be Snow White, but I drifted."

~*Mae West*

After rambling off my terms like a wannabe lawyer, Sid ran a long talon against the inside of his arm and kept his eyes trained on me as he said, "By my blood, I agree to these terms and swear to hold my end of the bargain."

He'd agreed to the deal—dancing for information. His blood slid off his skin and fell to the floor in a dark thick pool. It saturated the beige fluffy rug that had been my favourite at one time. Not anymore.

I partially shifted my forefinger into a sharp claw and repeated the action with my left palm, reciting the same words. I didn't cut as deep, though. Show-off.

Sid smirked as if he read my mind, and the air in the room buzzed with energy.

And the heavy mouth-breathing Witches behind me.

"Out," I said, not making eye contact with any of them.

I waited until my front door clicked and the strong smell of honey and vanilla dissipated, though some still lingered. *Witches gone. No witnesses.*

"You're overdressed for what you promised, little Carus."

I released a long breath. "I'm not little. I'm five foot ten for fuck's sake."

"You're little to me." True enough. The Demon towered over me at around seven feet. A complete guestimate gauging the distance between my ten-foot ceiling and the top of his head. I had no desire to break the circle to take a tape measure to him.

"Then what do you call women who fall below five-five?" I wondered out loud.

"Petite? Stop stalling, and get naked."

I rolled my eyes and walked over to the side of the room to stick my mp3 player into the docking station.

Go to the bedroom, I told Red.

But—

Go! I didn't want her to watch, either.

She snarled, but ran to the bedroom. My fluffy duvet crinkled when she nestled into the sheets.

Heck, I didn't want any of my feras to watch. The idea of witnesses made my stomach churn. If only I could send the feras in my head to the bedroom along with Red. My dancing wouldn't suffer too much without their influence. The animal magnetism on the other hand...I needed that.

Look away, I told the three feras cohabitating my mind.

The wolf snorted and curled up into a tight ball. The mountain lion yawned and continued to pace, just in case I needed her. The falcon cackled. She may as well have said, "Make me."

I released a long breath and scrolled through my music. After I found the right song, I pressed play.

The deep pumping bass filled my living room, and my body swayed automatically to the rhythm. My feras perked up as soon as the music flowed through my bones, ignoring my earlier command.

I loved to dance. Privately. Not with a Seducer Demon panting in a salt circle waiting to feed off my energy.

Shame bubbled up my spine, but I pushed it down. If I blocked everything out, maybe…maybe I'd enjoy this, or at the very least, not hate myself. I needed to know about the Demon, and not just to protect Wick from Lucien, but for my own safety. He knew me somehow, and I probably wouldn't like the reason.

I let my head roll back as I unbuttoned my shirt and moved my hips, letting the animals inside guide me in a dance as old as time. The melody rolled out and rushed around, lifting the hairs on my arms as I anticipated the upbeat. My hands floated up, my legs moved, and I danced out of my remaining clothes.

Lost to me, were the frustrations of the day, of not knowing the extent of my true nature, the hurt and fear of being faced with a Demon again, the anxiety of two possible mates, the Vampire liaison job from hell. Gone. Flowing out of my body with each twist and turn and swivel. I forgot the present and let everything just *be*. With each turn and swing of my hips delayed, I made each move more sensual and smooth, yet primitive.

When the song ended, the heat burning inside remained, my heart still beat with the tune, my body hummed and vibrated with potent energy, until slowly the sexual charge seeped out into the silent living room, feeding the Demon. It took a while to open my eyes, to ruin the mood and crash back into reality. My skin crawled as if an invisible layer of dirt moved to cloak every inch of it. I swallowed and turned to face the Demon.

Sid stood in the middle of his circle, muscles tense, eyes aflame, hard-on raging.

Shit.

The deal was to dance until fifteen minutes remained before dawn, or when he finished feeding. Looking at his tightly-corded, flexed muscles, and a posture clearly indicating he prepared to pounce, not drift off to sleep and start snoring, I knew the terms hadn't been met.

"Do I need to keep dancing?" I asked.

Sid shook his head.

Guess I was off the hook for more air humping.

Sid watched me, eyes glittering like shards of obsidian.

I waited.

When he finally spoke, his voice came out deep and husky, verbal rough sex. "I'd give you anything, anything you desired, if you allowed me out of this circle, little one."

"Not happening." I grabbed my robe and threw it on.

"Have I mentioned how…happy…I am that you summoned me?" Sid's seductive voice coiled around me like a lover's embrace.

"Shut up." I tightened the hold on my robe. "Stop trying to lay the sex mojo on me. Don't waste my time tormenting me."

"Oh my, someone's testy." Sid held his hands up in mock defense. "Not getting laid?"

"None of your business."

"No need to answer. I overheard your conversation

with the *neo-bhàsmhor* and know it's true." He leaned in. "I could help you out, you know. On the house. No one would know."

"I'd know. And I already feel dirty." I clutched my robe closer. "The *neo-bhàsmhor*?"

"The primary human servant to your Vampire Master."

"Clint?" Why'd Sid call him a…what the hell did he say? Sounded like neo-whore. Sid must've met Clint before.

Then, an ugly thought struck me. "Stop eavesdropping on private conversations. It's rude."

Sid crossed his arms. "I eavesdropped because you looked unhappy with the *neo-bhàsmhor*. I remained close in case you needed my help."

I narrowed my eyes at him. "Out of the goodness of your heart? You want me to believe you care about my wellbeing?"

Sid nodded. "I have a certain soft spot for you." He glanced down. "Or should I say hard?"

I glared at him. What the hell was he trying to pull?

"Relax, Carus. Despite what you may think of us Demons, we have our independent interests to pursue and protect. You happen to be one of mine."

"Looking for a life companion?" *Oh my Feradea! Please say no.*

Sid snorted. "No. If you want me in a physical capacity, I'd be more than happy to oblige, because I feed off sex and am always hungry, but my interest in you runs deeper than that."

"Explain."

He shook his head. "Not part of the deal. Ask your questions, Andy, the ones you summoned me for."

"Who is he? The Demon that sabotaged the Vampire summit."

"He has many names. Caacrinolaas, Caassimolar, Classyalabolas, Glassia-labolis, Glasya Labolas," Sid pronounced each word and name slowly, watching my face. "But I believe you know him as Bola."

No reply or retort escaped my mouth. Instead, a big exhale of air made its way out of my lungs as I fell, face forward, and hit the floor.

****

A throbbing pain stabbing my head behind the eyes brought me out of the fog. With my face planted against the floor, lips smushed into the rug and arms splayed to the side, only two reasonable explanations explained what had happened. Either an invisible Mack truck had barrelled through my living room and smacked into me, or I'd fainted.

Crap!

I hadn't done that in decades. Ever since my botched Clint assassination, my inherent awesomeness in badass-ery had dissipated. Like a slow leak in a tire, each day I lost a little of the brutality I'd counted on as an assassin.

Red's head butted mine, and she licked my face.

Gah! I swatted her away.

"I was beginning to think I'd have to leave before you would wake and give me a proper farewell," Sid said.

Groaning, I rolled over to find the Demon sitting cross legged in the middle of the circle. Naked. Thankfully, he no longer sported a raging boner. Instead, he looked calm and relaxed, as if seeing my head bounce against the floor was a completely natural thing. Maybe it happened a lot in hell. I hauled myself up and mirrored his sitting position, carefully tugging my robe down to ensure my lady bits weren't visible.

"What can you tell me about him?" I asked.

Sid tilted his head to the side. "I think you know him more intimately than I do."

Instead of heat spreading across my face, cold rage consumed my brain, prodding me to lash out. "How do you know about that?"

"Bola likes to kiss and tell. He often shares the intimate details of his conquests."

"He didn't conquer me." My skin froze as my already cold blood turned to ice. Bola had violated me as had every male in my previous pack. He may have conquered my physical being with the help of his host body and Dylan, but he never broke me. Never.

No one had.

Red jumped onto my lap, and I unclenched my fists to stroke her soft fur. I wanted to bury my face into her plush coat and tune out whatever crap Sid had left to dish. But I didn't. I needed to hear what information he had, so I ran my hands down Red's side instead, and forced my breathing to slow down, and even out.

Sid raised an eyebrow, and studied my lap for a minute. "No," he said. "Bola didn't break you, but he enjoyed you despite the restrictions of using a host body. Thoroughly. And frequently, if his tales are true."

I squeezed my eyes shut and took another deep breath. My hand clutched Red's fur. She yipped, and I released it. "Do you *relish* in sharing these details with me?"

"As they're not getting you off, not particularly, no. I'm a Seducer Demon, remember? You asked."

"Is there anything else you can tell me about him?"

"Yes. And I will do so for free. Bola is a powerful Earl of Hell and commands thirty-six legions of Demons."

"Only thirty-six?"

"Each legion contains anywhere from four to ten thousand Demons. Each general purposely hides their exact numbers. Always posturing for power and control, for favour with Lucifer."

I cursed. "Do you command any legions?"

Sid tilted his head at me, but remained silent. Right. Why would he answer that?

"What else?" I asked.

"He is the master of manslaughter and bloodshed, and can control people to make them either love or kill each other. I don't think I need to tell you which of those two options he prefers." Sid paused long enough I thought he was finished, but just when I was about to speak, he snapped his fingers. "Oh. And he has a hard-on for science."

"He always appeared human, taking one of the Were bodies when Dylan had him summoned. He wore the Were's scent, too." A shudder racked my body.

"He lacks a human form, and hiding his scent is one of his talents."

"Any weaknesses?"

Sid tsked and shook his head.

Technically, Sid had met his end of the bargain. But rah-rah for me, it didn't appear like he wanted a dismissal, and a little night remained for more discussion. Anything I could glean from him now would be an added bonus. Hell, after my performance, I deserved some sort of deal.

"Do you like Bola?" I asked. *That's it, McNeilly. Just sit back and chit-chat with a Seducer.*

"Like? Demons don't *like*, silly girl."

"Just a bunch of sociopaths, then? Well, that confirms a couple of things for me, at least."

"We don't emote wishy-washy feelings. When we feel, it is not done halfway. We hate, covet, lust, love—"

I snorted. Love? Who was he kidding?

Sid narrowed his eyes at me. "Yes, some of us are capable of love. It is an extreme, fevered emotion. We do excessive emotions, and we do them well. We don't *like*."

"Getting a little touchy over my word choice."

"Just making a point."

"Didn't *like* it?"

Sid pursed his lips.

"Fine, then. What *extreme* emotion do you feel when you think of Bola?"

Sid paused and then something in his eyes lit, ablaze with fire. "Hatred. I despise him to the very core and depth of my being. Death is not suitable for him. I wish him obliterated, ruined, destroyed, yet still alive to feel it all, to experience failure and pain so intense he can only scream soundlessly at the agony. I wish to—"

I held my hand up. "I think I get it."

Sid's lips widened in a slow smile.

"So if I needed to hurt Bola, badly, you'd help?"

"For a price."

"What? Even if it means you get what you want?"

"I want you to pay my price more."

"More naked dancing? You can't be that hard up for strippers in hell."

Sid's mouth, opened and ready to comment, snapped shut. He blinked a couple of times before speaking. "My, my, you're judgemental. I don't think you should make assumptions about people based on their profession. Would you want people to do that to you?"

Is a Demon really preaching one of the commandments to me right now? "No, I wouldn't want them to *judge* me, but it wouldn't mean they were incorrect. Are you going to explain your pricing scheme, or not?"

"My price will be different for assisting with Bola. Information for dancing is fair, but interceding with an Earl of Hell? That requires…more."

"Aren't you Satan's assistant? Doesn't that rank higher than an earl?" I had no clue. Demon hierarchy wasn't covered in any books I possessed, and they didn't have courses on the subject when I went to university. Maybe now? Demonology 101? *Mental note: look that up later.*

"Technically yes, but in some ways it means I am more accountable."

"With great power comes great responsibility?" I tried to quote comic books as often as possible.

"I've heard that from somewhere, but yes."

"It's from one of the best comic book characters ever." When Sid replied with a blank stare I waved it off. "So what would the price be?"

"Blood," Sid said. "I want your blood."

Chapter Nine

"I have measured my life with coffee spoons…"
~*T.S. Elliot*

After the dawn brushed Sid off the face of this realm and swept him back to the nether regions of hell like the dirty scum he truly was, I bribed Ben with a twenty-four pack of his favourite Canadian beer to scent-wipe my apartment, and after he finished, I took a nap. I'd learned long ago lack of sleep resulted in loss of control. I may have successfully beaten my beast twice without going on a rampage, but there was no guarantee I'd be successful again, especially if sleep deprived. Caffeine could only do so much.

My eyes closed, and my body sank heavy into my mattress. A weighted numbness overcame every limb, while the crickets and birds outside sang me to sleep with a melodic lullaby.

And then the buzzer sounded. *Wha? Ugh. No. Go away.* I pulled my blanket over my head, and buried my face into my soft pillow.

It's almost noon. Are you still asleep? Tristan's voice purred in my mind.

What? Oh no! I must've broadcasted my thoughts, and being a Were, Tristan heard it. Noon? My head bounced up, and I stared at the digits on my clock. Red and glaring, 11:49 stared back at me. I'd been asleep for almost six hours. *Crap!*

I swear I just closed my eyes, I said to Tristan before flinging back the cotton sheets. With a long stretch, my limbs loosened and relaxed.

Then I remembered what I'd learned last night from Sid. My shoulders tightened, and my feras became agitated. The beast stirred.

Fly away, my falcon demanded.

It's okay. I'll come back later, Tristan said, interrupting my panic attack. *You need to sleep.*

No. No. I'm up now, I said to him. No way did I want to be left alone with my thoughts right now. *Just give me a second. I need caffeine.*

I brought some. His words rang like magic in my head, and a loud sigh escaped my mouth. The tension from my shoulders released.

I think I love you, I said.

I hope you'll say that and mean it one day.

My heart spasmed before picking up the pace, pitter-pattering in my chest like a drummer's tambourine. The conflict of my warring emotions doused the momentary happiness caused by Tristan's words.

After throwing on the closest available sweats and T-shirt, I shuffled to the bathroom, ran a brush through my hair, admitted defeat in that department, and then brushed my teeth. I might not be runway ready, but at least I had minty-fresh breath—a must when around Weres and Shifters and our acute sense of smell.

"Tristan," I greeted the Wereleopard as I swung open the door. My breath caught in my throat as I took in the sight of him. Just under six feet tall, and built like a rugby winger, his body fit mine like the perfect missing puzzle piece. Bright sapphire eyes, porcelain skin and brown hair so dark, it looked black in most light. I wanted to rub my body against his, and purr.

With angelic good looks, his complexion made him appear youthful, maybe early thirties in age, but I knew from his ability to quickly shift and some of his previous comments, his age was much, much more. Just another mystery of Tristan.

Want, my mountain lion purred and pawed at my skull. She wanted the Alpha. I did, too, but I also harboured intense feelings for Wick. Tristan was reason number one why I wasn't with the Werewolf Alpha, and vice versa. I used to make fun of heroines falling for two guys. Now, I got it. But this couldn't go on forever. I needed to choose between these two dominant men, or turn them both loose and go solo. My heart constricted with the conflicting emotions.

"Andrea." Tristan leaned in for a kiss.

I hesitated for a fraction of a second before meeting him halfway. When his lips brushed mine, a zing of energy travelled to my toes. Only one other man had that effect on me.

"Come on in." I stepped back allowing him entry, but he handed me a steaming coffee in a takeaway cup before gesturing for me to precede him into my apartment. He paused to shuck his sneakers off. I wished he'd gone first. His ass in form-fitting dark denim provided a world-class view.

Instead of jumping him, I put my nose to my coffee's sipping hole and inhaled deeply. Cappuccino, topped with cinnamon. *Mmm.* My favourite.

"How'd you know?" I asked, referring to the type of coffee.

"I take an interest in everything about you. On our date, you ordered one for dessert."

Totally forgot that. "Huh," I said. I had no clue what type of drink Tristan liked. How bad a person did that make me?

Hell already had a place reserved for me. Falling for two men—who did that? I didn't even know them well enough to identify their favourite drink. My muscles stiffened, and my chest tightened around my heart.

Tristan stepped up behind me, caught both arms and pulled me into his body before wrapping me up in a delicious hug. The skin on the back of my neck warmed as Tristan leaned down and spoke into my ear. "I like lattes with full fat milk, cream is even better." His chest rumbled against my contracted back muscles as a purr filled the room. "In case you wondered."

Geez. Maybe Tristan read minds, too. He certainly knew magic. Instead of tense muscles, my body threatened to melt into a puddle of goo.

I turned around in his arms. "It freaks me out how well you read me."

Tristan smiled and spun me out in a dance move completely foreign and alien to me. I almost dropped my coffee on the wood flooring. When I danced, it was all instinctual, animalistic. I still had no idea why it appealed to Sid. I'd seen myself in a mirror. I looked like a possessed terrier chasing a squirrel. But the move Tristan just made? It screamed formal training.

Pursing my lips, I watched him take a seat, all grace, reflecting a prowling leopard beneath his skin. Not that I minded the view or the visit, but why was he here? At least I had enough sense to get Ben to scent-wipe and clean the blood-stained rug instead of waiting to bring in the professional Witch cleaners. My place looked tidy and smelled fresh instead of reeking of blood, salt and Demon.

"So what's new?" Tristan asked.

"You came all this way for a progress report?"

Tristan tsked me. "I came all this way to see you and use the 'what's new?' line as an excuse."

"Oh."

"So what's new?"

"Aside from a rampaging Demon running around slaughtering innocent norms and supes alike, and my dear old *master* ordering me to find out who it is?" I shrugged and ignored my racing heart. "Not much."

Tristan blinked and leaned back. "Maybe start at the beginning?"

"Right." I sat down beside him to recount the events, first at the Vampire summit and then when Stan called me out to the crime scene in Steveston. I skipped Sid. I had to tell him, but the words wouldn't come out. Sitting so close to Tristan made my skin hyperaware. Every movement, every breath, every facial expression of his sent my neurons into a tizzy, racing around and stirring up all sorts of things; things I shouldn't want or act on until I'd officially chosen a mate.

If Tristan sensed my conflict, he didn't show it. He'd reached for my hand about halfway through my explanation, but otherwise, just listened. He took it all in, occasionally drinking from his coffee cup, or stroking a finger down the top of my hand.

"What's your next step?" he asked after I finished.

"Tell Lucien the name of the Demon."

"You know it?"

"Yeah. It's Glasya Labolas." A sour taste engulfed my mouth as if saying Bola's name soiled my taste buds. Chills shivered across my skin, and my head became light and dizzy. I watched Tristan's face intently. Luckily, no flickers of recognition flashed across his face. Not sure what I'd do if he knew of him. Would it change anything between us? Not really. Maybe.

"How'd you find out about the Demon?" Tristan rested his elbow on the plush back of the couch, and propped his head on his hand.

I held my breath, gulping down air every once in a while to stay quiet. I had to tell him, but how? How could I word the truth and hide my shame? I released a long breath, and met Tristan's sparkling gaze. His eyes narrowed a little, probably picking up on my apprehension, but he waited, patiently, like a cat.

I squared my shoulders and spoke. "I asked another Demon. Turns out it takes one to know one."

Tristan hesitated before nodding. "Same Demon you asked about the Kappa?"

"Yup." I stared at my hands.

Tristan frowned. "Why do you smell wrong?" His nose flared, his hand dropped from his face and he straightened. "Guilt?" He stilled. "What price did you pay?"

I forced my shoulders down from my ears and exhaled a long breath, leaving my lungs dry and empty. "The Demon I summoned is called Sid the Seducer. He has some sort of interest in me, but I'm not sure what. Maybe it's just because I'm Feradea's chosen. He said something once about how Demons liked to defile the treasures of the gods."

"Defile?" His head jerked, his body tensed.

"I danced for him. Last night and the time before, when I needed information about the Kappa. That's all. No defiling. He doesn't get to touch me. He stays in the circle the entire time."

"But?" Tristan asked, not missing a beat.

"But I'm naked. When I dance. For him." *Smooth, Andy.* My skin flushed and trembled with heat, pores sweating. With my chest tingling and nausea roiling in my gut, I gulped down my shame and waited for Tristan's response.

His chin lifted, and his nostrils flared, tightness creased his face. His gaze grew distant, the beautiful sapphire replaced with leopard yellow. Quiet spread across the room, and the mundane sounds of life surrounded us: the distant hum of someone's washing machine, the rumble of light traffic in front of the building, the idle conversation of a couple walking their dog down the sidewalk.

Tristan drew in slow steady breathes. For a second, I worried he might combust, but then his expression softened, and his shoulders relaxed. The leopard yellow receded, and his brilliant blue eyes returned to normal.

"I'm not going to lie, Andy. I don't like it." His tone remained stiff, and a bit deeper than normal. "I certainly don't like that some Demon has seen all of you, and in a way only a lover should."

"But?" I asked, trying to keep the hope out of my voice, and failing. I still had a tough decision ahead of me mate-wise, but the idea of Tristan walking away right now stabbed my heart like a sharp blade.

"But…" He took another deep breath. "I get it. I'm not an idiot, Andy. I know you worked for the SRD as an assassin. I know you have an animal magnetism that appeals to norms, and even some supes. I feel it. You must've used it to your advantage to lure your targets. How could you not? Your body and magnetism is a tool, an advantage, and a deadly one."

Tristan stared at his hands. His dark brows pulled down, making his angelic face appear more severe and stern. What was he thinking? He seemed to understand, but that didn't mean he was okay with me dancing naked for a Demon. If he couldn't accept this, he'd never get past the rest of my history. And if Tristan, the most level-headed Alpha I knew in existence, couldn't come to terms with my Demon bargain, I had no chance Wick would.

Fear of losing Tristan wiped away any lingering dread I harbored after learning about Bola. I waited as Tristan seemed to collect his thoughts. The air hung heavy between us. *Please, please, please, be okay with it.*

Finally, he looked up, sapphire eyes burning intense holes into mine. "You have a past, Andy. Me, too. We've both done things, things I'm sure neither of us like, nor are proud of, but that's what makes us what and who we are today, makes us stronger. Do I want you to do it again? No. But if it will save your life? Yes. Absolutely." He clutched my hands in both of his.

Wow. Just...wow.

"Uh." My intelligent response tumbled out of my mouth as I fought breathlessness I'd never experienced before. Butterflies danced the Macarena in my stomach.

"Besides, I'm a Were, you're a Shifter. Naked is natural. What I don't like is he fed off your sexual energy." He leaned in and trailed his fingers down my arm before kissing a path along my collarbone. "If anyone is going to feed off you, it should be me."

Oh boy! The incinerator in my core kicked up a notch. I mentally fanned my face.

"Thank you? That's incredibly insightful. And understanding."

"I've been around awhile." Tristan winked.

"And exactly how long is that?" Weres and Shifters practically stopped aging at thirty. So if a Shifter looked old, he or she was really, really ancient. Tristan looked around thirty-five, so realistically he could be anywhere from thirty-five to a couple hundred years old.

"Not telling. It will scare you away."

Probably a couple hundred then, at least. I was almost eighty. He'd probably seen and done a lot. How long was he under Ethan's control? How many awful things did he have to participate in?

I looked into his blue gaze before my conscience started to crush me, and I had to glance away. I'd have to be as understanding as him. Two-way street. We both had skeletons. Looking at the creases between Tristan's eyebrows and the knowing look behind his smooth seduction and laughter, I suspected Tristan had a shadier past than me.

He'd killed my handler. Ordered by his Vampire Master, Ethan, Tristan had no choice. What else had he been ordered to do?

My scalp prickled as if new hair shot out of my head.

Then another thought crushed me. Did I even have time to spend on Tristan or Wick right now? I needed to find big, bad Bola and put him down like a rabid dog. I shouldn't be holding hands with a hot guy in my living room or digging my nose into Tristan's personal history.

My head started to pound, and my body sagged with an unseen weight.

Tristan stood up and drew me with him. Thoughts of the Demon flew from my mind again. Running his fingers down my face in a gentle caress, Tristan stared intently in my eyes, his sapphire gaze glowing with intensity. He clasped both my hands in his and leaned forward to press his lips against mine. "Thank you," he said.

"For what?"

"For trusting me. For telling me some of your past. I know it wasn't easy, but I hope…" His voice trailed off, and his gaze cast down to the side while his fingers tightened on mine.

I squeezed his hand and waited.

"I hope we can trust each other more. Unearth all our secrets. I know yours aren't all roses and daffodils, and I hope you understand mine aren't either." He returned my hand squeeze. "But I want no secrets between us. If you…If you choose me, that is."

He dropped my hands, pecked me on the cheek, walked out of the living room, down the hall and let himself out, quietly shutting the door behind him.

I remained standing, right where I was when he last touched me, my feet growing roots into the rug. No secrets? He wanted to know *everything*? And tell me everything? He'd said something like that once before. He must really mean it. Could he handle the truth?

Could I?

Then something weird happened. A jolt in my body

led to a flutter in my belly and a tingle in my limbs.
   Hope.

Chapter Ten

"I figure if I'm gonna be a mess I might as well be a hot mess."

~Mindy, The Mindy Project

The hope tingling through my veins from Tristan's visit quickly faded from my body as guilt took over, again. Guilt for my attraction to Tristan when I also wanted Wick, guilt that I'd spent an hour getting closer to the Wereleopard Alpha instead of researching the Demon, and guilt for taking an emotional hiatus from my current problems.

My phone vibrated in my pocket and jerked me out of my head. I fished it out to find a text from Mel, one of my few girlfriends and a fellow survivor of Dylan's pack. I tapped the screen and entered my password to read her message.

I'm thinking about getting banged, she wrote.

I laughed. I couldn't help it. After the high stress of telling Tristan part of my sordid past, the eggshell gently encasing my sanity cracked. Oh no! I slapped a hand over my mouth, but the giggles kept coming, tumbling around my hand. Mel and I, and most supes over the age of fifty, found the constant revolving door of new technology difficult to keep up with. Autocorrect was a bitch, and both Mel and I had declared war on her, having lost many battles already.

Currently, I held second place, having told Wick I planned to pick up cocaine instead of coffee and asking Clint to "watch" instead of "wait" when I planned to take a shower.

But Mel? She took first place. She'd asked me to get penis instead of pedis and to go crotch shopping with her instead of shopping for clutches. Wick came in at a distant third, I suspected he proofread.

Getting banged? Yup. Mel was a victim, again, and clearly winning the race.

Did you want help...or? I replied and then waited.

OMG! I meant bangs! My hair...getting bangs!

I twirled my bangs around my finger before texting back. *Well crap! I was on my way over.* I laughed again. Mel knew I didn't swing that way.

Do you think they still sell flip phones? I want my old one back, she lamented.

Suck it up, buttercup. I think both bangs and getting banged will look good on you.

Sometimes you can be a real bitch, she texted.

I'm being nice!

Whatever. I have a hair appointment tomorrow. Want to meet me after and go for coffee? 3pm...ish?

Sure. I might have a Demon to hunt down and destroy, but I needed my friendship with Mel as well, for my sanity, for my recuperation. Besides, I had to tell her about Bola. I wasn't the only one to suffer from his attention in Dylan's pack. She had the right to know. I just had to figure out a way to break it to her gently. *Where's your hair appointment?*

Lola's.

Of course. I should've known. Lola's, an expensive and exclusive hair salon in the West End, catered to the very trendy and very wealthy citizens of Vancouver. Clint had once booked an appointment for me there. Anticipating I'd fail to meet Lucien's demands and Clint would get me as a toy, Clint's first plan as my owner had been to send me in for a dye job. He liked blondes.

With jet-black hair, gray eyes and ethnically ambiguous skin tone, it wouldn't have worked. Me and a blonde bob? Not a good idea.

My phoned rang. Stan. I hit the "Accept" button and brought the phone up. The screen heated against my ear and warmed my palm. The summer sun streamed through the blinds as I flopped butt-first onto my plush sofa and braced for the Stan-tirade.

"Andy." Stan's cop voice cracked the air waves. "You've been avoiding my calls."

Crap! When did he call? I tugged at my shirt collar, suddenly feeling a bit hot. Then I remembered smacking my phone a couple of times before I drifted to sleep last night. Well, this morning, technically. It must've been Stan. *Oops.* "Have not. I've been busy." Liar, liar...

Silence. Then, "I know what *busy* means, Andy."

"Oh? What's that?" I leaned back on the couch and rested my head on a cushion.

"Whenever my wife says she's busy, she really means she's going to stay home, sit on the couch braless and watch television."

The mental image of a female Stan doing what Stan described flashed through my brain and burnt a number of brain cells. No logic. Stan's wife probably looked nothing like him, but I'd never met her, and my brain needed a face. Now, I wasn't too sure I wanted to meet her.

"Yeah, I think we have a different definition," I said. "So did I pass your sergeant's little test the other night? He didn't seem too impressed."

"On the contrary. He congratulated me on my initiative for roping in a supe for assessing crime scenes."

"Roping in?" My left fist twitched.

"His words."

"Better be," I grumbled. "So why are you calling? Got another crime scene?"

"More than one. Don't you watch the news?"

"Not after they lumped me in a group they dubbed 'the killing trio.' "

"We have a problem." Stan's voice took a tired edge, or maybe I just noticed it now. The crime scene like the one we'd been to would rattle even the most seasoned veteran. "The number of murders and violent crimes has increased one hundredfold in the last two days. One hundred, Andy! The politicians are getting involved. And that never works out well for anyone. They're calling it an epidemic, like it's some sort of fucking disease. They're questioning the professionalism of the entire force and demanding results."

He took a deep breath and continued. "The media's eating it up, and now we have reporters sticking their microphones up our noses while politicians stick it to us up the...well, you know what I mean. As if we're not working hard enough as it is."

"Stupid polis." I used the derogatory police term for politicians, not only because Stan and I were buds, but because he should know how hip I could be. I'd never heard Stan talk for so long. He was more of a grunter.

"Yeah," he muttered.

"Similar crime scenes to the one I sniffed out for you?" My stomach rolled at the thought. I clutched my belly. I might be a seasoned assassin and desensitized to violence compared to the average person, but these crime scenes were different. My brain started to throb behind my eyes.

"The scenes are similar," Stan confirmed. "But we have a different description. It's not a dog with wings, or any Demon for that matter. Half of the crime scenes were just pandemonium. Norms killing other norms by any means necessary for no apparent reason. No Demon present for any of them that we can tell, but we have linked the incidences to one consistent element using security cameras. Shows up about five minutes before all hell breaks loose. Pun not intended."

"What is it?" I asked when Stan's nanosecond pause threatened to kill me with anticipation.

"A man."

"A man?" I pinched the bridge of my nose, but the pain behind my eyes continued to spread out.

"Just a man."

"No other description? That's not much to go on." How the hell did the VPD expect me to sniff out one man in a massacre crime scene?

"Caucasian male. Five ten to six two. Average build. Light brown or dark blond hair. Wearing a black hoody and fitted blue jeans. No eye colour reported. No one got close enough to see and survive. Might've been wearing sunglasses."

"So average white guy? Again, not much to go on."

I dropped my head on the couch as I thought about it. The pain lancing through my brain cells behind my eyes dissipated as a thought came to me. "Could still be the Demon."

"How so?"

"I've identified the Demon involved in your first crime scene. He goes by the name of Bola. We have…history. He can possess anyone willing."

"Why would anyone willingly allow a demon to possess them?"

"You'd be surprised."

"Will you be able to tell?"

"Maybe. Even with a human hosting the Demon, the area could potentially contain the Demon's scent. At least according to the references I've checked. In the past, this Demon masked his stench when in possession of a Werewolf, which is not a typical occurrence among Demon kind. He has a special skill. We'll have to hope he didn't care enough to hide his scent this time." My heart hammered against my ribcage. The idea of going to another slaughter caused by Bola made the acid in my stomach bubble up my throat. My mouth dried out.

Stan needed me. I knew Bola, all too well.

"Can you come and sniff out one of the crime scenes?"

I squeezed my eyes shut. Yes, Stan needed me, but I also needed to relay the Bola information directly to Lucien before he got torture-happy and mutilated Wick. I wasn't taking chances with a simple text or phone call. Not when he refused to release me from a previous debt due to a similar technicality.

I glanced at my watch. Still four hours until sunset. My breathing evened out, and my muscles relaxed.

Plenty of time to get to the crime scene and assess it before my little "date" with Lucien. "I'll meet you there in wolf form and when I'm done, I'll call you with the information. Just tell your men not to shoot the wolf, okay?"

He hesitated. "Meet me in Chinatown."

The jerk hung up before I could ask where in Chinatown he wanted to meet.

****

When I arrived at Keefer and Main, in the heart of Chinatown, I knew exactly why Stan didn't need to give further directions. Chinatown, normally decorated with vibrant reds and golds to my falcon's sharp eyes, now looked drenched and stained in the dark colour of thick, clotted blood. It coated the walls, sliding down in clumps of matter. Internal organs squashed like road kill. Lifeless, limp bodies and various body parts lay strewn across the sidewalks and roads. A few of those parts lay across doorways or through broken glass, as if running to escape the horror.

Thank Feradea I'd left Red at home.

When I landed in one of the alleys and shifted into my wolf form, my senses were flooded with new information. Bola's Demon scent punched my nose, over and over again, with each drag of air. Without a doubt, the Demon from my nightmares had been here.

A growl ripped from my throat. The thick fur along my back rippled, and I made my way out of the alley to find the VPD.

Officer Stan and Sergeant Lafleur stood at the end of a particularly bloody pool, their faces closed off, but their scents screamed outrage and fear.

Underneath the acrid blood and cloy of sweet

sweat, something familiar niggled at my brain. Something other than Bola's cruel Demon scent, something other than death. Something…argh! I lost it. I clawed the ground to stir up more scents, but the nagging smell slipped away, feather light in the wind.

I sniffed around the mangled and burnt body parts, more to ensure due diligence than out of necessity. Scouring the gruesome crime scene didn't yield anything more than what I figured out in the first two minutes. Bola had struck again.

Trotting across the intersection, I skirted as much of the evidence as possible and made my way over to Stan.

Lafleur saw me first.

He stiffened. Then he reached for his gun.

I froze, one paw off the concrete. Escape route. Where? My gaze darted back and forth. I was in the middle of an intersection. The white crime scene van twenty feet to my right was the closest cover, and if the sergeant had a decent shot, he'd peg me well before I made it.

Stan looked over at his sergeant before following his gaze. Stan's steely cop stare met mine, and his shoulders dropped. He placed his hand over Lafleur's and stopped him from drawing.

I relaxed and set my paw down.

Leaning in, Stan whispered into Lafleur's ear. At this distance, Stan's words weren't discernable with all the other officers and investigators milling around, but Lafleur's hand dropped from his holstered firearm. I continued forward and closed the distance. The immediate threat of death by firing squad might've been over, but Lafleur remained stiff. So I remained wary.

What was his problem? He'd seen me in wolf form before.

Hopping over a decapitated body of a young man nailed it home for me. A crime scene like this would make even the staunchest veteran tense, and a bit trigger happy. Especially a norm. Super powerful supes freaked me out, and I had an advantage. If I was a norm…I'd pack semiautomatics everywhere.

"Did you get what you need?" Stan asked me when I reached him.

I slowly nodded my head like a good little dog.

"And you'll phone me?"

I nodded again.

"What if she's the one doing this?" Lafleur snapped.

My head snapped in his direction. With my teeth barred, a low growl escaped my throat. I took a step toward the sergeant.

A blast sounded almost instantaneously when something like a sledgehammer exploded into my hindquarters. *Fuck!* I yelped and spun away. Pain lanced through my body, followed by numbness. A police officer sighted me over his handgun from across the intersection. His eyes narrowed, and he leaned forward.

I hopped behind Stan and Lafleur, both barking out orders. My heartbeat thudded in my ears, the numbness faded, and shooting pains ran down my hind legs. Not waiting to find out who won that argument, I scanned the area quickly and hobbled to the nearest alley. I didn't need an entire police department using me as target practice, or as a supernatural scapegoat.

Scapewolf? Whatever.

As soon as I rounded the corner I willed the change, and beat my wings hard to take off. Landing might hurt, but flying didn't require the use of my legs or butt.

Why are you hurt? Lucien demanded as I soared in the wind streams, trying to shake the ache. Damn that Master Vampire mind-link thing.

I glanced at the setting sun. How was he up so early?

Andy?

Stupid cops, I answered.

Come to me, Lucien's voice beckoned in my head. He lay a compulsion down in his words.

Already on my way. A closer proximity to Lucien meant faster healing, but I had another reason to head for the base camp of the Vampire horde. I needed to dump a whole lot of info-bombs on Lucien so he'd leave Wick alone. His compulsion to make me "come to him" was a dick move and completely unnecessary.

Good. Clint will meet you.

I groaned. Guess Lucien technically wasn't "up." Talking in his sleep?

Somewhere over Granville Street, the bullet dislodged from my body.

It hurt.

A lot.

Had it been a less serious bullet wound, it would've popped out when I first shifted into a falcon, but the bullet had struck bone and took its time working through the tissues. Much bigger in relation to the falcon's body size, the bullet burned every millimeter it moved until my body finally pushed it through the skin and expelled it.

With the air soothing my sides and gliding around me, I lost myself to the freedom of flying while my muscles and tissues knitted together.

Chapter Eleven

"Get your facts first, then you can distort them as you please."
                                                            ~*Mark Twain*

Wrapped in a fluffy white bathrobe and trying to ignore Clint's leer from across the room, I waited for Lucien to rise and grace me with his presence. In the twenty minutes since my arrival, my body had healed the bullet wound, and now only a distant ache reminded me of the injury. Before Lucien blood bonded me, bodily damage like that would've taken weeks to heal, but now, less than an hour. The one benefit to Lucien essentially blood-raping me. That and added strength. If I could get my head back in the assassin game, I'd be super-duper badass now.

"Andrea." Lucien's voice preceded him as he swaggered into the room, modelling his Italian good looks. With his thick black hair immaculately gelled into place and his crisp, unwrinkled suit, he looked ready for a runway, not for his morning blood smoothie. His face remained placid and indifferent, as if threatening Wick held no importance, as if ordering me here like an owner called his dog was of little consequence, and as if he remained completely ignorant and ambivalent to the slaughtering epidemic going on in the city around him.

When he smoothly glided up his podium and sat on his wannabe-throne, he laced his fingers together and fixed me with his blank gaze. "Tell me everything."

I cleared my throat. "The Demon is Glasya Labolas. He has other names, but he usually goes by Bola. He's an Earl of Hell and commands thirty-six legions of Demons, each of which can contain anywhere from four to ten thousand lesser Demons. He likes manslaughter and bloodshed, and can incite love or homicidal rage in humans. He prefers rage."

Lucien sat motionless, taking it all in while stroking the smooth wood of his armrests. "And the pain I felt through you earlier? How were you hurt?"

"I was asked by the cops to help confirm a recent massacre was the work of Bola. One of the officers on site got a bit trigger happy and took a pot shot at my ass. It's already healed." My fingers dug into the soft white fibres of the bath robe.

Lucien drummed his fingers and pursed his lips.

"Chinatown?" Clint asked.

"Yes."

"Did they request your services for Steveston as well?" Clint asked, sharing a look with Lucien that told me nothing.

"Yes."

"Why did you not report this arrangement with the cops to me immediately?" Lucien asked. "Steveston did not happen today."

"No, it didn't. That was…two days ago, I believe." Only two? *That's it?*

"Again. Why wasn't I informed?"

I shrugged before pulling my robe closer around me. "I didn't realize I had to report *everything* to you."

Lucien smoothly flowed out of his chair to stand directly in front on me. His hand snaked out, and clasped my neck. Leaning down, his face inches from mine, he whispered, "You are *mine*. You report *everything*. Is that clear?"

In case it wasn't, he gave my neck a little squeeze before releasing it. Lucien had a thing for gripping my neck a little too hard. Nasty habit.

"Perfectly," I answered, rubbing my throat. I needed to shake this blood bond. *Screw this guy.*

"This Demon." Lucien flicked his hand up in the air. "This…Bola…he implied he knew you. Now that you know his name, is it true?" He leaned forward, dead eyes watching intently. Even if he couldn't scent a lie, he'd feel it through the bond. At least he couldn't read my mind.

"Yes," I said. "I know him."

"Why didn't you recognize him at the summit? His scent would've given him away, even if his appearance didn't," Clint reasoned. His voice came from my right, but I didn't dare take my focus off the seething Master Vampire whose fangs flashed inches from my face.

"Answer Clint," Lucien demanded.

My shoulders sagged, and I clamped the fluffy robe in my hands to avoid striking out at one of the douchebags in the room. "I've never seen his demonic form before. He always possessed one of the Werewolves when my previous Alpha summoned him."

"Dylan," Lucien said. His body snapped up, straight again, and he moved back to sit in his seat. "Yes, Wick has told me of this Alpha."

Apparently everyone knew my past, or at least the worst part of it. That wasn't humiliating. No, not at all.

"And his scent?"

"He smells different when he's in possession of someone else's body. I didn't know that was possible. I've only ever met two Demons. He masked his body odour in the past, because there's no way I would've forgotten that stench."

"But now?" Lucien asked.

"He didn't bother hiding his scent in Chinatown or Steveston. His particular brand of stank clung to everything. I think he possesses the male norm that's been linked to all the crime scenes."

Lucien's face took on a thoughtful look before he flicked his hand at me. When I didn't react or respond, he leaned forward and whispered, "You're dismissed."

I turned to go when a dark shadow slipped into the room. As tall as an average male, around six feet, with the body of a turtle, Tamotsu represented a present-day mutant turtle. Technically, he was a Kappa, and technically, I controlled him, though Lucien believed otherwise.

Carus, his voice slithered in my head like a slimy reptile.

Tamotsu, I replied. *How are you?*

I exist, Carus. That is enough, for now.

My heart started to pang. Maybe I should... Mentally, I slapped myself. I shouldn't feel bad for this supe. He slaughtered a whole slew of supes to feed off their energy, and killed a bunch of norms to do it. *Existing* was enough for Tamotsu, for now. And later? I had no idea what to do with him.

I nodded in his direction to acknowledge his point, before turning back to the Master Vampire, now glaring at me for delaying my departure.

Another thought from the days of the Kappa Investigation trickled into my awareness. I turned back to Lucien. "Before I go, did you find the mole in your horde? The one who dobbed me in to the SRD?" I'd lost my agent status because of the mole, but instead of firing me, Agent Booth made me an Ambassador of Vampire Relations. She pissed off a lot of the guys at the top with the move.

Lucien's whole body twitched.

"There must've been a bug planted," Clint cut in. "All present at the time have been interrogated and cleared."

"So you don't know?"

"No," Clint conceded. His gaze flicked to Lucien. "You'd better go."

Not liking the sound of Lucien's teeth gnashing together, I bolted to the nearest window before Lucien found some new use for me, or before he threatened Wick's life or limbs in some new perverse way to get me to do his bidding.

Not prey, my mountain lion hiss.

Not sub, my wolf growled.

I agreed.

Chapter Twelve

"I didn't ask to be hated; I just don't mind being a bitch."

~Courtney Love

Arriving home in the wee hours of "I don't give a fuck" in the morning, I kept with standing tradition: ignored all blinking, flashing and vibrating electronics, brushed my teeth, and fell face first into my firm extra plush pillow-top mattress. Red's warm body pressed into my side as a reassuring presence.

The next day, I greeted the morning with no less than fifteen voicemail messages and texts. Wick wanted to see me this weekend. Tristan purred. And one lewd message from Clint where he suggested something to do with pot shots and my well-rounded ass. The rest were from Officer Stan Stevens.

In Stan's defense, I had promised to phone him with the Chinatown sensory details as soon as I got back into human form, but in my defense, being shot in the derriere tended to mess with plans, and it definitely wasn't a part of the deal.

His texts and voicemail messages, filled with concern and apologies, only served to piss me off more. I'd told him to brief his fellow officers. His negligence nearly cost me my life, or at the very least, my left butt cheek.

Taking a deep breath, I found Stan's contact information in my phone and tapped the "Call" button.

He picked up immediately.

"Andy!" His voice near hysterical. "Are you okay? Where are you? Do you need medical assistance?"

"It takes more than a bullet in the butt to take me out, Stan. Make sure to tell your fellow officers that next time. You know, when you forget to tell them NOT TO SHOOT ME."

Red yipped in agreement.

He paused and then let out a big gush of air. "Oh, thank god. You're okay."

"No, thank Lucien. His blood healed me." I didn't explain exactly *how*. Stan didn't need to know about the blood bond. Not even *Preternatural Science* or the SRD laboratory doctors could explain why blood bonds promoted accelerated healing in human servants. They just did.

"Look, I'm sorry, Andy," Stan said. "I told the other officers. I really did. The guy who shot you…he's a rookie. He didn't mean to."

"Anti-Supe?"

"No. Just scared shitless of anything and everything, really. And you were a wolf, which news flash, freaks most people out. He saw a wolf step toward our sergeant, and he didn't think."

"No, he didn't. I want a name."

"Absolutely not."

"I'm not going to hurt him, Stan." *Much.*

"Then why do you need it?"

"Just want to show him the friendly face behind the fur. So next time he will stop and *think*." I jabbed my finger into the side of my head a couple times, even though Stan couldn't see me.

"That's a bad idea. The guy's been suspended for discharging his firearm in an active crime scene without provocation. He's probably going to lose his badge, or at least get sent to therapy."

"Well, fuck you, Stan. I got shot in the ass. Make sure it doesn't happen again."

"I will! I will." A tapping sound from the other side of the line came through, and I got a mental image of Stan sitting on his desk clicking the end of his pen repeatedly on the desk. "So…"

"Yes, it was him. The Demon. A lot of the deaths were actually caused by the norms, though. The Demon's inciting homicidal rage and sitting back to watch the action unfold. Apparently, it's his MO."

"Don't say MO. You sound like a B-list actress trying to be a tough cop. Same goes for that polis term you used yesterday. I don't think a cop has used that term in two decades."

"I'd make a badass cop," I grumbled.

Stan snorted, and I stared at my phone. When I didn't say more, he cleared his throat and asked, "Anything on the human he's possessing?"

I shook my head. "No. Too much blood and emotions clogged my nose. There was something familiar about it though. But I couldn't put my finger on it."

"Don't you mean paw?"

"Oh har de har, Stan. You're so funny." Like I haven't heard that one before. Red snuffled at my feet before curling up.

"My wife thinks so."

"Well, that just confirms there's someone out there

for everyone."

"Then what's your excuse?"

"For what?"

"For not getting laid."

I hung up to the sound of Stan's laughter.

If I didn't like the guy or respect him as a cop, I'd block his calls and send the Witches after him for some practical jokes.

My phone rang again, and I jumped, nearly tripping over Red. She yawned at me when I shot her my death stare. I tapped the screen without looking to pick the call up. "You're an ass!" I growled into the phone.

"Good morning to you, too, sunshine," Mel replied.

I held the phone back and looked at the screen. Sure enough, not Stan. "Err. Sorry. Thought you were someone else."

"Obviously. We still on for coffee?"

****

Although I loved Mel with a fondness I normally reserved for chocolate, regency movies and swimming naked in the ocean, part of me secretly hoped Mel version 2.0 with bangs would resemble the Barbie dolls I gave "haircuts" to throughout my childhood. Not the case. She rocked the look.

Breezing into the small café on the corner of Denman and Haro, near the ridiculously expensive Lola's, she slid into the iron-wrought seat across from me and gently tossed her hair around in a manner that would make any shampoo model turn green with envy. "How's it look?" she asked.

"So good I'm debating whether to throw my coffee on your shirt or scratch your face off with my nails."

Friends should be honest, after all. My words came out snarky, but they sounded hollow to me.

Mel giggled. "That good? Sweet."

"Special occasion?" I asked, pushing the skim vanilla latte I bought for her across the table. Red settled beside my right foot and pressed against my leg. Her presence sent warm reassurance along my skin. I needed it to tell Mel about Bola.

My mouth dried out, and I took a couple of deep sips from my coffee cup.

She leaned forward, grabbed the cup with both hands and brought it close to her nose to inhale. "It's my anniversary today. With Dan."

"For when you met, went steady, or mated? Or are you such a hussy, that they're all the same?" My skin grew clammy. Maybe I should just skip the small talk and get straight to the point? Rip the bandage off.

Mel ignored me, and took a sip of her coffee. "Mmm. That's good."

Well, she didn't plan on elaborating, maybe this was my chance to tell her. I cleared my throat and drew my shoulders back. Now or never.

"It's the day we mated," she said, interrupting my planned speech.

It took a moment to realize she'd answered my question after all. Today was the anniversary of when she's finalized the mate-bond with Dan.

Some of the tension knotting my neck drained away, and I smiled on the inside. Mel had a calming effect on me.

"I'm glad you're happy," I said. "I worried after. When I destroyed the hold Dylan had on me and killed those sadistic wolves…I thought…" I gulped as old fears dredged up and clamped onto my heart. "I thought I destroyed the women, too. A backlash from killing their mates." Part of the reason I'd lived as a mountain lion for over three decades was because I couldn't face the guilt of killing the pack's women.

Mel shook her head. "We survived. The women didn't sink into depths of despair, not like those who lose their true mates. I guess it's different when the mating bond is forced."

I nodded, having thought along the same lines.

"I'm very thankful I found Dan."

"Well, it helps that you're smoking hot."

Mel reached out to whack me, but I jerked out of her way. "You're not so bad yourself," she said. "You have two hot Alphas panting after you."

"My animal magnetism is the only reason Wick and Tristan and other men of their calibre are attracted to me. It's my feras, not really *me*." I patted my chest.

Mel scowled. "You don't give yourself enough credit."

"I give myself plenty of credit. I've got legs for days, and my boobs aren't half bad."

"You're more than that."

"You're right. I'm also ethnically ambiguous, so not only do I get to field intrusive questions from nosy supernaturals about what I am, but dumbass norms as well."

Mel's lids drooped into a smarmy expression. "Hey baby," she said in a voice several octaves below her natural level. "You have a unique look. What are…er…what's your…ethnic background?"

We giggled.

You women are weird, Red said. She curled up and

tucked her nose under her hind legs.

"Men are idiots." Mel snorted and took another sip of coffee.

We clinked our paper coffee cups in a silent toast.

"How'd you meet Dan, anyway? I don't think you've told me the story." I mentally shushed my inner voice, the one demanding I tell Mel about Bola.

"I haven't had the chance. You've been too busy running around with a rampaging, incurable death wish."

"I didn't really have much choice, Mel." My heart sped up, knowing I could only stall for so much longer.

Mel puckered her lips. It should've twisted her face up into something ugly, but she looked like a pouting lingerie model.

Mel scanned my face while I took a big swig of cappuccino goodness. "You're right," she said. "But I'll save the story for another day. He took me by surprise. Let's just leave it at that."

"Why not tell me now?" My gut rolled. Dammit, I didn't want to tell her. I didn't want to see fear on her face again.

"Because I know the line between your eyebrows represents more than your continued neglect of a healthy skincare routine. You want to talk to me about something. Something you don't think I'll like."

I forced my shoulders to relax. "Fine. You're right. But I don't *think* you'll dislike the news. I know it."

"Spit it out, already. I plan to get laid tonight and if you stall anymore, you're going to kill my mood."

"It's going to kill it anyway," I warned.

Mel fixed me with a half-decent death stare.

"Bola." After all the warm-up conversation and

practice speeches in the car on my way over, and I still spat it out like a socially-inept teenager. Forget my ground game. I needed to work on my interpersonal skills.

The colour drained from her face. She gulped and put her coffee to-go cup gently down on the counter. "Bola?"

My body tensed as I watched Mel's reaction. The scent of sweet sweat wafted off her skin and stirred my feras. The wolf growled, demanding I protect her. My mountain lion hissed at her fear. She should be safe, always. I took a deep breath and continued. "I'm sorry. He showed up three nights ago at the Vampire summit, sabotaging a vote they held to decide on a Demon-Vampire alliance. Then he started a bloody rampage."

"Steveston and Chinatown?"

I nodded. "He took possession of someone's body, and apparently the Witch who summoned Bola forgot to limit his access to the mortal realm, or didn't care enough to. I thought you should know."

Mel nodded before she stared at her cup. Her breathing shuddered a couple times on exhale, but then her posture loosened. Mel had been one of the luckier women in the pack, if such a thing existed. She hadn't suffered from Bola's attentions often because she'd accepted the forced bond between her and David. As a sub, she hadn't acted out or been as defiant as some of the others. She still had to watch though. Watch as Bola was used as a form of punishment to teach the more dominant females a lesson. Like me.

Her hand flashed across the table to grip one of mine. She squeezed. "How are you doing?"

"I've been better." I hated the shake my voice took

on. It was always hardest to hide my true feelings from Mel. Like she said, she knew me well, including my past and all my tells.

"Do you want to talk about it?"

"Not really." I squeezed her hand back as images from the past slashed through my memory.

The first time I said, "No," and Dylan forced himself on me…

The first time he raped me in front of his pack…

The first time he ordered the other male pack members to join in…

The first time I gave up fighting and distanced myself from the pain and humiliation…

The first time Bola was present and participated…

My heart clenched in my chest. A wall of shame traveled up my body as nausea sloshed in my guts. Stomach acid bubbled up my throat.

I swallowed, mouth dry.

I needed to face my past. Some of the shame and guilt would never go away, but what happened wasn't my fault. Yes, I was a victim of Dylan's horrific and perverted abuse. But I survived. Dylan paid the price. They all had.

Except Bola.

Mel sat across from me and held my hand the entire time my emotions waxed and waned. Surely, she smelled the changes, reading my mental process as if I spoke out loud, but she remained still and silent, her presence provided welcome and reassuring company.

This visit wasn't supposed to be about me. As a dominant Shifter, I protected the subs and the weak. I was supposed to be the rock. My wolf vibrated in agreement.

"It will be okay," Mel finally said.

"What makes you say that?" I attempted a smile, but it probably looked more like a grimace.

"Because you'll get him," she said. The truth of her statement, her belief in its accuracy, warmed my heart. Mel smiled at me and squeezed my hand yet again. Her eyes hardened and narrowed. "You'll get him. For all of us. And you'll make him pay."

Truth, my wolf growled.

Chapter Thirteen

"The only thing that will be remembered about my enemies after they're dead is the nasty things I've said about them."

~*Camille Paglia*

My phone vibrated, and the ringtone's volume increased in strength. A female rock star belted out her classic song of love and battlefields. The iconic music blasted from my phone as I left the coffee shop and a shaken, but ever-confident Mel. I dug the noisy device out of my pocket, and glanced at the screen. Blocked caller. Only a handful of people had this number.

Not even telemarketers had caught on yet.

Are you going to answer? Red asked.

Nope, I replied and hummed along with the song. An ugly thought wound its way into my lyrical paradise. My pace slowed. What if Bola had struck again? What if he planned murder and mayhem right now? He could be walking on this very street.

My falcon screeched and demanded I shift to fly home. My wolf growled and the hairs on the back of my neck tingled like rising hackles. I froze on the sidewalk.

Stop it! I told my feras. *Be calm.*

The time of Dylan and his sadistic sidekick Demon was over. I would not allow fear to rule me again.

Never again.

I clenched my fists and started walking again, this time with a bit more stomp in my gait.

The song finished, and my phone stopped vibrating. If the caller had legitimate reasons for calling me, they'd leave a message. I shoved the phone back in my pocket. More relaxed, I strolled to where I'd parked the Poo-lude. Destination: Home. Time to make a list of my priorities before Lucien called me back and ordered me to take care of Bola.

My ringtone started again, shrieking from my pocket about heartaches.

I shimmied my phone back and forth to wrench it from the clutches of my jeans just as the chorus started. I might have to rethink skinny jeans. Not only impractical for quick shifting, they made accessing my phone extremely difficult. I looked like a contortionist every time I had to pull it out. *Why'd I let Mel talk me into them?*

I stared at the phone. Blocked caller. Again. A persistent unidentified caller.

What's the worst they could do over the phone?

With my index finger, I jabbed the "Accept" button and said, "Hello?"

"Ambassador McNeilly?" a familiar voice asked.

Where had I heard this smooth, yet grating voice before? The kind that shredded nerve endings. "Yes. Who is this?"

"This is Agent Tucker." He paused for effect, and boy did he get one.

My phone creaked as my hand convulsed around the plastic in a death grip. Fucking Agent Tucker. If a zombie apocalypse or a second Purge left only me and this guy on the planet together, I'd rather swap spit with lifeless corpses or dance naked for the entire demonic realm than remain alive with him as my sole companion.

When he'd asked me for the location of my fera, I'd reacted by trying to strangle the life out of him—a completely natural and understandable reaction from any Shifter's point of view—and now he seemed hell bent on making my existence on Earth miserable.

I'd rather sit braless with Stan's wife watching cop drama reruns than speak to this guy. *Fucking Agent Tucker.*

"Ambassador McNeilly?"

Oh crap. He'd been talking. "What?"

"Did you hear anything I just said?"

"You had me at hello."

A pause. "I didn't say hello."

"I know."

"McNeilly, do you know the whereabouts of Agent Booth?"

Amusement bubbled up my throat. Agent Booth had been my previous supervisor at the SRD. I liked her. She'd turned out to be an Egyptian goddess searching for her long lost husband, Sobek. After she used me to run him down, she'd left the SRD. Pretty sure she was off somewhere doing the dirty with Sobek. Did I know her *exact* whereabouts? "No."

"I don't believe you."

"Are you going to haul me into the SRD headquarters and strap me to your machine?" I'd pass that question with his stupid norm lie detector with flying colours.

"Don't tempt me."

If I didn't have a hectic life, I'd antagonize him on a full-time basis. Let him bring me in and waste taxpayer dollars. Maybe Daddy, the Director of the SRD, would have to have a stern word with his son about the appropriate use of taxpayers' money, instead of feeding him everything on a personalized, gilded spoon.

"I'll try not to," I said.

"Did you know she was missing?" Tucker asked.

As I continued walking, I turned down an alley, and my canary yellow car came into view. It looked different. Something bright red now adorned the side and faint waves of spray paint floated on the light breeze.

Motherfucker!

I stood beside my crappy car, and limply held my phone. Tucker's irritating voice screeched out of the speakers, but I ignored him to stare at some wannabe-hoodlum's attempt at creating an artistic rendition of male genitalia on the side of my car. Bright-red cock and balls.

The artist took time detailing the veins and...er, fluids, but the image wasn't remotely close to being anatomically correct

This was the last time I parked this hunk-of-junk in an alley.

"Andrea?" Tucker's nauseating voice cut through my rising anger. "ANDREA!"

"What?" I brought the phone back up to my ear. Oh right, he'd asked if I knew Agent Booth was missing. "Agent Booth is gone?"

"Yessss," Tucker said. The way the "s" slithered out, I got the impression he'd lost patience with me.

Maybe he clenched his jaw? Maybe he ground his teeth? Good. I hoped he broke a tooth.

"She wasn't in her office the last time I came in for a visit, but I didn't think anything of it." Truth! I fingered the red paint. Dry. Dammit. I'd have to drive through rush hour with this.

"Of course not." Something crinkled in the background. It sounded like Tucker balling a bunch of papers in his fist. Then he released them and exhaled a quiet breath, as if relaxing.

Oh crap.

"Due to Agent Booth's recent disappearance, I've been promoted within the organization."

Double crap.

"Part of my promotion is to assume some of Booth's previous responsibilities."

Triple crap. I could hear his smarmy smile from across the phone.

"I'm now your acting supervisor."

And there it was. The nail in the proverbial coffin. What harm could answering my phone cause? A massive brain hemorrhage, also known as a headache. It started behind the eyes, making my vision blurry, before radiating out to start a deafening throb at the back of my skull.

"Ambassador McNeilly?"

"What?" I snapped.

"I'd like you to come in to discuss some of your recent activities."

Oh goody. This got better every second. "Do I have a choice?"

"Of course not."

"When?"

"Now."

I rotated my wrist to check my watch. Four in the afternoon. Dang it. He'd have me for at least an hour before the end of the day. "I can get there in half an hour."

"You can get here in ten."

"I'm not shifting in front of you." No way did I want Tucker to see me naked. Plus, I didn't know if he was aware of my multiple shapes. No need to let the Carus out of the bag.

"Your phone GPS indicates you're in the West End. You're a couple blocks away from the downtown office. Leave your crap car and walk over. I'll see you in ten." *Click.*

I glared at my traitorous phone. GPS? He'd tracked my phone? How'd he even get this number? Stan? Sergeant Lafleur?

Red's beady little eyes stared up at me.

Looks like we're making one more stop, I told her.

Chapter Fourteen

"I like long walks, especially when they are taken by people who annoy me."

~Fred Allen

With heavy feet and a heavier heart, I dragged my body through the main floor of the downtown SRD office with Red close behind. The entrance and hard tiles seemed more expansive than the last couple of times I'd been here. The sterile smell, more irritating. Talking with Mel had been emotionally exhausting, and the prospect of sitting down to "talk" with Agent Tucker drained any extra energy I possessed.

Ben and Matt glanced up from their post at the main desk. When I'd first met them, I thought they were the most boring SRD Witch guards in existence. Now, I knew better. Now, I loved that I had friends who worked security at the SRD.

"Hey you!" Matt greeted me with a smile. "What brings you in?"

"Agent Douche Nozzle," I grumbled.

Matt's eyes widened before confusion consumed his plain facial features.

"Agent Tucker?" Ben asked in a whisper.

"I think I love you a little more now." I leaned against the counter and flapped my hand, palm up, for the clipboard. "You guessed right."

Ben snorted and gave me the sign-in sheet. "You're not the only one to call him that," he said. "Well, actually, your choice of words is more creative, but the staff around here has several names for him."

"You, too?"

Ben tsked and shook his head. His gaze cut to the security cameras. He'd probably said too much already. Of course, Tucker would monitor the staff.

I shrugged and exchanged the clipboard for a "Guest" name tag. I clipped it to my shirt and inhaled a deep breath, trying to relax my muscles. "Great finale last night. 'I want to know What Love Is' sounded pretty awesome with all of you belting it out together."

Matt's chest puffed out a little. "Thanks! My pick. I love Foreigner."

Ben squinted at me. "Cut the crap, Andy. We sucked, and Matt couldn't hit the right note if we spelled him—"

"Hey!" Matt said.

Ben turned to him quickly. "It's true. Get over it." Then his full attention swung back to me. "Why the compliments?"

"Just buttering up the security."

"What for?" Matt asked at the same time Ben groaned.

"In case she loses it and attacks Tucker," Ben explained, confirming his spot as my favourite Witch. He *got* me.

"Oh," Matt said.

"Don't worry." Ben turned to me and leaned forward to whisper with a conspiratorial flourish, "We'll let you finish the job before apprehending you."

"Oh, I know," I whispered back. "I'm being nice so

you don't fling any of those nasty curses at me."

"Tucker's taken Booth's old office. I trust you know where to find it?" Ben asked in a loud voice.

"Yes, thank you for your assistance," I said and flounced through the metal detectors before making my way to the elevator.

****

The Wereleopard receptionist with a petite curvy body looked up from her desk when I entered the main office area on the tenth floor. Angie, or Angelica as she liked to be called, and I had history. I suspected she loved Tristan in more than an I-respect-you-as-my-leader way, but so far, nothing had come to blows, or scratches. Just a few silent hisses. She wasn't his mate, and they'd never been involved intimately.

"Ambassador McNeilly. Agent Tucker is expecting you," she said. "Please go on through."

Huh? Since when did Angie act like a proper receptionist? When I stood gaping at her, Angie widened her eyes and jerked her chin toward Booth's old office. Ah, since Booth left and Tucker replaced her. What did that mean for Angie?

I nodded, and walked down the hall to Tucker's office.

Fucking Agent Tucker. Propped against Booth's former office doorway stood the average-looking norm with hazel eyes and expensive cologne. He directed a condescending look mixed with hatred at me. "Ambassador McNeilly," he said in a smooth voice that scraped against my nerves.

"Agent Tucker."

Without another word, he spun around and sauntered into his office. Guess he expected me to follow? I did. No point in running away now, but the idea I kowtowed to this prick set my back into a straight line.

Can we kill him? Red asked. My other feras growled and shrieked their approval.

No.

Walking into the room, the sharp contrast of Tucker's style compared to Booth's struck me sideways. With the exception of a few random trinkets on her desk, Booth's office had been sparse and professional. Within the same space, Tucker managed to alter the room into a shrine to, well, Tucker. No standard certificates or awards mounted in a tasteful manner. No. Instead, a large realistic painting of himself in a quasi-Thinker pose hung on the wall. On the shelves, intermittent between books I'd never heard of—*The Stranger*, by Albert Camus, *Portnoy's Complaint*, by Philip Roth and *Infinite Jest*, by David Foster Wallace—were strategically placed photos featuring Tucker with famous celebrities, politicians and his dad, the Director of the SRD.

The acid from my stomach bubbled up my throat. Maybe if I threw up, he'd cut this meeting short?

Not wanting to make eye contact with Tucker longer than necessary, I continued to analyze his bookshelf while he rummaged behind his desk looking for something.

Catcher in the Rye, by J. D. Salinger? What? Did Tucker feel misunderstood, like Holden Caulfield? I shuddered. I didn't plan to be the first person to delve into that hot mess of a brain.

Part of me wished Tucker horded a collection of regency romance novels. It might make him a tad more tolerable.

Tucker made an "Aha!" noise, and I turned to face him. He'd taken a seat and pulled out a file from his desk drawer. My file. The one Angie had told me disappeared with Booth. The one I'd never looked inside, with all my personal details and most likely information about my family prior to my adoption. The one with all the coffee mug stains. The little circles somehow endeared me to the beige parchment. The errant papers that had poked out last time must've been reordered, because the file looked neat, tidy…and thinner?

"Have a seat, Ambassador McNeilly. We have a lot to discuss."

I bit down hard, and did as ordered.

"You've been working with the VPD," he stated.

"I have."

"You don't feel that's a conflict of interest, working for a competing agency?"

"First off, I don't view them as competition. I view the VPD as an agency of equal standing from the norm side of the law. I think we should work together more often and pool resources."

"That would put a lot of people out of jobs."

"I disagree. As long as assholes continue to exist, there'll be work for us."

Tucker blinked. "Sharing resources and aiding them in an active investigation without approval is not only a COI, but against our regulations and policy. Information that protects the best interests of supernaturals should remain private."

Somehow Tucker hadn't learned repeating things like a parrot didn't make them any more true.

"Well, if a supe breaks the law, I see no reason to continue protecting them. But that aside, as I am no longer an agent, I'm no longer bound by the SRD's rules and regulations. I'm an ambassador between the SRD and Lucien's court. COI's don't apply to me. I'm a contractor."

"Your contract and ambassadorship can be revoked if you don't fulfill your duties, you abuse the position, or your integrity has been compromised. It's made very clear under article 15.3a of the SRD's Code of Ethics. I can have a copy sent to you, if you'd like."

"Sure. Please send it along with the code of ethics that defines abuse of power, particularly the section pertaining to supervisors in the SRD."

If looks could kill, I would've died instantaneously from Tucker's glare. "Your file's been cleaned. Know anything about that?"

It took me a moment to process Tucker's words. *Thank you, Agent Booth!* She must've removed some information before she left. So I hadn't imagined it, the file did look considerably thinner than last time.

Tucker cleared his throat.

"News to me. Shouldn't it all be electronic nowadays anyway?"

"Can't trust technology."

"It appears you can't trust your filing system either."

Tucker pursed his lips. "So you know nothing of this?"

"Nope."

"How convenient." He didn't look like he believed me, but I didn't care. I glanced at the clock on the wall. Despite Tucker's demands, I'd taken my time walking here and only fifteen more minutes remained in the work day. Tucker struck me as the type to sign out right on time. No need to put in the extra effort. He'd get the promotion anyway.

"Is there anything else you'd like to discuss?"

My mountain lion hissed. *Claw his face off.*

Tucker pursed his lips. His fingertips turned white as he clutched his pen. He glanced at the clock. "No. That's all for now."

Part of me wanted to comment on how he'd wasted my time, calling me in for such trivial questions, but the other part wanted the hell out of his office before I actually did something to jeopardize my position with the SRD.

Fly, my falcon squawked at me. *Be free with the wind.*

"Then have a great day," I said, wearing my best fake smile.

"You, too," Tucker replied. He didn't bother smiling, nor did he bother trying to add false sunshine in his voice. No, he spoke with evident hatred, and his eyes told me he wished the exact opposite of what he said.

Right back at you.

Chapter Fifteen

"The truth will set you free, but first it will piss you off."

~*Gloria Steinem*

With my head nicely rested on an extra soft pillow, I lay on the couch in my living room and flicked through the channels in a pathetic attempt to distract my errant brain. Every time I thought of ways to introduce Bola to my fists, knees and elbows, nausea boiled in my gut and chest. In order to take the Demon out, I'd have to get close to him, and the very thought… My stomach churned again.

I thought I'd faced my past, and aside from a couple flashbacks, conquered it. Apparently not. Opening myself to the possibility of love and stronger friendships must've opened the floodgates to other feelings as well. With my knees drawn to my chest, I wrapped myself in the fetal position.

I didn't need to confront Bola. Yeah, he was on a killing spree and a lot of good, innocent people were dying, but it wasn't my job to save the world, right? The bigger, badder supes in the area, or heck, even the authorities, could handle it, right? I could just sit this one out…right?

I took a deep breath.

Maybe I looked at this the wrong way. These

resurging feelings of fear needed to be converted into something useful. Every time Bola entered my mind, I reverted to my old self, the one from over five decades ago who stayed with a psychopath and became weak, abused, and scared. I needed to confront my past, and this time, vanquish it.

Weak? Fearful? Not me. Not anymore.

A switch inside me flipped. The fear rolling through my veins in waves dissipated, soon replaced with something much warmer and deadlier. With a shake of my head, I clenched my fists. I should track down this piece-of-shit Demon and gut him repeatedly for what he did to me. Not roll up in a ball and tuck my head.

The beast stirred.

Revenge. Her growl vibrated my whole body making me sit up.

Hunt, my mountain lion hissed.

Kill, my wolf growled.

Devour, my falcon screeched.

Red yipped and jumped on the couch to snuggle into my stomach.

Well, at least my feras were on board for some retribution.

One of my favourite songs blasted from my pocket. I dug my phone out and accepted the call, knowing the caller by the personalized ringtone.

"Mel? What's up?" I spoke into the phone.

"Something's not right," she whispered. The phone line crackled, and I missed what she said next.

"What? You're breaking up." My thoughts of revenge fled, and my senses tingled, now hyper-alert.

"Something's…no…ight…t…ack.   F…ting.

Get…er he…ow." Her voice clipped off, and the dial tone rattled my ear.

The blanks didn't matter. I needed to get to the pack house right away. I jumped off the couch, threw open the window and shifted into a falcon. As my clothes drifted off my smaller body, I took to the night in a seamless transition. Only when I was aloft in the air did I realize I'd have to deal with whatever I found at Wick's place without any clothes.

****

When I flew through the window and shifted to my human form, I tensed into a fighting crouch. Werewolves everywhere. Some still in human form with blazing yellow eyes, some half-shifted and snarling, some in full wolf form growling with their hackles up. They had turned on each other, and almost every Were in the building was fighting. Ripped clothes and overturned furniture littered the floor.

Looking more like a Spring Break episode on 'roids than a pack house, everyone had gone to the left side of coo-coo. The room filled with the smell of burnt cinnamon and foggy smoke. Sounds of growling and yipping flooded my ears. My teeth tingled and shifted into fangs; the taste of blood burst into my mouth.

John bumped my shoulder as he and another male wrestled in human form passed me. I hissed at them without thinking. *What the heck?* I shook my head, and stepped back until my spine pressed against the wall.

Blonde hair to my right snagged my attention. Mel cowered in the corner, her face creased with concern.

I jogged around the snapping Weres, and knelt beside her. "You okay?"

She nodded. "It's only affecting the dominant

wolves."

"What is?"

"Whatever this is." She waved her hand at the chaos.

"Is anyone hurt?"

"No, but I think Steve and Ryan are working hard to change that." She pointed across the room. Sure enough, Steve and Ryan rolled around on the floor, with red, strained faces, clutching each other's necks.

"I can't get them to stop," Mel said.

"Where's Wick?"

"He left before it started." She turned away.

Huh? What did Mel avoid telling me? "Where did he—oh screw it, I'll fix this first." I stomped over to the two Weres, one who despised me and the other who didn't.

I thumped Steve in the side with my foot. "Oi! Stop it."

They kept rolling and ignored me. The lycanthropic virus made Weres stronger than Shifters, so I couldn't use physical means to pry them apart. Not unless I shifted to the beast, but that seemed a bit…excessive. I watched as they continued to squeeze.

Ryan's normally freckled pale face turned a darker shade of red. Steve snarled something unintelligible. His café-au-lait skin looked severely burned, and his gem-green eyes bugged out of his face. Maybe if I poured something on them?

The front door slammed shut. "What the hell is going on?" Wick boomed.

Everyone went limp. At least, everyone within my field of vision. Steve and Ryan sagged to the floor, and rolled away from each other. They got slowly to their feet and cast confused, yet wary glances at each other. My skin prickled.

"Well?" Wick demanded.

Ryan scratched his head. When he caught me looking, he scowled and dropped his hand. Well, I deserved that. I had used my "feminine wiles" on him to escape the Were house back in the good ol' days when Wick held me captive for Lucien. I'd sprayed dog repellant in Ryan's face, to buy enough time to shift into a falcon and fly away.

He hated me.

Understandably.

Wick growled, and his espresso irises flashed yellow. The power of his dominant Alpha wolf steamrolled through the room, making me want to crawl on the floor and grovel.

Not happening.

The Weres in the room dropped to their knees, and bowed their heads. I locked my knees and braced. My inner wolf mewled, wanting to flop in front of him, belly up.

"Answer me, Ryan," Wick repeated, this time making it a command. I'd never seen Wick use his power in such a direct, brow-beating way. Heat spread across my chest, and I squashed the urge to cross the room and rub against him. His dominance was super sexy.

Want, my wolf growled. I shushed her, and waited for Ryan to answer. His face had drained away the flushed red. Now, his skin looked pale and pasty.

"I'm not sure what happened. One minute we're watching our zombie show on television, the next, Steve was in my face," Ryan said. Sweat broke out along his nose and forehead. As Wick's second in the pack hierarchy, he stood accountable for anything that happened in Wick's absence.

"How?" Wick asked. "How did he get *in your face*?"

"He, uh, he started making fun of me. Telling me a real man wouldn't have let Andy escape."

I flinched. Ouch. Even I knew that was a low blow. My stomach dropped. I wasn't proud of my actions with Ryan. Despite trying to escape an unknown fate with Lucien, Ryan deserved better treatment.

Wick's eyes narrowed, and he turned to Steve. "Is that true?"

Steve nodded. "Yeah, I said something like that. But only after an underwear commercial came on, and Ryan made fun of my job. Said the reason I got cut from the HOM campaign was because my junk wasn't big enough to fill the briefs properly."

I grimaced. Damn! These Weres fought dirty. Plus, I'd seen Steve naked after a shift. Not true.

Wick's face pinched, and his mouth flattened into a thin line. "This isn't like either of you. What happened?"

Ryan hesitated. "I just had enough and got angry."

"Me, too," Steve said.

The others in the room joined the discussion, agreeing they felt the same.

Unease flittered in my stomach. Did Bola have something to do with this? He'd controlled Weres in the past. Had he targeted Wick's pack on purpose, or was he nearby causing murder and mayhem, and this just demonstrated the side effects of close proximity?

"Is the anger still there?" Wick asked.

"No," Steve said.

"It's gone," Ryan agreed. "It dissipated when you arrived."

Huh. The pack must've been caught up in a wave of Bola's power, but Wick's Alpha power dissipated the effect when he came home. What was Bola up to?

Wick's facial expression relaxed, but the tension in his shoulders remained. "Clean up," he ordered. Then he turned to me, his gaze flickering quickly to take in my naked state. "Not that I dislike the visit, but how are you mixed up with this?"

"Mel," I said. My one word answer was enough.

Wick nodded. "Let's go upstairs and talk."

My gaze darted to Mel. She shooed me away with a wave of her hand before turning to her mate. He appeared okay. Dan looped an arm over Mel's shoulders, and pulled her into a hug. She'd be okay, too.

Wick let me walk up the stairs ahead of him, but for once, I didn't suspect him of checking out my ass. Bleach with a hint of sweat filled the stairwell and eliminated any need on my part to ask Wick if he worried about what just happened. He was worried, all right, a lot.

When we stepped into his room, Wick closed the door behind us, and turned to me. I'd planned to discuss the implications of tonight and the possible involvement of Bola. But Wick's gaze changed from worried to predatory lust.

He took a step toward me. Coconut and musk, heavy in the air, announced his intensions. Something niggled at my brain. Since I arrived, something rubbed against the grain, something other than the weird anger consuming all the Weres, something Mel had said…or didn't say.

"Where were you?" I asked.

He stopped short, his body snapping straight as if slapped. "What?"

"Just now. Where did you go? Mel said you went out, but she hid something from me. I could tell. She gets all pensive between the eyebrows."

"I drove someone home."

Immediate understanding slammed through my veins like ice. Only one woman in the pack would cause this avoidance and evasion by both Mel and Wick. The one shewolf bent on having Wick for herself. "Christine?" Why did I ask? The expression on his face told me the answer.

"Yes, but—"

I held my hand up. "It's not what it seems, or looks like? I feel like we've had this conversation before."

Wick growled. The muscles in his neck tensed as his shoulders rounded. He leaned forward. "We have. And if you gave me a minute to explain, you'd realize how unnecessary your anger is. Again."

I folded my arms over my chest, and forced my breathing to stay even. "Fine."

Wick hesitated before rocking back on his heels. "I drove her home because she turned up in wolf form and needed a lift. She's still in my care. I have to protect her."

"So you drove a *naked* Christine home?"

Wick shoved his hands in his pockets. "No. I gave her clothes."

"Why couldn't she just run on home as a wolf?"

Wick's gaze remained locked with mine. "She was

too injured."

"What? How?"

The smell of blue cheese and alcohol filled the room. I narrowed my eyes at Wick. Shame? He kept his gaze unwavering, not able to look away because of his Alpha dominance, but hurt sliced across his face.

My heart thumped around in my chest, and I wanted nothing more than to run to the window, wrench it open and fly away. I didn't want to hear what Wick would say next.

Fly, my falcon whined.

"I banished her," he said.

My heart stopped.

"I banished her," Wick repeated. "From the pack house. I didn't want her to sabotage any chance I have with you, so I told her she couldn't come to the house anymore. A few of the pack join her for a separate run during the full moons, so she's not alone. She has our protection, but otherwise she has no member status in the pack."

My breathing stopped. "When did this happen?"

"Day after." His dark brows framed large chocolate-brown eyes. Currently, his molten gaze beseeched mine for understanding.

And he had it. My heart swelled with it.

He didn't need to name the event he banished Christine after. The last full moon, I'd run over to the pack house to let him know the identity of the Supe Slayer, only to find Christine mounted on his lap, gyrating against him. He claimed to be a victim of Christine's plotting, that she'd heard me approach and pounced on him. But his hand had been firmly clenching her right buttock. He hadn't looked like a victim, and his actions spoke louder than words. Things had been strained and weird between me and Wick since, hot and cold.

"So she just showed up?" I asked.

"Yes."

"And you drove her home."

"Yes," he said slowly.

"Why does the room reek of your shame?"

"Because I ordered the women to discipline her."

Ah. Understanding hit me like an unexpected knee to the abdomen. Wick would rather take a punishment than see a woman harmed, but when Christine actively and blatantly disobeyed his direct order, he'd had no choice. Christine's actions undermined his authority. If he hadn't acted, his dominance would've been compromised. Every dominant Werewolf in his pack would have their internal wolves pushing for a challenge, regardless of their personal feelings. Alphas couldn't show weakness. Even his most loyal pack members would struggle not to challenge him for control. Running a Werewolf pack was a precarious position.

Either Wick had Christine disciplined, or more wolves would get hurt.

I bit my lip. Of course, Wick chose the whole over the individual. That's what made him a great Alpha. But it went against his personal beliefs. In his mind, women were for protecting, loving and cherishing.

Why did *he* have to drive her home? He had a lot of other Weres in the pack he could've asked. I could demand an answer to that question, but I already knew what he'd say.

He drove her home out of guilt, and his strong

sense of responsibility.

Wick stared at me, like he expected an answer.

"I see," I said and winced. Was that the best I could do?

"Is that the best you can do?" Wick echoed my thoughts.

"Well, it's difficult to go straight from self-righteous and pissed off to understanding and sympathetic," I said. "Give me a second."

Wick rocked back on his heels again put his hands on his hips. "One Mississippi, two Missi—"

I surged forward and planted my mouth on his to shut him up.

It worked.

Strong arms enveloped me, pulling my body closer as his tongue stroked mine. I pressed against his hard muscles, and enjoyed the heat lancing through my body. His hands drifted down to clutch my bare ass. This man could do wonderful things with his mouth. I'd know. His mouth had been on me before.

I stifled a groan and pulled away. "I've got to go."

"You sure?" Wick traced circles on my back.

No. Not at all. "Yeah."

He pursed his lips and let his hands fall from my body, freeing me to run away. I'd love to spend more time in Wick's arms, but the feeling of guilt tugged at my spine. It wasn't fair to either Wick, or Tristan, for me to keep flip-flopping between the two of them. I had to pick one.

And soon.

How could I choose between two amazing men? Two guys I'd developed feelings for, not just because they'd both win male beauty pageants, but because they had something to set them apart. Something unique and touching, strong, yet compassionate. Something that made them...

Mine, my mountain lion hissed, referring to Tristan. She sent the memory of how his sapphire gaze had twinkled in the moonlight before he kissed me for the first time.

Mine, my wolf growled, flashing images of Wick's naked body.

The two feras squared off in my mind, and grumbled at each other. The falcon flapped her wings, and squawked.

Shush, all of you.

Wick, probably sensing my inner turmoil, led me to the window and slowly slid it open without saying a word.

"Andy," Wick said. He reached out and stroked my cheek with his thumb. The rough, calloused skin sent my emotions back into a tailspin. "You need to make a decision."

My chest ached at the words because he was right. This couldn't go on much longer. My muscles ached for no reason besides despair sinking into my bones. I didn't know what to say, so I nodded.

"I think your pack may have been targeted by a Demon, tonight. The same one that's massacring norms around the city."

"We'll be careful." Wick reached out again, but this time, he pulled me in for a hug. I sagged into the strength of his arms, and allowed myself a minute to enjoy the security of it before pulling away once again.

"I'll see you soon," I said.

Wick nodded, and stepped out of the way.

I shifted to a falcon and flew into the night air. Aloft in the dark sky, a wispy thought accumulated at the base of my skull, like something was wrong, or off, and not just my love life. Like someone following me. Bola? I screeched and circled multiple times, but didn't see or sense anything.

Maybe it was just my conscience.

Chapter Sixteen

"Know what? Bitches get stuff done."

~*Tina Fey*

With the day gone and my head pounding, I stared down at the sheet of paper in front of me. I'd spent the last half hour at my desk scribbling random thoughts, trying to make sense of a world gone crazy. Traces of cinnamon, nutmeg and caramelized sugar from the banana loaf I baked last night for emotional therapy mixed in the air with my half-assed attempt at breakfast. The cushions of my couch beckoned, tempting me to lay down for a quick cat-nap to recuperate some of my lost sleep. A half-finished coffee sat beside me and demanded I reheat it in the microwave. I reread my list instead:

My To Do List:

- Find and banish Bola. Or destroy. Utter destruction preferable, if possible.
- Review local university course selections. Demonology 101?
- Find out what the hell Clint is and how to kill him (might come in handy).
- Sing in head when around Allan, it annoys him and helps shield thoughts.
- Allan's mind reading has limits, find them all.
- Find and remove the mole in Lucien's horde.

- Expel Lucien. He's an ass.
- Avoid Sid. He's a freak.
- Confront Agent Tucker. Or maybe get him fired. He's a dick.
- Pick a man and get Laid.

Why is laid capitalized? Aside from questioning my strength in grammar, reviewing my list acted as a calming balm to sooth my errant brain waves. Previously skittering around like a bolting new colt, they'd now settled down to a rhythmic throb, indicating an impending headache. *Awesome.*

After tapping away at my computer, and managing to only curse a few times about the new operating system, I discovered nearby Simon Fraser University did, in fact, offer a Demonology course, but for fourth-year students. I needed to be an accepted undergraduate with a declared major in Supernatural Studies in order to register for the class. Hmm. What if I contacted the professor and requested special permission? Or maybe I could audit the course. They couldn't prevent me from slipping into the back of the room, could they? Things couldn't have changed that much in sixty years.

A couple more clicks and I discovered the summer session had already started, and was well under way. I didn't have time to wait until September for the next course offering. I jotted down the time and location, and added to my mental notes to go to class and sit in. Couldn't hurt.

Bam! Bam! Bam!

I jumped in my seat. Someone pounded on my apartment door. I pushed away from the desk, and rose from the faux-leather office chair. With arms reaching for the ceiling, I arched my back and stretched. My mountain lion purred.

The backs of my legs, sweaty from the chair, stuck to my track pants. I peeled the material off and shimmied a little.

The pounding continued.

"Okay, okay. I hear you. Settle down," I yelled at the door as I walked down the hallway. Who could it be? And how'd they get past the building's front door? Maybe Ben needed something.

A familiar vanilla and honey scent seeped beneath the crack of the door, and swirled around the entrance of my apartment. Witch. Male. Christopher?

Ugh. I sucked in a deep breath, and flung my head side to side to crack my neck. *What did he want?* I unlocked the deadbolt, and swung the door open.

Christopher braced his body across the doorway with one arm on each side of the frame. His bent posture gave me a perfect view of his unruly brown hair. The disheveled black hoody, wrinkled blue jeans and tang of body odour told me he hadn't showered in a while. Did he come here straight from his liaisons? *Gross.*

Sniffing as discreetly as possible, I detected something else. Blood?

"What do you want, Christopher?" I crossed my arms, and leaned my hip against the opened door.

Christopher raised his head, and his glassy red gaze met mine.

A slice of ice slashed through my body.

Christopher was possessed by a Demon.

Even with fear riding my body, and my feras demanding action, neurons fired in my brain. Connections were made, conclusions drawn. The "normal" man the witnesses reported at every crime scene, the demon host, the familiar scent I couldn't quite trap or detect—Christopher.

That meant…

"Andrea," Christopher said, in a voice that wasn't his. No. This voice I knew. My muscles tensed, my body straightened, and my nails dug into my palms. Bola's voice.

I stepped back as Christopher's body lunged forward. In one swift move, he turned toward my retreating body and swung the door closed behind him, letting it slam, the sound echoing through my apartment. I continued to back away.

"It's been so long," Bola said. "No hug for an old friend?" He held his hands out wide, inviting. He must've abandoned his control over his scent, because his Demon defiled-almond stench barrelled down the hallway and slammed into my face.

"You were never a friend."

A slow nasty smile spread across Christopher's face. "But I was something."

"Just another perverted rapist." My words might've sounded strong, but inside I shook. My brain wanted to replay memories, ones I tried to locked away, ones Bola starred in.

No.

I wouldn't go back there. I'd promised myself never to be a victim again. And I meant it. Time for some revenge. I just had to figure out a way to take him down.

"You'd be an expert on perverts, wouldn't you?" Bola grinned, making Christopher's face contort into an unnatural expression.

"How did you find me? Did you steal the information from Christopher's memory?"

"No. I followed you."

"From where?"

"From the Werewolves' lair. My, they were easy to find. Easy to stir up. Their pack isn't whole, their leader is unmated. Imagine my surprise when I discovered you're neighbours with my host?"

"You purposely incited violence amongst the Werewolf pack to draw me out?" All the signs were there. I should've seen it. Why hadn't I?

A gaze of melted chocolate flashed through my memory. Wick. I'd been so focused on what he did or didn't do with Christine I'd missed the obvious. Idiot!

Bola's mouth twisted again. "I knew you'd be linked to them somehow. You never could stay away from the dogs."

Did he plan to go back and harm them? The blood rushing through my veins heated as my vision stained red. "What an original insult. Why wait to follow me home?"

"I want you all to myself this time. No sharing."

Though Bola's essence might control Christopher's body, it was the Witch's mouth moving, his eyes leering and his body leaning in. The fluttering in my stomach started to churn the emptiness. Small at first, but it grew stronger with every heartbeat banging against my chest. My skin prickled, wanting to be touched as my knees weakened, and my legs turned to play dough. My tongue tangled in my mouth as I tried to speak. I wanted to run to Christopher, jump him, wrap him within my strong legs and take him to the ground to mount his body.

Something niggled at the back of my mind. Christopher? I wanted to bang Christopher?

No. Make love, sweet, sweet love. Make a child with him, and build a home. White picket fences.
I shook my head. *Whoa.* I took another step back, and met Bola's, not Christopher's, calculating gaze straight on. "Must be getting rusty on the love mojo. It's not working."

Bola shrugged. "Never was my favourite emotion. Too sappy."

The stomach flutters faded away, leaving my gut an empty pit, the walls radiating sharp stabs of pain as if the lining dried up and shriveled, transforming my core into a hard rock. Bola walked toward me in slow motion, but the movement occurred too fast for me to react. I was helpless, unable to flee, unable to defend myself. Bola would rip me to shreds while I stood performing my best statue impersonation.

Statue impersonation? Really?

"Fear?" I asked, shaking off Bola's influence. "Also, not your forte. What do you specialize in again? Right. Inciting violence and rage. Bloodshed and war. Why not give me those? I'm already pretty pissed off."

Bola paused, as if he considered my question. "Detrimental to my health?"

"Scared?"

"Of you?" Bola scoffed. "Of course not."

Fear darted through my tissue cells as Bola laid his influence into me again. Images of past events, the rapes, the abuse from Dylan's pack overloaded my mind. The old, dirty, shameful feelings spiralled up, and threatened to choke me. I staggered to the side.

Bola's body smacked into mine and sent us both

reeling to the floor. The fear still racing through my veins became a distant throb. I blocked Bola's fist and elbowed him in the nose. Blood sprayed across my face and the floor.

Bola used Christopher's body as a giant paper weight, and I flailed my arms around trying to find some leverage to throw him off while my mind fought to kick his mental influence. He snared both my wrists in a one-handed, vise-like grip. I bucked my hips trying to dislodge him, but he pinned my arms above my head, negating the effect as he braced himself.

My heartbeat raced like a herd of elephants. This could not be happening. My feras screamed in my head. A flash of gray to my right told me Red had attacked Bola. Probably his leg. Not that it would help.

Bola's breath hit my face. Tomato sauce and meat. He reached down, snagged the elastic band of my track pants with his free hand and pulled with his Demon strength. A loud rip filled the room along with our heavy breathing. He flung my shredded pants across the room.

No. Not this. Anything but this.

I squirmed under his body, but it did little to deter him. He pushed his hips against mine, forcing his hard erection against the sensitive skin between my legs. I stilled. He still wore clothes, but the feeling of him, down there, even with the barrier of my underwear sent cold chills streaking through my body. My stomach turned to ice.

"Don't fight it. You might enjoy it," Bold said before he ripped off my underwear. Instead of flinging them away like my pants, he brought them up to his bloody nose and inhaled deeply.

Stomach acid bubbled up my throat.

"Mmm, Andy. You're a naughty girl. Who got you so turned on today?" He shoved the panties in my face, covering my mouth and nose. The stale effect of my earlier arousal filled my nose before he pressed the material harder against me. I couldn't get any air in. I thrashed my arms around, trying to strike Bola. He deflected the blows, but the pressure on my face eased. I turned my head to the side to cough and gag for breath. The air laden with Bola's stench flooded into me.

Bola laughed. He brought my underwear to his face, took another long drag of air and then chucked them over his shoulder. "Maybe one day I will inspire that response."

"In your dreams," I spat. "You'd rather inspire pain and fear."

"Too true," he said. He thrust his jean clad hips into me again. "You give such a delicious response."

His hand reached down again, and I squeezed my eyes shut. The sound of his fly being unzipped reached my ears and my limbs began to shake.

No. Not again. Never again.

The beast stirred.

Blood pounded in my ears, and time slowed down. My vision clouded. An edgy feeling vibrated through my core, flowing out to my arms and legs, giving me strength, feeding me with energy.

Should I risk it?
Did I have a choice?

Taking a deep breath, I called on my beast.

She answered, barrelling up from the deep, dark place inside where I kept her chained. I met Bola's smug expression, and *roared*.

The beast rose with rage and I embraced her, as I would any of my feras, accepting that she was just as much a part of me, and my soul as the other forms. I willed the change. Skin stretched, bones snapped, teeth elongated, claws protracted, scales replaced fur. My shift forced Bola to release his grip. He stumbled off me, and scrambled out of the way.

I pushed off the ground, eyed the fragile mortal shell Bola wore in front of me and roared again. Saliva flew from my mouth and splattered against his face. One of my picture frames fell off the wall, and shattered against the floor.

Instead of cowering or running away as I expected, Bola's smile grew. "You've learned new tricks, Carus," he said. "You've come into your own, finally. Dylan was never strong enough, good enough, to hold you for long."

I stepped forward to throttle him. His wide red eyes reflected my menacing shape like a mirror. Resembling a dragon-human-demon hybrid, my beast body stood over eight feet tall, with hard obsidian scales running along my back and legs. The only soft part of my body was where the impenetrable scales gave way to my face and to the soft black fur that covered my stomach and chest. Large, black wings with almost translucent webbing spread out from my back as extra appendages and a long, spaded tail swished around my feet.

What caught my attention and the beast's was my vaguely familiar facial features. Surrounded by my straight black hair and two short horns protruding from my forehead, my reflection stared back at me through dragon-slit eyes.

I blinked.

The beast nudged my mind, prodding me into action.

Destroy. Destroy this weak husk, this shell housing a Demon, and then destroy them all, she hissed. Her compulsion settled into my bones like a lead-paint coating.

Bola.

The Demon who wore Christopher's body. Time for revenge. I barred my teeth, and stepped forward.

Bola waggled his forefinger at me and tsked. "Would you harm this vessel I wear?"

I stopped.

My beast growled in my head and threw her control forward.

I locked my knees and narrowed my eyes at Bola. I didn't like Christopher that much, but I liked his roommates, his brethren. I owed them not to take him out, not yet, anyway. There must be another way to destroy Bola.

The beast wailed in my head, raking her sharp talons against my brain.

Bola walked to my sliding glass doors, and opened them. Before stepping out into the night, he turned to me. "This will make things more interesting; my victory, more sweet."

I growled, but Bola was already gone, taking Christopher's body with him.

The beast roared again.

Chapter Seventeen

"When angry, count to a hundred; when very angry, swear."

~Mark Twain

Rain pelted the bay windows in my living room as a not-so-rare summer downpour moved through the neighbourhood. I lay in a heap on the floor and fought the beast for control of my body. The struggle seemed to go on for hours, but when I finally stood on two human feet and checked the clock, it told me it only took half an hour, max.

With past success, and more notches on my belt, the transition from beast to human became easier each time.

How did I feel about that? *Not sure.*

Beast form still didn't come naturally to me. The day it became comfortable…might be the day I take out another Werewolf pack. Only this time, they might not deserve it.

Or maybe I no longer had to fear the beast. Maybe she was like a super duper ass-kicking fera I could use at will?

No. She was still a bitch and dug her talons in every time to prevent me from regaining control. I should only use the beast form when necessary.

Almost becoming a Bola victim? Definitely

necessary.

Bola. Invisible grime coated my skin. My stomach turned. My arms ached as if invisible hands still gripped them and held me down. My throat warmed as if his hot breath still scraped the sensitive skin.

I found my underwear and what remained of my clothes. Bola and Christopher's scents wafted off each piece, embedded in the material. I snatched them off the floor, and threw them in the garbage.

My mind raced with all the things I needed to do, but one item kept popping up at the top of the list.

I needed to get *clean*.

****

Night fragrances of japonica and honeysuckle flittered around, but Bola's stank still clung to my nostrils. No amount of air freshener would get it out. Not that I snorted the stuff, but I'd sprayed my apartment three times and took an hour-long shower to scrub my skin. Bola's attack left me angry and confused.

Mad cow disease? There had to be a logical explanation for the recent abundance of male interest directed my way. "*When it rains, it pours*," sure, but this was ridiculous.

Tristan and Wick wanted me as a mate because of the connection between our animals; Clint wanted to dominate me; Sid had no qualms over feeding sexual energy off me and hinted at wanting something else, something more; and now Bola wanted a piece? My animal magnetism explained this a little, but there had to be more to it than that. I might be horny as all get-out from the lack of sexy time, but that was nothing new, and my raging pheromones had never incited this level of male attention before.

Tristan and Wick, I understood. Might not know what the hell to do with that situation, but at least the "why" part was taken care of.

Clint? I only appealed to him because I came close to killing him. He wanted to dominate me to assuage some inner self-esteem issues. Like getting on top of me meant he was superior somehow. I definitely didn't fit his type.

Then there were the Demons. I didn't get the sense this had anything to do with me, at least not with me as a woman. Something else was involved. It had to do with my status as the Carus, but what? Nothing in the *Encyclopedia of Supernatural Beings* hinted at reasons Demons would stumble over themselves to possess me.

Maybe I should ask Feradea? This must be her mess, somehow.

I could call on Booth to help.

Did I want to use my one and only deity favour to find the answer? I'd planned to use it to find my birth family instead. If they still lived.

Men and deities aside, I had something else to do first.

You coming? I asked Red.

She leapt onto my bed, and curled up.

Guess not. I threw on a robe and stalked over to my neighbours' place. Their large identical-to-mine door stared back, and I paused to take a deep breath. When the adrenaline evaporated from my bloodstream, it left my limbs heavy and my energy sapped. I tapped the faux-wood with my knuckles and waited.

Ben opened the door. He brushed his shaggy hair out of his face and beamed at me. "Andy! Just in time.

We were about to get started." He looked down at my robe. "Uh. You might want to put some proper clothes on."

"You." I jabbed him in the chest with my forefinger.

Ben took a step back.

I followed and jabbed him again. "You. Better. Explain." Jab, jab, jab. "Why Christopher just showed up in my apartment, possessed by the masochistic Demon." JAB.

Ben fell back onto his couch, and stared at me with wide eyes. I'd poked him all the way to his living room.

Matt and Patty poured out of the adjoining rooms, Patty carrying a carrot microphone and Matt with a pink feather boa wrapped around his sandy hair like a turban.

"What's going on?" Patty asked, blue eyes wide. When he realized he spoke into his "microphone," he scowled at it and threw the carrot away. Like we didn't all just see that.

"Ben, here, was going to explain how Christopher has been running around town possessed by a Demon."

Ben gulped. "I didn't know!"

"How could you not?" My hands flew to my hips. The scent of his truth softened my anger only a bit. "Don't tell me you thought he was banging Witch groupies this whole time."

Ben's laced his fingers together and started twisting them around. "No. I was getting worried. The locator spell failed. I planned to go over to your place tomorrow and ask for help."

I grunted.

"I didn't know!" Ben said again.

I leaned forward. "He couldn't have summoned the Demon on his own. He can't speak and he's not strong enough to complete the ritual without vocalizing the mantras. Only you are."

Ben's shoulders sagged.

I waited and stared at his dirty-blond hair, several weeks past due for a haircut.

About to demand more talking, less air sucking, Ben's breath hitched.

I shut my mouth.

Ben's whole body tensed, and his hands balled up into fists. His gaze slid to the side and looked over my shoulder.

I followed his glare and turned to find Matt and Patty looking as guilty as a personal trainer caught eating fast food take-out. Matt clutched his boa, pulling it down around his face, in a classic hear-no-evil pose. Patty swayed back and forth on his feet. He reeked of sweat, parmesan cheese and musk oil—fear and guilt. Well, I knew which one would run, if it came to that.

"Start talking," I said.

"We summoned Bola because of his science knowledge. He promised to give Christopher back his voice in exchange for freedom from the circle," Matt said. His green gaze darted away.

"He promised no harm would come to us or our den," Patty quickly threw in. His lithe frame still sweating and swaying.

"Congratulations, the four of you are the only ones safe in this entire world," I said with a flat voice. My skin warmed, and my falcon demanded I peck at their faces.

Silence blanketed the room. Patty looked ready to

bolt.

Hunt, my mountain lion hissed.

"You forgot to specify the length of time." Ben's voice broke the strained silence.

Matt nodded.

"We forgot to specify the length of time," Patty mimed.

Unlike a Demon in a summoning circle, the rising sun didn't send a Demon possessing a host body back to hell. The Witch fledglings had majorly messed up.

Silence settled on the apartment as the Witches exchanged puppy-dog "I didn't mean to do it" looks.

"If you guys come together for a group hug and commiserate about this learning opportunity, I'm first going to puke on your carpet, and then I'm going to knock your heads in."

"So violent," Patty said. He stopped swaying.

"He tried to rape me." My throat grew thick, and my face tingled. I swallowed and pursed my lips. No. I refused to feel this way. I gulped back some more spit and lifted my chin.

Matt made a small squeaking sound and covered his mouth. Patty's face went white, and he looked at his feet. Ben turned to me, mouth agape with soft light-brown eyes.

"Are you okay?" Ben asked. He took a step forward. For a hug? Fuck that. Voluntary touching was so not happening right now.

I waved him off and backed away. "I'm fine. I would've killed him then and there, but it wouldn't be Bola…"

"It would be Christopher," Ben finished.

I nodded. "You and your den owe me. This

mayhem could've ended tonight. If anyone else gets slaughtered, it will be on us. We'll have to live with the knowledge. I risked many lives for the life of one. For you guys."

Ben winced. The other two looked away.

"Especially you two." I pointed at Matt and Patty in case they misunderstood. "You guys should have told Ben right away when you realized your mistake. Instead, you've been running around as if things were normal. People have been *slaughtered* because of your mistake."

"We thought we could fix it," Patty mumbled.

"How long?" I asked.

They tensed, but remained quiet.

"How long were you going to wait before you fessed up?"

They refused to meet my death stare, which provided answer enough. They were going to wait awhile. Maybe forever, hoping someone else would solve the problem. Cowards. Did they even care whether Christopher walked away unscathed?

I jabbed Ben in the chest one last time. "Discipline them."

Chapter Eighteen

"If you can't fix it with duct tape or beer, it's not worth fixing."

~Redneck slogan

I bolted upright in bed, tangled in sweaty sheets. My heart bashed against my chest cavity so hard it drowned out any other sounds. I gulped back some air and forced myself to breathe evenly. The smells of my room flooded in—laundry detergent, soap, shampoo, coffee. And something else. Not so much a scent, but an absence of one, like I needed to find it.

Come to the forest, a husky voice filled my head.

I flung back my cotton sheets and jolted out of bed, the urge to listen to the voice undeniable. Which of my feras spoke? I shrugged. Did it matter? A compulsion hadn't pushed me like this since…I glared down at Red.

What? she asked, all innocent.

"Again?"

She curled up on her spot on the bed, tucking her nose under her hind legs.

"Ahem."

One fox eye popped open and she said, *Go to the forest, Carus. You need control.*

I sputtered. "Control? I need to—Argh! Didn't I just stop myself from eviscerating Bola? Where's my gold star?"

The call of the wild pulled my body, and my stomach dropped. I staggered and steadied myself, one hand on the headboard.

"I don't have time for this," I said, to no one in particular, as I straightened and attempted to shake the sleep from my limbs.

Make time, Red said.

I clenched my fists and released; clench and release, clench and release. Screw this. I needed sleep more. Sure, I needed all my feras in a row, but what if I lost control? When I gained Red, the added animal in my head had almost caused spontaneous combustion. Could I afford to risk that right now?

No. I needed sleep. Maybe I'd deal with this new fera tomorrow night. If I didn't bring my A-game to the bonding, this animal might be the straw that broke the Carus' mind.

I closed the window, and flopped back into bed. My head sank into the pillow. *Ahhh. I missed you, pillow.*

You're losing it, Red remarked before snuggling into the back of my legs.

I agree.

****

In a fog, I ran backward looking over my shoulder. Five men with Kiss masks ran backward, yet chased me at the same time. What the heck? If they wanted to catch me, why wouldn't they run forward as I ran backward? I'd plow right into them. My heart rate kicked up a notch, and I tried harder to get away, but I kept running backward. Or did we all run forward, and some divine entity hit the rewind button to play some awful joke on us?

I'm so confused.

Suddenly, I ran into a house that looked vaguely familiar. People partied all around me, dancing, drinking and having fun. Was that Mel? I waved my arms frantically at her as I kept running backward. Up some stairs. Passed some weird masked guy in the corner.

I paused, mid-stride, frozen in place, forced to watch as the man in the corner pulled off his mask.

Tawny, thick brown hair, hazel eyes, full lips twisted into a cruel sneer.

Dylan.

I jolted up in bed. Again. My head swam with the quick movement, my vision went fuzzy. My hair flopped into my face, and I ran my hand through the rat's nest. I turned and groped my nightstand to find my phone, still blasting out the song I'd set for Mel's calls. That was it. Mel was getting a new ringtone. When my dreams resembled music videos, it was time for a change.

"Hello?" I said as I hit the "Accept" button. Or at least I think I said that. It sounded more like a zombie's war cry.

"Did I wake you up?" Her near-cackle told me she already knew the answer.

"Uh huh." I rubbed my face and stretched.

Mel said something, but I missed it. Sometimes stretches were so good, I tuned out everything else.

"Sorry, what?" I asked.

"You need to tell Wick about Bola," she said. "All of it."

"Um," I stalled, not liking the idea one bit. Mel didn't know the most recent Bola events, she only referred to my history. Still half-asleep, exhausted brain cells fired repeatedly, trying to get the message through to the rest of my body. A chill ran along my spine. Nope. Still didn't like the idea.

It's not that I feared Wick's reaction, not really. The idea of discussing one of the most traumatic and...

I swallowed some more air, and stared at the ceiling.

The ceiling provided no answers, either.

"Andy?" Mel spoke softly. "He knows something's up with me. He can feel it through the pack bond. I can't hide it."

Blood rushed through my veins and a heavy weight fell in my stomach, knocking the air from my lungs. "What happened?"

A pause. "He asked me what was wrong."

I held my breath. Such a simple question could crack open my tightly-woven defenses against my past. I'd sealed those memories for a reason—a fear if opened or revisited, I'd return to the weak, damaged soul Dylan had turned me into. I'd plunged into the fear time-capsule a couple of times already.

My head started to throb. Wick already knew some of my past. So did Tristan. They'd both been sweet and understanding, but this... If I told Wick, this might set his wolf into a fit, and that would jeopardize his whole pack.

"I didn't say anything," Mel continued, filling the silence with her trembling voice. "But I couldn't lie to him either. He's my Alpha. I told him it was your story to tell. I'm sorry." Mel spoke so quickly, her words blurred into one long run-on sentence. "I know it's not something you like to think about, let alone discuss, but

Wick should know. I think it will help him understand your…you better."

"It's okay. I get it." The pillow cushioned my head, but my brain still pounded against my skull. Wick had been patient and understanding with my need to go slow, but with only a few puzzle pieces, he didn't know the extent of the "why" for the situation. Wick never pressed me for information, and his confusion never changed his demeanor toward me—loving, caring, and patient—he was the perfect boyfriend…until Lucien used him against me, repeatedly.

"Dan knows," Mel continued. "He agreed not to say anything until you talk to Wick. Please do it soon. He would never use his power to order us, but he deserves to know. And you might not believe me, but it actually helps to tell someone else. You shouldn't bottle this all up."

Well, crap on toast. I knew that, but it didn't make the thought of revealing my inner, darkest secrets any more digestible. Besides, Mel may have gone through similar trauma, but she didn't have to worry about containing a rampaging beast hell-bent on destruction. Yeah, I'd successfully reined in the beast a few times, but that didn't mean the next time would go my way.

"Thanks," I muttered. "I'll get on it."

"Let me know how it goes. I'm here for you," she said.

I grunted and hung up.

Chapter Nineteen

"I think all men should have to spend one day possessed by evil, hungry, emotionally expressive Demons so they can forever understand PMS."
~Olivia Wilde

Under settings on my cell phone, I hit the "Save" button and cackled. Now every time Mel called, I'd hear the theme song to an old video game. That always brought a smile to my face. And I'd dreamed of being in the game countless of times, so I knew it wouldn't weird me out like last night's experience.

It also helped, momentarily anyway, to take my mind off talking to Wick, and what had almost happened in my apartment last night with Bola.

Someone knocked on the door. I jumped. Coffee sloshed out of my cup and landed on my hand. *Gah!* I never functioned well when I woke up early or unexpectedly. Caffeine should come in an intravenous option.

Red yipped and ran to the door like a frenzied Chihuahua. I walked through my home, bare feet digging into my plush rugs and then plodding against the wood flooring. All the while my brain snagged on the possible marketing campaigns and coffee labels for intravenous coffee—IV League Coffee, Down the Drain, Tubular Coffee.

Rosemary and sugar wound its way from the entrance, announcing my guest before I reached the peephole. I squared my shoulders, took a deep breath, and swung the door open.

A giant-sized Norse god greeted me.

"Hi," I said, rocking back on my heels.

Wick smiled. "You always smell like coffee."

"That's because I run on the stuff." My smile faltered a little. Too forced.

Wick's eyes narrowed, but he didn't comment. Instead, he leaned down and planted a gentle kiss on my cheek. Despite the innocent gesture, my face warmed.

"You need to take better care of yourself. Get proper meals in you," he said.

Red wound around Wick's feet.

"Come in," I said.

You know you're not a dog, right? I said to Red.

Vaguely aware she growled at me and stalked off toward the bedroom, Wick's face held my attention.

His mouth softened, and he brushed past me, his chest to mine, as he stepped into my place. My nipples pinged at the contact. Brat! He did that on purpose. His light denim jeans clung to his powerful legs, and the bright orange soccer jersey he wore showed off his impressive pectoral muscles.

I stepped back to close the solid door when someone else entered the building, just down the hall from where I stood. Warm air rushed in. Citrus and sunshine flooded my nose. I hesitated, my bare toes curling into the wood flooring.

Only one man I knew smelled that good. Had Mel contacted them both to get them over here at the same time? Two birds, one stone, and all that. I wouldn't put it past her, but I doubted she had Tristan's number.

"Andy," Tristan purred as he approached. He wore a close-fitting T-shirt and dark-washed blue jeans that accentuated his lean, muscular build. His white sneakers matched the stitching in his pants.

I said "hi," but the deep growling coming from behind me drowned out my voice. I flung my arm out to stop Wick from charging out to confront the Wereleopard Alpha. Wick pressed his solid chest against my sleeve, and then took a deep breath. His muscles relaxed, but he remained close, his body heat seeping through my clothing and licking my skin.

Tristan reached me and darted in to peck me quickly on my cheek. He wrinkled his nose as he withdrew, but didn't comment. He probably smelled Wick on my skin. Awesome. Another awkward moment. There'd been one like this before, but the order of arrival had reversed.

"Tristan," I said. "Please come in."

Wick stalked farther into the apartment before Tristan entered. Wick's feet thumped against the wood flooring. The sound disappeared once he got to the living room with the large rug. His decision to leave me with Tristan avoided the uncomfortable scenario where one of the Alphas would have to give the other his back. That wouldn't happen. Ever.

The silly image of them trying to walk side by side down my hallway and getting stuck flashed through my mind. They'd never fit with their broad shoulders.

Tristan hung back at first and then gestured with a sweeping hand that I go before him, and when we rounded the corner to the living room, we found Wick pacing. He stopped at our arrival.

"Does anyone want something to drink?" I asked.

"I'll have water," Tristan said. "Thanks."

I looked over at Wick, and he nodded.

"Will you two behave if I leave you alone together?" A justified question. Last time they'd attacked each other and made a disaster of my living room.

"We'll be good," Wick said. He held his fingers up to his forehead.

"Scout's honour?" I guessed.

"Sure."

When I brought out the waters, I sat down on the couch with Tristan. Wick apparently, preferred to pace. I should enjoy the male attention, but the bubbling nerves in my core prevented it.

"Well, since you're both here, I may as well get this over with," I said. The cushions of my couch provided little comfort to my nerves.

"You've made your choice?" Wick asked.

Tristan sucked in his breath.

"No. I need to tell you about Bola."

Both men relaxed, and then tensed again, as if dancing a choreographed number.

Tristan reached out and placed his hand on mine. With a gentle squeeze he said, "You don't need to. Not if you don't want to."

I shook my head. "It's a need and a want. You both need to know what baggage you're dealing with, and what…personal history I have with Bola. He might comment on it, and I'd rather you be prepared than blindsided."

Wick moved around to sit on my other side, and

Tristan kept his warm hand on mine.

"In the final days, when he got really desperate to complete the mating bond, Dylan summoned a Demon to inspire love within me. It failed. Not even Bola could incite such a reaction from me at that point. But I don't think he tried very hard. He got what he wanted regardless of his success."

"And what was that?" Wick asked, his voice quiet and rough, no longer whiskey poured over warm cream, but gravel churned in a cement mixer.

Images of dark rooms, reeking of sweat, blue cheese and alcohol—fear and shame. The candle light illuminated the circle formed with blood soaked salt.

I squeezed my eyes shut against the memories, but they kept coming, hitting my brain cells in wave after wave.

A male pack member with the red eyes of the possessed. Naked. Hard.

Strong arms holding me down, pinning me open for the Demon host.

The penetration, the panting, the smell of his twisted pleasure, and the drain of my energy as he fed off my pain and humiliation.

Deep breath.

Sweat dripped down my back as I struggled to put my past into words. After my short talk with Mel, I decided on the direct method; verbally spew out the truth, like ripping off a bandage. It worked with Mel, right?

I continued, "Bola became a part of the raping tag team. That was the price he named when Dylan summoned him and requested his aid, and that's what Dylan granted."

The glass in Tristan's hand shattered, and the smell of his blood flooded the air. At the same time, Wick jumped off the sofa and kicked over the coffee table. My drink sprayed across the floor.

My throat grew thick again, my face tingled. If only the flooring would surge up and swallow me whole. "I lost count of the times Dylan, his pack, and Bola violated me. By the end, I learned how to distance myself from my body. They could have my flesh, but not my mind. It was the only way to protect myself."

Silence.

I cleared my throat. "Bola wasn't there the last time, though. That much I remember. I'd had enough. The…beast had enough. When it was my turn, again, something inside me snapped. The beast took over, and I annihilated the pack. I lost control and ripped them to shreds."

My chin dropped, and I stared at my hands as my gut twisted in knots.

More silence.

The room buzzed with energy. Outside, cars drove by my building and a couple argued about who should pick up their dog's poop on the sidewalk. The living room, which had smelled nicely of fresh flowers and laundry detergent, now stank of burnt cinnamon, hot metal and manky snakeskin. My nose wrinkled up on its own.

"I'm going to kill him," Wick seethed.

Tristan plucked the glass out of his hand, and watched the gashes in his skin heal. "You'll have to beat me to it."

Wick growled. Tristan growled. Their eyes flashed yellow. The couch dipped as Tristan's weight shifted, and he prepared to lunge.

"Neither of you can kill him. Yet. He's in the body of my Witch neighbour." My chest grew tight, and my stomach sank into my core. Why couldn't things be easy? Why did life continuously throw these choices at me with no desirable outcomes and no clear solutions?

Tristan squeezed his bloody fists together, and Wick went back to pacing.

Silence dropped over the apartment again. It stretched and stretched and stretched. I had no interest in who picked up the dog poop outside, or how many cars passed. I wanted... What the heck did I want? Comfort? No, not really. Talking about my history left me raw. I wanted acceptance. I wanted these two strong men to hear the truth in my words, hear the horrors of my past and tell me they still wanted me, that everything would be okay.

"Well, that went well," I said. "Look, I've had forty-eight years to get over this, to deal with the hurt, pain and humiliation, and it still pisses me off. I understand this information upsets you, but you need to support me right now. Not the other way around."

Wick's shoulders heaved as he struggled to get his breathing under control. His fists clenched and unclenched. "I can't..." he said.

I crossed my arms over my chest and looked sideways at Tristan. He'd wrapped his hand in the base of his shirt to soak up the blood. With Were healing, the wound would've mended already, but he kept it twisted in the blue cloth. When he caught me looking, he untangled himself and reached out to hold my hand. He squeezed.

The burnt cinnamon grew stronger and came off

Wick in waves, my gaze snapped back to him. He shook his head. "I can't even console you. Not with *him* here. Why did you tell us together?"

Fair question and it took me a moment to consider why I dropped this landmine on them in such a way. It was easier. For me. More distance. "Maybe I don't want to be held. Maybe I just want you to listen," I said.

Wick grunted and looked away. "I hate this."

"Not getting to hug me, or my history?" I asked.

"Both."

I nodded, not knowing what else to say. "If I could erase—"

Wick held up his hand. "Stop right there. You have nothing to be ashamed of."

Tristan nodded. "Dylan was not your fault."

Wick grunted in agreement. He shot the Wereleopard a dark look, like Tristan stole his line. "The truth of your past is hard to hear. I want to kill Bola, or do *something* to make the pain inside you go away."

My lungs constricted. I opened my mouth to object. I had over forty years to deal. My past no longer pained me.

Wick settled me with a flat stare.

"We can smell it," he said.

Well, damn. He had a point. My emotional pain stained the air. The cushions on my couch wouldn't swallow me whole, even if I wished it.

"You have nothing to apologize for," Wick continued.

I nodded.

Tristan squeezed my hand again, and I turned to smile at him. His full lips parted to say something, but

Wick's voice cut him off.

"Unlike this guy," Wick said.

"What?" I asked. My neck stiffened. Not that it always had to be about me, but geez, if any moment should be centered on me, it would be this one. What did Tristan have to do with my painful past, anyway?

"Tristan has a lot to answer for." Wick folded his arms

The Wereleopard Alpha released my hand, and got to his feet slowly. "What do you mean by that?"

"You killed Andy's handler. From what I hear, you gruesomely gutted him in his own home without mercy."

"That same handler used Andy and was a wanted fugitive," Tristan said. "He had a kill bounty on his head."

Wick's eyes narrowed, and he stopped pacing to square off. "What else have you done?"

"Excuse me?"

"If you killed a defenseless norm for Ethan, what other dirty work did you do?" Wick took a step closer to Tristan.

Part of me wanted to rip Wick a new one for using this opportunity to take a dig at Tristan. The other part wanted to know the answer, too. What else had Tristan done for Ethan? What was he capable of?

Would it change things for me?

I'd done some pretty heinous things myself.

Tristan's eyes narrowed at Wick. "Like your hands are clean? Are you going to stand there with this lofty act and pretend you haven't done any tasks for your master? Weren't you the one holding down Andy as your *master* blood-raped her? We both had masters, we both know what that means, and we have to live with it for the rest of our lives." Tristan took a step toward Wick. They stood inches apart. "The only difference is I no longer serve a master. And you do."

The truth sent an arrow to my heart. I cared for Wick, but his actions were often not his own. They were Lucien's. I tended to forget this harsh reality whenever we were together because my reaction to him was so overwhelming, but Tristan's reminder acted like a cold rag to the face.

Wick jerked to attention. His mouth flattened into a grim line and his muscles tensed.

What the hell? I told these men my deepest, darkest, dirtiest history, and they turned it into a pissing match.

Heat spread from my chest, up my stiff neck and across my face.

"Guys," I said.

They ignored me and leaned toward each other, arms out.

"Guys!" I shouted. They both hesitated and reluctantly turned their heads to me. "I'd like you both to leave."

Wick's eyes widened and Tristan flinched. They both moved toward me. I jerked to my feet.

"I have a lot to think about and a lot to do. I'm emotionally exhausted, and I can't do any more of this right now. If you really want to scrap like frat boys at a mixer, then take it outside." I shouldered past them, and stalked to my bedroom. I slammed the door behind me and fell face first into my soft duvet.

The men left quietly without a single word. I don't know how they did it without tearing each other apart or without one of them turning his back on the other, but they must've made a silent agreement to get the hell out of my space. Good.

****

With a heavy heart in a hollow chest, I sat on my bed after Tristan and Wick left and stared at nothing, letting the tangled emotions flow out of me. An empty husk.

The beast stirred.

She pushed for power.

No. Not happening. My inner bitch could calm down.

As if I spoke to her directly, which I kind of did, the beast settled, nestling back in my core.

I hadn't lied to the men. After forty-eight years, the past usually held little power over me. With the reappearance of Bola, however, old fear, weakness and humiliation resurfaced. Less sharp, the pain didn't slice as deep, but it still cut.

Spilling my history to the men had slapped a bandage on the old wound, but now something else coiled up my spine. The thought of Bola made another emotion surge up to rattle the beast and put me on edge.

Anger.

No longer an empty husk, red hot rage boiled in my veins.

Maybe I needed an emotional timeout. I had no desire to let the beast take over and rampage through the Tri-cities in destructo-mode.

Instead, I got off the bed, made a tea, took a deep breath and dug out my phone.

Forget the timeout. I needed some answers.

The old man's voice crackled over the phone.

"Ambassador McNeilly, what a pleasant surprise."

Alone in my living room with only the lingering scents of Wick and Tristan, I relaxed on the couch, and rested my head on the back. Agent Donny O'Donnell, the coyote Shifter. I'd first met him when I'd tried to choke the life out of Tucker and since Donny did nothing to stop me, I'd considered him a friend ever since.

"Cut the crap, O'Donnell. You always seem to know when I'm going to call, so this shouldn't be such a shock."

O'Donnell cackled, and I wanted to smack my phone to see if it would hurt him on the other side.

"Good point," he said. "I guess the real surprise will come when you tell me why you are calling me. There's such an array to choose from."

"How do you detach a Demon from a host's body?"

"Ah, so it is about Demons, then. Is the host willing or unwilling?"

"Unwilling. No wait. Willing, sort of."

"Is it you?" he asked.

"No, you old coyote, it's not me. The host was originally willing, but the Witches botched the agreement and forgot to specify a possession time limit."

O'Donnell whistled. "There's a lot of botching going on in your life, isn't there? First the failed attempt on Clint's life. Now this?"

I glared at the phone.

Donny cleared his throat and continued, "As long as the host is alive, the Demon is tethered to the realm of Earth and cannot be banished. You will need to either kill the host or catch the Demon outside the host's body.

"Both of those will be difficult." Technically, killing Christopher wouldn't be difficult aside from tracking him down, but morally the decision sucked. Christopher would be dead and Bola sent back to the demonic realm, free to return on his next summoning.

"No other options?" I asked.

"Well…" he said.

"Anything." My fingers dug into the couch's soft material.

"There's always divine intervention."

I snarled into the receiver and held the phone back to jab the "End" button with my index finger.

"Wait!" O'Donnell said.

My rigid finger paused millimetres from the screen. "What?" I asked. "I'll say thank you when I get over my dire circumstances."

"Whatever." Donny vocally waved off my comment. "Divine intervention isn't as outlandish as it sounds. Think about it. And before you hang up on me, I wanted to ask how things are going."

"Really? Did nothing from our conversation give you a hint?"

"With your feras," he clarified. "How's your fox? Have you had any other…?"

My eyes narrowed. "Donny O'Donnell, if I catch you sneaking around my house at night playing Peeping Tom, you're going to be sorry."

The Shifter chuckled. "I'll take that as a yes. Have you met your newest fera yet? What is it?"

This time my finger didn't falter when it hit the button to hang up. Donny took way too much enjoyment from the debacle of my life. I could just picture him wheezing in his office with that laugh of his, slapping his leg.

Chapter Twenty

"Apparently, my greatest achievement for today was keeping my mouth shut."

~Andy McNeilly

The warm summer air clung to my skin with scents of lilac and jasmine. A perfect night for flying. Unfortunately, my destination was Lucien's manor, and as soon as my bare feet hit the expensive Italian marble, the Vampire lair sucked away all the enjoyment from my short flight. As if Lucien tapped an emotional vein and fed.

I stood in a fluffy white bathrobe, compliments of Allan, and waited for Lucien to finish his meal in the other room. Soft sucking sounds and smells of decay and the dregs of a wine barrel wafted through the grand receiving room to scratch the inside of my nose.

I hated this place.

Judging by the increasing pitch and rate of moaning from whatever woman Lucien used as a blood bag, my wait would end soon.

I stood on the red rug in front of his throne-like chair in the giant, empty room. All of Lucien's minions were preoccupied with running errands, but the air in the vacant room hung heavy with layers of Vampire scents. The room closed in on me.

Need to be free, Red whispered.

I stared down at the ghost-like fera wrapped around my leg. Her soft belly pressed against the top of my foot, and her cold snout tickled the skin behind my ankle. I'd left her at my place, but somehow she'd winked back into existence once I landed at Lucien's. I needed a fera operating manual.

I can't dispel him, yet. He can still kill me, I told her.

If he keeps ordering you around, he might kill you anyway.

She had a point.

"Andrea," Lucien crooned. He swaggered into the room looking ever the Italian model, the red rug his runway. "Thank you for coming."

Like I had a choice. I bit back the snarky comment, and plastered a fake smile on my face. "What do you want, Lucien?"

"Straight to the point, little Carus. All work, no play."

"If you asked me over for a play date, I'm leaving."

Lucien smirked, and stepped up to his chair. He gracefully turned and sat on the padded cushions. "I have no interest in you that way. Your Alphas can relax."

I bit down on my response. Apparently, my greatest achievement for today was keeping my mouth shut.

"I want you to rid the city of this Demon Bola."

"Already working on it." My skin itched to shift, and my falcon screeched her encouragement.

Fly! She demanded.

"Not fast enough. Kill the host," Lucien ordered.

His voice wrapped around me and tugged.

"That's only a temporary solution. I'm looking for a more permanent one." The fluffy white material of the robe scraped against my skin. My body warmed and sweat started to form in the dip of my lower back.

Lucien leaned forward. "It's not a request."

He didn't need to remind me of the blood bond or his willingness to torture those I cared for. Wick's safety and health were constantly at risk whenever I balked at Lucien's demands. The Master Vampire might make decisions for the best interests of his horde, the supernatural community, and hell, even the norms, but his continual choice to use me as his workhorse sucked.

"This Demon is hunting me. I'll find a fast resolution." *And I'll do it for me, not for you.*

His eyes narrowed, and he probably sensed my defiance, but he eventually nodded. "Good."

A knock on the door interrupted whatever Lucien planned to say next.

"Enter," he said.

The door opened, and Tamotsu walked into the room. A Japanese supe, the turtle-like Kappa became bound to whoever filled his bowl with water. I'd handed him over to appease the high-and-mighty blood sucker. At the time, I'd hoped it meant Lucien would leave me alone after doing his bidding.

I was wrong.

Carus, his voice rasped in my head.

Tamotsu, I replied.

"You are dismissed," Lucien said to me, breaking up the possibility of further conversation. Fine with me. I didn't have anything to say to the Kappa anyway.

"Okay," I replied and walked to the large window, leaving sweaty footprints on the Italian marble.

"And Andrea," Lucien said.

I looked over my shoulder at him. "What?"

"Remember the consequences for tardiness."

And there it was. The imminent threat. I'd expected it, but Lucien's words still sent a shiver slicing down my spine.

****

I bolted upright in bed. This was becoming all too familiar. My heart hammered in my chest. My thin white summer sheets clung to my body, slick with sweat. The fragrance of night-blooming flowers hung heavy in the night air, but something else tangled with the smell, something tantalizing and foreign.

Berries and earthy scents wound around my body like a lasso and tugged. I staggered out of the bed, bringing my sheets with me. I peeled them off and stumbled to the window. When I flung it open, the smell grew stronger. It beckoned. It seduced. I needed to go to the source.

I clambered out my first-floor window, bumping my knee. Pain rushed up my leg, but I didn't care. The scent claimed me and *pulled*.

Dressed in cotton pajama shorts and a white tank top, both plastered to my body by sweat, I made my way to the river. Bare feet pressed against rough cold concrete, then dug into soft summer soil, then plodded against the pebbles and sharp rocks used for the part of PoCo Trail running along the forested river. Crickets buzzed and hummed. The eerie call of an owl flowed with the rushing water and rustling leaves.

A couple of homeless living in the woods called

out to me, but I ignored them. Let them make cat-calls and innuendos. I could always circle back in animal form and scare the crap out of them.

When my feet hit the icy river water, a sense of calm washed over me. The cuts and scrapes on my bare feet numbed in the cold. I flung my head back, stretched my arms wide and closed my eyes to the full moon above. My heartbeat slowed to match the natural rhythm of the forest.

Wick would be out running with his pack.

I shooed the thought from my mind. Tonight wasn't about Wick. Or Tristan. It was about me and whatever animal had called. Her presence pricked at my nerves, tingling my skin like a homing device. She lumbered through the woods, brushing passed bushes and stomping on twigs. A couple of the homeless people shrieked and scurried away.

The water flowed over my feet as I turned to greet my new fera.

A lot of humans believed bears stunk. A common misconception. In actuality, all the ones I've come across were fresh and clean. Not even their poop smelled bad unless they'd recently eaten meat or lots of insects. This bear smelled divine. Like strawberry shortcake.

Hi, I said, lamely.

Carus, she grunted.

Red chose this moment to race out from the underbrush. She must've followed me from my apartment. She wound around the legs of the two hundred and fifty pound black bear, as if she was a long-lost litter mate. I knew what she'd say before she said it.

I am you. You are me. We are one, Red said. When we'd bonded, she'd recited the same thing. They all had. My other feras chimed in, repeating the phrase over and over again in my head as I walked toward the bear.

Her cute little ears perked up and pointed forward.

I am you. You are me. We are one, the bear said, joining the chant. Her deep gravelly voice somehow made the choir in my mind more grounded.

I nodded and stepped out of the river, closing the short distance between us. I reached out to rub her silky nose. The moment my skin touched her, she shimmered. Wavering in my vision, the bear lost all colour as if my finger formed a magical straw and sucked it out of her. Her energy flowed into my body, filling me with power and strength. The now translucent bear's eyes met mine, big and doe-like, before she completely disappeared.

In tune with the flowing river, her energy streamed into my body, my brain, and into my very being down to the cellular level. Then, it ballooned out, pushing against my skull and rib cage. I crumpled to the leafy ground as all my feras shrieked inside and battled for dominance. Red sat by my face. Her ghost-like body, perched inches from me, but I couldn't reach out to her. I couldn't move as my head pounded, and my bones ached.

The beast stirred.

Too much, I said. *It's too much.*

The beast stretched.

Dispel the bear, Red whispered, and prodded my face with her nose. As if that would help.

The beast pushed against my control.

My skin stretched and pulled, bones cracked and my hold on the beast slipped. She surged up, wanting control, wanting to break free. I rolled on the ground and screamed, the pain like cold icicles shearing through my flesh.

Help me! I yelled.

The beast roared.

My feras stopped squabbling and as one, tackled the beast inside my mind and pushed her down. She slashed at them with sharp talons, but the other feras ducked, weaved and slipped by her.

I tightened my hold on the beast and shoved her back, deep inside my core.

She rumbled and spat curses at me.

Sweat poured off my face, I wiped at it and stared at my hand. It was covered with blood. My nose continued to gush, and the world around me spun.

My mountain lion hissed at the bear, and my wolf growled. They circled the new fera as she stood her ground, just as dominant. She growled and swatted at them with her large clobber-like paws. I needed to act fast before they started going at it again.

Bear! I mentally yelled. *Leave my mind. I dispel you.*

She stopped swinging at the mountain lion and wolf and focused on me. Her love warmed my body as if I lay on a tropical beach and basked in the sun. Then the heat disappeared, slowly, like cooling prey after a successful hunt, leaving me cold and empty. I opened my eyes to the dark summer's night and shivered.

A ghost-like bear sat beside a ghost-like fox.

Sleepy, the bear said, opening her pointed snout to yawn.

Me too, I replied as I staggered to my feet. "I'm calling you Baloo."

She snorted at me. *I am you. You are me. We are one.*

Yeah, I get it. But I need something to call you. Too awkward any other way.

We lumbered back to my apartment. I plucked leaves off my sweaty skin and tried to brush the dirt from my damp clothes, all the while replaying Donny's words. He'd once said feras would present themselves as I needed them. How the heck was a giant black bear going to help me with my current predicament?

And how would I fit all these feras in my place? Baloo was massive, and if Donny was correct, she and Red were only the beginning of my fera add-ons. I'd have a zoo in my place before long.

You're not going to fit on the couch, I told the bear.

She clicked her tongue at me.

Chapter Twenty-One

"I never made one of my discoveries through the process of rational thinking."
~*Albert Einstein*

The university smelled of hope, stress and raunchy freshmen sex. Not much had changed since I attended.

The bold blocked room number WMC 3260 stared at me before I took a deep breath and slipped into the auditorium.

The double doors slammed shut and slapped my ass, pitching me forward. Thirty heads swiveled in my direction. I stumbled a couple steps, and my cheeks warmed. Maybe my grand idea of attending class undetected wasn't so fabulous after all. I froze, ready to turn around, but it was too late.

I should've brought Baloo and Red with me for invisible support.

Then again, they'd probably laugh at me.

Thirty pairs of blinking eyes continued to observe me. A couple of mean girls smirked, and a few hipsters yawned, but most looked incredibly nosey.

"Umm," I mumbled and looked around. "This isn't Women Studies 102, is it?" Why couldn't this be an afternoon class? Who wanted to study Demons at 9:30 in the morning? Who functioned this early in the day?

The professor's head popped up. Tall and lanky,

with sinewy muscles, he moved like a willow tree branch in the wind, circling around the podium to stand at the end of the aisle. With dark brown inset eyes bridging a long pointed nose, his stare could intimidate even a snotty post grad student.

"No, it's not," he said as his dark eyes narrowed. "This is Demonology 421. But I suspect you knew that. You can join us, if you'd like. Please, have a seat." He waved his hand at the empty seats in the front row, fanning out his long fingers. "I'm Professor Westman."

I cleared my throat. "Oh. Okay. Busted."

Each step I took down the steps echoed in the small room as the students watched in silence, their bobble-heads and glasses swiveling to track my movement to the front of the auditorium.

"Maybe you should introduce yourself, tell us what you already know? We're a small class," the professor said as I slid into a plastic chair by the aisle. My neck hairs screamed at my exposed back. Too many people behind me.

The vanilla and honey Witch scent wafted off the pale professor and curled around my body before filling my nose. Maybe he could help me. Did he know what I was? Witches didn't have as keen a nose, but they had other ways of telling, of protecting themselves. My nose involuntarily flared, taking more of his scent in. There was something odd about it. Tainted. Maybe he practiced black magic? That would explain his starving-student look—dark power tended to take more than it gave. Magic had a price.

"Oh, umm," I stuttered. Truth? Or lie? Opening my senses to the room, I registered more supe smells: Weres, Shifters, a few more Witches, a lot of norms. A lie wouldn't work here. "My name is Andy McNeilly," I said.

The professor's eyes widened in his elongated triangular face. He'd heard of me. How? The news, maybe? "And what do you know of supes, Andy?"

"I, uh, work for the SRD."

A collective gasp sounded in the auditorium, bouncing against the padded walls and vibrating my eardrums. Really? How sheltered were these students? Working for the SRD had never been prestigious.

Well, if they knew I'd been one of the assassins, the gasping would be warranted. We had a pretty good reputation, or bad, depending on how someone looked at it.

The professor's smile twisted, warping his face into something almost ugly, before he widened it, showing bright white even teeth. "And what type of supernatural being are you?"

"A Shifter," I stated. Thanks to the Channel 5 news who recently did a piece on the local ambassadors, I no longer clung to the secrecy of my identity like I had in the past. The exposure left me feeling like someone had ripped away my baby blanket.

"But you smell of the forest." A man leaned in behind me.

I turned my head slightly, and took in the burly man with a patchy beard and professor sweater. His Werelynx scent—fresh snow and tree sap—clogged my nose. A sweater? In summer? Probably took pictures of all his meals and posted them on social media, too.

"Just came back from hiking," I said. When his breath kept hitting the back of my neck, I flashed him my teeth over my shoulder. "Piss off."

The man grunted and leaned back in his chair. My mountain lion yowled, leaving my head ringing. She wanted to claw his face. So did I. No Were or Shifter liked having a stranger approach from behind, let alone lean close enough to feel and smell their breath. Werelynx boy needed a breath mint. And he should've known better.

"A Shifter. How interesting," the instructor interrupted, giving the Werelynx behind me a pointed look. "And in what capacity do you work for the SRD?"

"I'm a liaison," I answered. My forehead prickled, the urge to wipe the beading sweat strong.

"For who?"

Geez. This guy wasn't letting me get away with anything. I eyed the emergency exit. If he could tell me something to help bring down Bola, this little information sharing would be worth it. I no longer worked as an assassin, and my identity had been revealed already. *You've already let go of your anonymity*, I reminded myself. *Relax.*

"I'm the liaison between the SRD and the Master Vampire of the Lower Mainland."

Some more gasping. *Really?* These were fourth-year students majoring in Supernatural Studies. Obviously field work wasn't a requirement.

"Lucien Delgatto." The professor's mouth curled into a half smile, telling me nothing.

"That's right."

The instructor nodded before sauntering around to stand behind his podium. "Well, we're pleased to have you with us, Ambassador McNeilly. I'd appreciate it if you stayed behind after class so we can discuss what brought you to my domain."

I dipped my chin slightly. This might work out after all. How'd he know my title? Not all liaisons of the SRD had the Ambassador title. And his *domain*? Talk about arrogant. Mentally shrugging, I slouched into my seat, settling in to do some learning.

****

Today's lecture was on a Demon known throughout history as the Slender Man. Professor Westman ran through various accounts of the Demon's transgressions, including historical references from ancient Egypt hieroglyphs, Brazilian Cave paintings and German woodcutting. The Slender Man got around, making numerous appearances in the twentieth and twenty-first centuries as well.

Westman's pale face took on an unhealthy sheen as he outlined his "favourite" sightings. Seemed the Slender Man really got off on rending animal flesh, including humans. But why take fifty minutes on one rather minor Demon with relatively little power or influence?

Thankfully no one asked questions and on the fifty first minute, Westman dismissed his class.

I remained seated, fighting the urge to turn around and hiss at the movement behind my back as each student filed out of the small lecture room. My feras didn't fight too hard, though; the professor rated higher as a threat to them than thirty undergrads. I agreed.

Why did I want to run? Black Witches, capable of extreme power and destruction, never put me on edge like this in the past. Except maybe that creepy voodoo priestess I had to retrieve over a decade ago when I was new to the job.

I kept my attention trained on Professor Westman, and he watched me right back, our gazes locked together in some secret battle no one told me about. I almost missed the shuffle of feet in the aisle beside me.

One deep intake of breath told me what I needed to know. Musky coconut, burnt sugar and canned ham. An unfortunate mix. I'd met enough professor groupies to recognize her type right away—completely infatuated with Westman to the point of desperation. No need to attack. She would self-destruct on her own by the end of her fourth year.

My lips twisted up.

"Professor Westman?" Her high-pitched, breathy voice made me think of Smurfette in a porno.

"Not now, Jane," the professor said, not sparing her a glance.

"But," she stuttered.

Westman broke eye contact with me to settle his unnerving gaze on the woman. I won!

"Not now," he repeated.

A petite woman with a naturally puckered pout stiffened at the steel in Westman's voice. Her eyes widened.

"Go," Westman said.

With trembling lips and a short sniff, she swiveled around and jolted up the stairs, a wake of sour air trailing behind her.

"I apologize for the interruption." Westman's smooth tone caressed the air as he moved to stand in front of me, effectively closing me in and forcing me to remain seated.

To hell with that.

I slowly rose to my feet. Would he take a step back

or stay put?

He didn't budge.

We now stood a foot apart, and the height difference pissed me off.

"May I call you Andy?"

"May I call you Westy?"

"You may call me Takkenmann."

Standing this close, his scent burrowed deep into my respiratory system and scent memory, the vanilla and honey Witch smell overpowering. And wrong. There was something about it, something off. My nose flared again. Something familiar. "An unusual name for a...Witch, isn't it?"

"Oh, I think we both know I'm not your average Witch."

The source of the wrongness hit me. His scent reminded me of teenaged boys, loading on strong-smelling cologne to mask their body odour. My face went cold, as if all the blood drained from it. My hands grew clammy.

Fake. The Witch scent was fake.

There, underneath, lay something else, something sweet and much more deadly. My heart punched against my rib cage, pumping so hard the throbbing echoed in my ears. I identified the smell.

Almond.

Chapter Twenty-Two

"Hit a tripwire of smell and memories explode all at once."

~Diane Ackerman

The Demon's grin widened. Standing a foot away from him with no room to maneuver and nothing to separate us, the serrated details of his shiny enamel glared at me.

My fingertips tingled as I started to shift.

Not fast enough.

The Demon lunged. His long nimble fingers closed around my neck as I shot my hands out, inside his arms, and dug my claws into his face. My elbows pushed against the insides of his arms. His hold should've weakened, but this Demon possessed uncanny strength. His frame stretched, growing to almost eight feet in height and giving his body an emaciated appearance. He pulled me close, his nose touching mine. I wrenched to the side, but my toes dangled above the floor.

"Bola sends his regards," he said, his breath hitting my face.

My gums stung as fangs protruded, and I hissed at him, ready to make the full change and get my fight on. I yanked on the mountain lion and spurred her into action.

"By all means, little nugget, shift into one of your

animals." He gnashed his sharp teeth together. "I love to rend the flesh of livestock, to mutilate the bodies of creatures and to smash the bones of beasts."

Then, I got it. I stilled and released my hold on the mountain lion. The energy vibrating my skin seeped away. My brain shuttered as if jump-started by a diesel generator. He spent fifty minutes of his lecture talking about himself, taunting me. I'd been staring at the Slender Man the whole time.

The Demon squeezed my neck.

My throat constricted. Sweat beaded on my forehead and ran down my face. My skin grew hot and clammy. He was too strong. Too strong for my human form. Too strong for my mountain lion. I'd have to let the beast out. I reached down and held my breath. I'd need all my energy to keep control. The beast woke and stretched.

Over his shoulder, something large and black charged across the room. Baloo leapt over seats.

You can't help, I told her.

She kept running, straight for us. Instead of bowling into Westman, she dove low and slammed into me. Her essence filled my body. Before any of my feras could react, she seized control and my skin stretched and snapped.

Underneath Westman, I shifted into a two hundred and fifty pound black bear. His eyes widened. I rolled and flung him off. He scrambled to his feet and ran toward the exit behind the stage.

Never run from a bear.

I barrelled into him before he reached the halfway point to the exit doors. With a deep-throated growl, I let my claws rake his back. He bellowed and flopped down beneath me. My nails dug into his flesh, and I flipped him over.

A pulsing sound vibrated from deep within my throat, and I bellowed into the Demon's face. His expression scrunched up and drool from my muzzle splattered against his cheeks. He recoiled, and tried to squirm away. My claws dug in more, and he whimpered.

I shifted back to human form and gripped his hair in my hands. My bear, instead of retreating into my mind, dispelled herself and sat ghost-like beside me.

What the hell just happened?

Focus, Baloo said. *Control the Demon.*

I didn't know what freaked me out more—what just happened with my fera or that a translucent black bear was the voice of reason.

Westman groaned beneath me. With a fistful of hair, I smacked the back of his head against the ground. "You'll tell me what I want to know or I will do the rending. Got it?"

Westman grunted and went limp underneath me. I took that as a yes.

"Can we talk like civilized supes, or do I need to keep you pinned for your good obedience?"

"We can talk, Carus. I will no longer fight you."

"Your word." I bashed his head against the ground again for good measure. "I want your word."

"I promise."

"Be more specific."

"I promise not to attack you or seek to harm you in any way, and will answer your questions."

"Not good enough."

He grunted. "I promise not to attack you or seek to

harm you in any way, either directly or indirectly, and will answer all your questions fully and to the best of my ability."

"Good." I released him and stood up."I can't believe the university failed their background check on you."

"Oh, they know," the Demon said as he clambered to his feet.

"What?"

"Who do you think summoned me and supplies me with the Witch scent charms? How do you think I'm present in daylight?"

"That's messed up."

"Not at all. You're just prejudiced." He took a few steps back, probably to distance himself from me. The shadows lay over him like a blanket, as if he pulled them over his body. I squinted for a better look. Now that I knew he was the Slender Man, certain things stood out. His body had a distinct rope-like quality to it, his long arms appeared boneless. The shadows embraced him like a dark cloud at midnight. He had the creepy factor down, and if I'd ever woken up to find him lurking in the shadows of my bedroom, I'd have screamed like a little girl.

Now, after beating him in a fight, he just appeared weak.

I glanced down at my shredded clothes and then surveyed the room. "I need clothes."

He pointed to the podium. In the cabinets beside it, I found some old alumni sweaters and track pants. Perfect! I clambered into them while keeping my gaze on the Demon, and my back to the wall.

"Let me guess," I said. "One of your agreements

for exiting the circle is to remain in your human form. Brilliant."

"My human form is essentially my demonic form, only more compact. What you see, is what you get."

"Weak?"

He snarled at me, but I ignored him. He'd threatened to rend me to pieces. I didn't care if he thought I was a bitch.

"What did you say your name was?" I asked. "Taco Man?"

"Takkenmann, Fear Dubh, Thief of the Gods…the Slender Man. My name doesn't matter."

"You're right. It doesn't. Where's Bola now?"

"I don't know."

"When is he outside of his host's body?"

Westman hesitated.

"Do I need to bash your head against the floor again?" I asked. "When?"

He winced. "Sometimes when he feeds, but it's not a given. He doesn't need to take his true form."

"How does he feed? Wait, what does he feed on?"

"He feeds on bloodshed and war. Fear, sometimes. You can find him near any location where that's happening. Hospital is a good bet. Or you could wait until he stages his next massacre."

Since I only found out about his demolition derbies after the fact, the latter suggestion wasn't an option. Not to mention it meant a lot of death. "I'd rather avoid another of those."

Westman nodded and shifted his weight from foot to foot.

"You're not going to run, are you?"

Westman shook his head. "My deal with the

institution forbids me to leave without permission."

"Good to know. So if I have further questions, I can find you here?"

Westman nodded again.

"Why do you look so cagey?"

"I'm providing information on Bola. Do you have any idea what fate awaits me if he finds out?"

"You're both Demons. Wouldn't you sell each other out for advancement? Surely, he knows I could summon one of his brethren and get information on him." Not a bad idea.

"The Demon realm is not as simple as you think."

About to chastise him for not providing a full answer as our deal entailed, I stopped. I didn't have time to fully research the demonic realm. If it didn't pertain to kicking Bola's ass, I didn't need to know about it right now. Time for that later.

"I'll be in touch," I said and walked out of the room, leaving the Demon with his shadows for company.

Chapter Twenty-Three

"As a child, my family's menu consisted of two choices: take it or leave it."

~*Buddy Hackett*

With plenty of day left and my ghost feras close on my heels, I barged through the SRD agent's office doors, not caring if I took out interns, minions or the devil himself. "Donny!"

The room smelled of dust, old parchment and coyote. Nothing but trouble. My lips shut on a mouthful of floating fur, and it stuck to the back of my throat. I staggered forward and bent over in a coughing fit.

I swallowed the surprisingly tangy fur and straightened. Good thing I gave up all pretenses of professionalism already.

Donny's coyote familiar lay on a dog bed in the corner of the room. Ma'ii's greeting consisted of popping one eye open and flashing his teeth at me before curling up to go back to sleep.

The old man looked up from his desk with a smirk on his face. "Yes?"

"How the heck am I going to keep my sanity if I end up with the entire zoo following me around squabbling?"

"You've lost me."

"After I dispel a new fera, they follow me around

like transparent ghosts. And they're chatterboxes. Way more than my first three feras."

Baloo made some sort of mooing sound, like a cross between a howl and a roar, without any malice. She nosed the back of my leg, and I had to fight to stay upright.

Donny frowned. "You mean to tell me there's a transparent ghost fox in the room with us right now?"

"And a black bear."

"A black—?" Donny wheezed. He doubled over and shuddered. I stumbled forward, reaching out to help him. A heart attack, maybe? Stroke? Then he started slapping his knee. I snatched my hand back and frowned. It took me a full minute to realize the old man laughed at me. Again.

I should've known better. My hands flew to my hips. "It's not funny."

Hah, cackled Ma'ii in my head.

"Oh," Donny gasped, "I disagree."

I flopped in the chair on the opposite side of the desk, and a cloud of dust and fur bloomed into the air. The particles slowly fell back to the floor as I waited for Donny to finish his laughing attack. Honestly. Nothing about this situation was humorous.

O'Donnell wiped his watering eyes with his shirt sleeve and took three long breaths before he sat back and focused his attention on me. "Have you tried asking them to leave?"

"Wouldn't I lose them forever then? I'm not about to give up parts of my soul like that."

Donny shook his head. "You can't lose what you've found. If they're 'ghost-like,' maybe they have ghost-like abilities, such as dematerializing. Maybe you can send them away and then call them back when needed."

Red and Baloo had both flashed in and out of existence already. I narrowed my eyes at the agent. "And *maybe* you know a little more about me than you let on, old man?"

He winked, the bastard.

Donny's wise, like his fera, Ma'ii gloated.

I squeezed my eyes closed and gripped the armrests. If Donny couldn't or wouldn't help me, I was screwed. What was I going to do? I couldn't walk around with a bulldozing bear loping behind me. Ghostlike or physical, it distracted the hell out of me. Red was easier to disregard, being smaller and less obtrusive, but Baloo acted like a battle-ax and took up entirely too much bed space.

"How much do you know about Shifter history?" Donny asked.

I shook my head and tried to shed the itchy feeling of despair. "Whatever I can find on the internet."

"Then you don't know much. Most Shifters choose to keep our history private, sacred, especially after the Shankings. We've always passed it down, generation to generation, by word of mouth."

"Well, you know my history and I'm ignorant, so cut to the chase and tell me what I need to know."

Careful, Ma'ii warned.

I leaned back and forced the tension from my shoulders. If Ma'ii thought I gave too much attitude to Donny or stressed him out, he'd sink his teeth into me. Usually the fleshy tissue of the calf muscle, or the sensitive skin on the back of the ankle. Not exactly fatal injuries, but the bites stung.

Donny sighed, as if he followed the dialogue with Ma'ii. Maybe he did. "It is believed we were once all like you," Donny said. "Descendants of Feradea and her human lover, we could take any shape without a fera. More like Angels and Demons, we had a human form and a divine one. The divine form resembled your beast, the Ualida, or something close to it. The animal feras came later, when we became tied to the land. Our history is unclear on why we lost the ability to take the shape of different animals, why all but the Carus lost their beast, or why we bond to only one physical animal familiar now. Some say jealous Demons tricked us, some say we defied the beast goddess and she punished us, reducing our gifts. Some say the feras exist as a reminder of what we once had, and some say simple evolution is at play. The Feradea hasn't answered my prayers. But our history is clear on one thing."

After a long dramatic pause, I took the bait. "And what's that?"

"You. The Carus is our salvation. Our path to redemption."

My vision wavered, and my brain became light-headed. A chill racked my stiffening muscles, and my hearing tuned out, overtaken by a weird wave-like sound—as if the sea crashed against my ear drums. "You bastard!"

"Excuse me?" Donny aimed his right ear at me.

Ma'ii's head snapped up, and he flashed his teeth at me.

"You told me there was no prophecy. I remember the exact moment. You made some cutting remark about how that was a good thing because I wasn't prophecy material."

"There's no prophecy."

"Then what the heck do you mean when you say I'm the salvation for Shifters? Sounds like prophecy to me."

Donny shrugged. "There's nothing specific about what will happen or who will do it. Remember, Carus, you might be unique, but you're not one of a kind. There have been Caruses before you, and there will be Caruses after. All we know is the Carus has the ability to save us."

"From what?" I groaned. "You also told me there was no doomsday plotline to my life. How could you flat out lie to me without smelling foul?"

Donny shook his head. "I never lied."

I pinched the bridge of my nose, but it did little to stem the increasing ache behind my eyeballs, beating in time with my heart—thump, thump, thump. "Donny. I need you to explain very explicitly what you're talking about."

"I wish I could, Andy. The fact is we don't know much. The Carus has abilities the rest of us Shifters don't. The lore passed down from generation to generation hints that one of those skills has the potential to mend the bridge between Shifters and Feradea. Most discard the stories as old legends to remind young Shifters to be wary of Demons, to explain our tie to Earth and to revere our patron goddess. Some believe the myths though. I do. Others… Well, others have different ideas."

"Like what? What do the *others* think? That I can destroy everyone?"

"Well, no. We already know the previous Caruses went insane and had to be put down. Your beast form is not invincible. No. The others think the Carus can break our tie to the earth; make it so all of us will have the same ability to shift into multiple animal shapes."

"What do the feras say? What does Ma'ii say?"

"The wily old beast clamps his jaws shut and refuses to answer any time I ask. I think it's a part of their nature not to comment on their origin or the tie that binds us to them."

Ma'ii cackled in my head again.

Will you tell me? I asked the fera.

The coyote snorted, and then coughed. His furry body recoiled as he choked on the air.

I leaned forward with concern, but Donny waved me off.

Ma'ii staggered to stand and hacked up a giant wad of saliva-coated fur.

Gross.

Ma'ii flashed his pointy teeth at me.

I turned back to Donny. "Would you pass on being bound to Ma'ii for the chance to gain my abilities?"

Donny paused, and a slow smile spread across his face. He glanced at the old coyote, currently licking up his own fur from his bed. The fera had so much gray around his eyes and snout, his whole face appeared ghost-like.

"Not in a million years," Donny said. "Ma'ii and I...we are one. It's unlikely anything you do will impact current Shifter bonds, but perhaps those of future generations."

"That's what I mean. Knowing the awesomeness of the fera bond, would you want future generations to miss out on that in order to become like me?"

"Are you saying you don't have a connection with

your feras?"

I am you. You are me. We are one, my feras chanted.

We sat in mutual silence. O'Donnell looked like he might be meditating, while I… On the outside I might look calm, but a battle waged on the inside. One half wanted to be pissed off and verbally rip Donny a new one. My other half wanted to run free in the forest, away from all this nonsense, away from all of life's complications, just be, just run.

"So you think I should just ask my ghost feras to leave?"

"Dematerialize."

"And then what?"

"Ask one of them to come back."

"What if she doesn't? What if she takes too long? What if it drains me of energy somehow? What if I can't do it?"

"You remind me of my daughter," he said. For a moment, sadness flickered across his face. I didn't comment on it, or ask about his daughter. With most of the Shifter population killed off during the first few years of the Purge, the probability spoke so Donny didn't have to. He cleared his throat. "She…she kept asking for guitar lessons. For her sixteenth birthday, her mother and I got her a package deal at the local music store."

He paused, but I didn't rush him. Instead, I reached across the table and clasped his hand. Donny's shoulders sagged.

"She kept going to those lessons, expecting to get better, but when she came home, she never practiced. When her package ran out, she only had a few songs to show for it." Donny's tone developed more steel as he spoke. When he finished, his eyes bore into mine.

"Hey!" I snatched my hand back. "What's that supposed to mean?"

"It means you should practice."

"How?"

"Try stuff out. Have you ever tried to re-embrace your fox and then shift into her form? Have you tried to do it in one fluid motion? After you tell her to dematerialize, try getting her to reappear when you call, then re-embrace, then shift."

Huh. As crazy as O'Donnell's suggestion sounded, that might work. It would explain what happened with my bear when I fought Westman.

"You look like you've thought of something," Donny observed.

"I think I've already done it once."

"When?"

"Today."

Donny's face morphed into a thoughtful expression. A little too calculating for my taste. "What happened?"

I quickly recounted my visit with the spawn of Satan and how Baloo had crashed into me. The size and strength of the black bear gave me the advantage I needed against Takkenmann.

The knowing look didn't leave Donny's face the entire retelling of the story. When I finished and leaned back in my chair, silence consumed the small office.

I cracked first. "You're not going to drain my blood and use me in some pagan death ritual, are you?"

Donny laughed, and shook his head. But he didn't answer the question.

I scowled at him and his cackling fera before letting myself out of the office.

Chapter Twenty-Four

"The hardest thing to learn in life is which bridge to cross and which to burn."
~Bertrand Russell

The hospital cranked the air-conditioning due to the daily influx of people and the sweltering heat outside, but no amount of disinfectant could mask the odour of unwashed bodies, dirty hair and an assortment of bodily fluids in the cool air. I hated medical buildings. Did Westman know that? Had he purposely led me to these buildings to torture me? I kept twisting my lips around in an effort to straighten out my wrinkled nose.

The automated emergency entrance doors parted, and I stalked toward my car.

Turned out, I'd wasted a day trying to track Bola down in hospitals. I'd visited all the ones in the Lower Mainland, and the sun set on another day of failure. I wanted to drive back up the mountain to the university and bitch-smack Westman for leading me astray, but he'd been truthful. Bola had been in this hospital, probably for an in-between-massacre-snack. But his scent ran cold, covered with layers of other filth and disease. Bola was nowhere in the building, and had he appeared in his true form, it wouldn't have gone unnoticed.

The sun beat against my black hair as heat rose in waves off the parking lot's pavement and cooked my bare legs.

Plan A: Find Bola outside his host while feeding and vanquish, rapidly disintegrated in my mind. It wasn't worth the risk to keep wasting valuable resources, like time and sanity, when other options existed. Plan B looked inevitable. Divine intervention. I'd have to call in a favour. My chest tightened, and I forced my lungs to exhale. I wanted to make this call about as much as I wanted to renounce chocolate.

I'd been saving my favour for my own personal interests—namely finding my birth family, but saving my hide, and potentially Wick's as well, rated higher in importance.

The bright red penis spray-painted on my canary-yellow Poo-lude glared at me as I wrenched open the door and flopped in, instantly sweating in the summer temperature. The thirty-minute commute home seemed to take three times as long, but when I checked the clock it appeared I made record time. I threw my purse on the counter and retrieved the weird miniature sculpture of a cobra-headed Egyptian goddess.

The last time I'd seen my previous supervisor, Agent Booth, she'd handed this ugly figurine to me and said to hold it and say her name, her true name, Renenutet, and she'd appear to pay her debt to me. That had been months ago. Would it even work?

I flopped on my couch, and turned the statue around in my palms. The energy drained from my limbs, and I couldn't quite make myself say the four-syllable name. Even if it would solve my problems. Articulating "Renenutet" meant saying goodbye to the last lead on my parents or any surviving family. Brothers, sisters, aunts or uncles. What familial relations waited for me to find them? My parents supposedly died in the first year of the Purge, but part of me held on to the belief they gave me up for adoption to save me from the Shifter Shankings.

If they'd died, why didn't I go to family instead of the adoption agency?

Then again, I'd survived almost eighty years without knowing. If family existed, they could've tried to track me down as well. No one had knocked on my door. No one called to inquire. That I knew of, at least. Working for the government gave me a new understanding of "the truth."

I squeezed my eyelids shut on my blurry vision and took a deep breath. "Renenutet."

At first nothing happened. I sat alone in my living room with the summer smells of hibiscus and bullileia. Then the air in the room stirred, and a woman appeared in front of me. I wasn't sure what to expect. I'd only known Booth in her business appropriate attire, not as Renenutet, the Egyptian goddess with a cobra head who could destroy her enemies with a single gaze. But when the mist settled and the figure turned to face me, I found myself oddly relieved to see Booth's familiar face.

A middle-aged woman with graying black hair and a large hooked nose, she no longer wore her trendy purple-rimmed glasses, and her eyes distinctly looked like those of a snake. She remained scentless, but this no longer made my skin crawl. With a double plumed headdress and a white, Grecian dress, she looked more like a goddess and less like an SRD agent.

Her lips pursed into a straight line. "Calling your

favour in so soon? You mortals are so hasty."

My shoulders sagged. "I need some divine intervention."

Her eyebrow quirked up. Then she swayed back and forth, reminding me of a snake poised to strike. This must be how mice felt. "Speak," she ordered.

"A bunch of newbie Witches summoned the Demon Glasya Labolas and allowed him to take possession of one of their bodies in exchange for his help."

Booth snorted. "I fail to see how requires my aid."

"They forgot to specify the length of time."

Booth's mouth dropped open to form a perfect "O."

"And now Bola has been busy causing mayhem all around town."

"Let me guess. Lucien commanded you to deal with it?"

"So you have been paying attention up there?" I pointed to my roof, in case she needed a reference. "Why'd you make me explain all this, then?"

Booth shook her head. "Silly child, I have better things to do than keep tabs on you mortals. It doesn't take a lot of intelligence to figure out your situation. I bet the Master Vampire threatened that yummy piece of Werewolf ass to provide extra motivation, too."

"Well, you definitely have his number."

Booth nodded.

I waited.

She stared.

I stared back.

"I'm afraid I can't help you," she said.

"What?"

"Glasya Labolas is too powerful for me, or Sobek for that matter, to intervene."

"How is that possible? You're an Egyptian goddess. I looked you up on the internet. You guys are badass!"

"We *were* badass. Sadly, we're only as strong as our worshippers, and not many worship the ancient ones anymore. Especially not in comparison to those who practice demonic worship. Bola has quite the following of perverted groupies."

My head swam. I'd hoped this would solve my problems.

"Why not kill the host?" Booth asked. "That will send Bola back."

"Last resort. The Witch is a…well, he's not *my* friend, but he's a friend of my friends. And I'd rather destroy Bola once and for all. I despise him."

Booth nodded, as if I made all the sense in the world. Maybe I did to her. Maybe she knew everything about me with her special goddess powers, whatever they were.

"Is there nothing you can do?" I asked like a whiney eight-year-old.

"I will try to help behind the scenes. Sobek and I might not be powerful enough to help, but there are others who are. And no one likes Bola. He's an ass." Without another word, Booth disappeared. Like the time before, she left no trace and gave no warning. My feras screeched in my head, and the beast stretched.

I stood in the middle of my living room with only my thoughts and nattering feras to keep me company.

The mountain lion paced in my head, back and forth. I didn't need to ask her what she wanted. She didn't have to say. She wanted to sink her claws into something—the tender underbelly of a deer, the bark of a tree, the soft soil of an old growth forest. She didn't care which, she just wanted *out*.

Me, too, growled the wolf and bear.

Me, four, yipped Red.

The falcon remained silent, but she sent me images of a calm night under a full moon and over a rolling ocean, the air laced with salt and pine, the wind currents perfect for soaring.

I ignored them all and focused on what Booth had said.

Did this mean I used my favour, or not? Had it been a good investment? Booth hadn't really committed to anything. My heart pulsated in my chest, so hard it hit my bones and lanced pain across my chest. I might've given up my hopes of family for nothing.

And if Booth couldn't help me, who could?

Chapter Twenty-Five

"Housework can't kill you, but why take a chance?"
~*Phyllis Diller*

After scouring the internet and SRD databases for hours, searching for clues or sightings of either Christopher or Bola, I admitted defeat. Besides, I only researched to avoid the inevitable. I had to take my momentary failure at locating Bola during his feeding frenzy as an opportunity to face Donny's advice.

Time to practice.

Time to clear my head of some of the extra voices.

With saggy jogging pants, an oversized T-shirt and flip flops, I trudged to the nearby forest with Baloo and Red in tow. Still early in the evening, people strolled along the sidewalk. The black bear lumbered along, snorting and huffing as she kept pace.

How could no one see or hear the ruckus behind me? How could Baloo not trample the elderly couple I just passed? When I looked over my shoulder, the norms walked straight through Baloo. The old man shuddered and Baloo snorted, but otherwise no adverse effects.

Only I could touch her. Only I could be squished when the two hundred and fifty pound black bear thought she was a lap-dog. As great as she was to cuddle, my life needed simplicity.

Don't be sad, Red told me.

I wiped my nose with my sleeve. *Who said I was sad?*

Your tears, Baloo said.

Well, okay. I'm sad. What if this doesn't work? What if I lose both of you?

Can't lose what's been found, Red said.

I better not. You're both a part of me.

I am you. You are me. We are one, Baloo and Red crooned the fera mantra. The ones in my head joined in. I rubbed my temples.

You won't be mad when I send you away? I asked.

Why would we be mad? Red asked.

We are always with you, Baloo said.

Right. Like that made a lot of sense.

As we walked away from the murmuring din of the city, the sound of the rushing river ahead carried through the quiet night. We entered the forest and made our way down to the river where I'd met Baloo for the first time. Red ran around like an overstimulated toddler on a sugar high.

Why are you so excited? I asked.

Why not? she replied.

I needed an operator's manual to deal with my split personalities. No wonder the previous Shifters with this "gift" went nuts. If all my feras were me, did that mean I talked to myself? How'd that work exactly? And how did the feras seem to know more than they let on. If they were me, are me, wouldn't I know what they know? See what they see? Why would I keep secrets from myself?

The wheels in my head wobbled off their hinges with each step. Once my feet entered the cool river, I stopped.

Could've done this at home, Baloo muttered. She lumbered into the water to brush up beside me.

I know. I like the forest.

Baloo yawned and flopped her gargantuan weight down on her haunches. I reached out and scratched her nose. Though I hadn't had much time to know my most recent fera, a couple nights spent spooning in bed, and the knowledge she represented part of myself, made me feel close to her anyway. I stopped scratching, and flung my arms around her. Face deep in bear fur, I inhaled her fruity scent. She rumbled and wheezed. As far as I could tell, the sound was the bear equivalent to a purr.

Okay, Baloo. I hope this works, I told her.

It will, Carus. Ask me to go.

I squeezed my eyes shut. *Baloo, please dematerialize.*

I am you, you are me, we are one, she said. Her body shook, and my arms, still wrapped around her, got closer and closer together, until I held nothing but the night air.

My eyes pinged open and took in the empty space in front of me. *Well, that was easy.*

Told you, Red grunted.

Baloo, I said. *Baloo!*

The night air blew through the trees, rustling the drying out leaves and bringing the smells of late summer; autumn just around the corner. But no Baloo. No berries or strawberry shortcake, no grumbling or ambling black bear.

Baloo!

Try something else, Red suggested.

"BALOO!"

That's the same thing, just louder, Red said. She pressed against my legs and shuddered.

Baloo, come! I tried, pouring my so-called will and inherent love for the fera into the two words.

A beastly bear call ripped through the night and a two-hundred-and-fifty pound black bear materialized two feet in front of me an instant before she rammed into me. I flew through the air and landed with a splash in half a foot of river water. Baloo landed on top of me, and a cold wet tongue slurped my face from chin to forehead.

Ugh! I pushed her shnoz out of the way.

It worked, Red exclaimed and sprinted circles around us.

It worked, I agreed. Now what?

I scrambled to my feet, and eyed the black bear. She mooed at me again.

Did it hurt? I asked her.

She cocked her head at me. Her cute little ears pinged forward.

Did dematerializing hurt? I repeated.

Baloo snorted. *No, Carus. No pain. All I felt was your love for me.*

Where did you go? Did you like it there?

She nuzzled my hand. *Yes. Big forest. Lots of berries. Room to sleep. I liked it very much.*

I squeezed my eyes shut. So dematerializing my feras put them out to pasture? She said she liked it; did that make it okay? This situation probably called for some epic pangs of regret or guilt, but none of that flashed through my mind or my heart. The truth of her words flowed through my veins and warmed my body.

She liked it there.

Would you like to go back? I asked.

Baloo sat up, eyes big and mouth opened in a toothy grin. *Yes. Please send.*

I reached out and stroked her beautiful, fuzzy face. Her ears flicked forward and I wound my hands around her big head, and scratched behind her ears. Her eyes closed, and her chest rumbled.

I'll miss you, I said.

Her eyes popped open, soulful and deep brown. *If bad, call me back.*

I nodded. *Baloo, please dematerialize.*

She leaned forward and slurped her giant tongue along my forearm before she vanished.

Red zipped around my feet, yipping, *Me, too. Me, too. Me, too.*

You, too? I gaped down at her. *Is my company so terrible?*

She stopped running around and blinked up at me. *No. You can call me when you need me. Baloo sent me images. I want to go.*

Something tightened in my chest. As if someone slung a belt around my heart, and yanked tight.

Let me go. Red wagged her tail at me. *Please?*

A long, tired breath escaped my lungs, my shoulders dropped. She wanted to go. I could call them back anytime I wanted. My mind would get some peace and quiet.

The tightness around my chest loosened.

Okay, I said. The words probably didn't need to be said, now that I sort of had a hang of it, but I spoke them anyway. *Red, please dematerialize.*

I vote for the Wereleopard, she said with a toothy

grin before blinking out of existence.

My mountain lion purred her approval.

I stumbled back to the path and sat down. Empty and alone, yet still carrying around a head full of feras.

RED! Come here! I bellowed, throwing command into my voice.

The little fox shimmered into reality a foot in front of me. Body tense, eyes bugged out, stance ready. *What? Where's danger?*

Just checking. I half-shrugged.

Red cackled, sounding a lot like Ma'ii. *We're here for you, Carus. The forest is divine.*

I nodded. With command in my voice, I spoke again. *Okay. Go back.*

She winked at me before disappearing.

Chapter Twenty-Six

"Don't judge me because I'm quiet. No one plans a murder out loud."
     ~*Darynda Jones, Fourth Grave Beneath My Feet*

After dragging myself out of bed at the embarrassing time of ten in the morning, the need to make another list hit me in the face like a cold fish. I turned the coffee maker on, and once I possessed a steaming cup of joe, I curled up on my couch beside the bay windows, mug in hand, and started scribbling. With my tongue coated in the delicious flavour of java and cream, my nerves calmed and my mind focused.

Plan A: Find Bola when he's separated from his host and kill him. FAIL.

Plan B: Summon Renenutet and Sobek and request divine intervention. FAIL.

Plan C: Kill Christopher and return Bola to the demonic realm.

I put the pen down. A heavy weight pressed against my shoulders. I shouldn't feel this sad. A few months ago, Christopher tried to kill me by blowing some toxic mumbo jumbo powder in my face. At the time, I wanted to kill him. Had Ben not stopped me, I would have. Why should the realization I needed to take out Christopher now fill me with sadness?

Why? Because I liked the Witches.

Even if Christopher's days were numbered, even if the Witches knew it was the only way, they would never forgive me. I'd lose them. And their killer karaoke nights.

Oh, be honest, McNeilly, you're scared to lose Ben. Next to Mel, he was the closest thing I had to a bestie.

My phone rang. Officer Stan Stevens calling. My chance to procrastinate ripped away. I knew without answering the nature of the call.

Bola had struck again.

****

Bola hit the beach. Literally. This current massacre so deadly and prolific, I arrived in White Rock while the killing still took place. The media vans that had parked at a presumed "safe" distance, now overrun with blood-frenzy-induced norms, kept the cameras rolling. No one was in their right minds to turn them off, and even if they were, they'd probably leave them on anyway. Bloodshed equalled great ratings.

The overly enthusiastic I'll-take-any-opportunity-I-can-to-wear-my-bathing-suit-in-public beach goers strangled and hacked at each other as I circled above and assessed the situation. When a woman tried to murder a man I presumed to be her husband with the picnic basket butter knife, I dove into her. She screeched, and flailed her arms around. She missed clipping my wings by a fingernail's width. Maybe the husband deserved some ass-kicking, but Bola's ability to incite homicidal rage told me the punishment didn't fit the crime.

For once, I couldn't waste time to take in the blood and guts or general horror of the scene. I visually tuned it out. Bola stood in a small clearing of bodies in the middle of the mayhem. With his arms spread wide, his head tilted back, and eyes closed, he looked like I did before I willed the change to falcon—absolute abandonment of humanity's constraints.

The open air filled with salt and sand vibrated with energy as Bola pulled it in his direction, draining his victims as they robbed each other of life, feeding off their rage and the tragedy of their deaths. I pulled my wings in and dove toward him. At the last moment, I flung my wings out.

The air rose and pushed against my slate feathers, bringing my little falcon body parallel to the ground, saving me from colliding into the hard packed white sand with my head. I willed the change again, ignoring the brief flash of pain that came with shifting. With the change completed, four tawny paws hit the blood-soaked sand.

As soon as I entered the clearing, Bola's head snapped forward, and his eyes opened to focus on me. He must've sensed my energy.

His lips twisted up into a smirk and I vaulted in the air, targeting his face with my wide open mouth and mountain lion fangs.

A bulldozer of pain slammed into my side. I never reached Bola. My body flew as an invisible power barreled into me. Like being T-boned in an intersection, my head snapped sideways in a whip-like action from the sheer force of impact.

My body hit the hard packed sand and everything went black.

****

My eyelids fluttered open, scratching my eyeballs with gritty sand. The air stank of blood, bodies and guilt. My human vision focused and a familiar face leaned over me.

"I'm sorry, Andy," Ben wheezed. "I couldn't let you. Christopher is my friend, my responsibility."

I grunted and rolled to my side. Sand stuck to my back, ass and thighs. Ben had covered my naked body with someone's towel. "Was," I said. "Christopher is no longer home."

"He's in there."

My head spun like I'd gone around the merry-go-round one time too many. The power of Lucien's bond flowed through my veins. Bones and muscles knitted together with little snaps of pain. "Yeah, he is. And he'll have front row seats for our deaths."

Ben's gaze cut away.

"Or at least mine. I keep forgetting your den is safe from his wrath. Maybe that's why you don't give a crap that he's mutilating the entire Greater Vancouver Regional District."

"I care."

"Really? What's one man's life worth? One Witch's?" I struggled to my feet and wrapped the towel around me, clutching it at my chest. "Did you at least trap Bola in some magical hocus pocus spell?"

"He got away." Sweat ran down the side of his face, and he wrung his hands together. "There's got to be another way."

"I've tried the other ways. Do you think this was my first choice? I'm not a complete asshole. I've run out of time for alternatives. Lucien will start taking my failures out on Wick. You haven't been running around with much urgency to solve the problem."

"I have so! I went to the Elders."

"Oh." The notorious Witch Elders. Damn. "How bad is it?"

Ben ran his hand through his thick blond hair. "Bad."

I nodded.

"I don't know what to do."

About to say, "Me neither," I clamped my mouth shut. There had to be another way. Some other way to separate Bola from his host. And fast. "I know someone who might know what to do. You're coming with me."

****

The Poo-lude died halfway up the hill to the university. I got out, clutched my towel and kicked my front tire. As if that would make a difference. Ben got out of the passenger side and looked at me over the car's canary yellow roof.

"Like that's going to make a difference," he echoed my thoughts.

"Not helping."

He shrugged. The yellow paint made him look pale and sallow. It also accentuated the dark bags under his eyes. I hadn't noticed them before. Leave it to my car's crappy paint job to make a point. Ben really had been trying. He probably slept less than I did.

"Doesn't help that you magically boosted it earlier," I grumbled.

"This again? I already apologized. None of us have a car and I needed to get to you in time."

I let my angry glare speak for me.

"What do we do now?" Ben asked. "The elders told me they'd put a hit out on Christopher if one more massacre happens. That means they're issuing orders as we speak. I don't know who they'll hire for the assassination, but we don't have much time."

Christopher's death warrant had already been signed and sealed. I could've saved the Elders an assassination bill, but Ben had slapped me with a spell to buy his friend a few hours, maybe a day or two. Precious time to find an alternate solution.

I opened my mouth to rip into him when I met his desperate gaze. Blood shot eyes, pale complexion, turned down mouth as if he needed to throw up.

The tension flowed out of my shoulders along with my anger. What had Ben said? We didn't have much time. I nodded in agreement. "Bola has to know his time is running short. Not everyone cares about the host, and he knows that. He'll want to go out with a big bang."

"Bigger than White Rock?"

"Bigger."

Ben stretched his arms out over the roof and then rested them. He twisted his head to look down the road. "Don't think anyone's going to head this way. Should we walk?"

I shook my head. "No. I'll fly. You wait here, and call someone for a tow."

"Fly—oh." Ben averted his eyes.

With a flick of my wrist, I removed the towel and chucked it in the backseat. "You're such a prude."

"Doesn't it bother you?"

"Being naked? No. Nudity doesn't bother me at all," I said. Vulnerability did. "Most guys don't have a problem with my nudity, either."

Ben shook his head and studied the pavement. "I'm not a Were or a Shifter. Not everyone is as comfortable with others strutting around in the buff as you guys."

I shrugged. If Ben was so uncomfortable with my nakedness, he should've brought me clothes. Then again, probably too much to ask for Ben to sit in the car with my hot pink panties.

"Do you think this professor Westman will be there?" Ben asked.

"Oh," I said. "He'll be there." *He's got nowhere else to go.*

I stretched my arms out, and willed the change. After a brief flash of pain and quick shift, I flapped my wings and launched into the sky. Ben waved, and got back in the car. He'd probably plug in his mp3 player and sing to himself. I hoped not.

Sitting in a dilapidated, canary-yellow Poo-lude with an emblazoned cock and balls spray-painted in bright red to the side...no one would stop for that hot mess.

****

After nabbing an oversized sweatshirt from an unwatched gym bag, I marched to the West Mall Complex to hunt down the Demon professor. The sweatshirt barely covered the private bits, but with some of the outfits undergrads wore these days, no one seemed to notice.

The office was easy to find and without hesitation I pounded on the door. When Westman's familiar voice bellowed, "Open," I turned the knob and stepped into his office. He looked up from his desk with a haughty expression, then his eyes widened and he visibly stiffened. "Carus!"

I resisted the urge to yank down on the sweatshirt. "Expecting some impressionable undergrad?"

He slowly released his pen on a mountainous stack

of papers, and pushed back from his desk. "As a matter of fact, yes. You have a way with interfering with my personal life."

His long lanky arms slid to rest on his chair, but the relaxed gesture didn't fool me. His dark brows arched over his inset eyes.

"If you're waiting for an apology, you're not going to get one. Those girls are looking for an easy A, not doggy-style with a Demon."

Westman sneered. "If you don't do doggy, you don't do Demon."

I held up my hand, palm out. "Please, stop there. You Demons really need to grasp the concept of too much information."

His mouth opened to say more, and I shushed him.

"Is there another way?" I blurted out. "Any other way to rip Bola from his host?"

Westman hesitated.

"Tell me." I slapped my hand down on his desk. My heart beat rapidly.

Westman jumped. "When he's summoned," he sputtered. "If you summon him, his incorporeal form will be wrenched from his host."

Of course! How could I have missed it? How could Ben? The solution was so easy.

"But you'll have to fight his true form, and he won't be vulnerable from feeding."

Well, okay. Not *that* easy.

I needed to call for some backup and summon a Demon. How could I possibly best Bola in his true form? None of my feras were strong enough.

Except one.

Air caught in my lungs.
The beast.

Chapter Twenty-Seven

"A woman's mind is cleaner than a man's: She changes it more often."

~Oliver Herford

Smelling of sweat, pork rinds and hot sauce, Ben and I ambled into my building. My arms hung limp at my side, my head weighed more than a garbage bag full of diapers, and my soft pillows and duvet called out to me. Wanting nothing more than to answer their summons, I grabbed Ben's phone and checked the messages. Yup. The boys were on their way.

"I can't believe that tow truck driver drove us all the way home, fixed your crap car and left without any payment," Ben said when we got to my apartment door. His eyebrows dug trenches in the skin above his nose.

"Oh, with the feast his eyes got of this," I made a large sweeping gesture with one hand, while the other kept a firm hold on my towel for Ben's sake. Maybe I should've kept the oversized sweatshirt instead of returning it. Regardless of my wardrobe, the tow truck driver had fallen victim to my powers and instead of requesting payment, he'd spent most of his time staring at my chest and drooling. The thirty-minute drive home had been a harrowing experience. "He got paid."

Ben snorted. "Sorry, Andy. I've seen the girls, and they're not *that* special."

I punched him in the arm, and he squeaked. Ben clutched his shoulder and scrunched his lips up. I didn't mean to hit him that hard. "You're a Witch. You're not susceptible to my charms like norms."

"Your animal magnetism, you mean?" He massaged his arm.

"Yeah, that."

"Ever get you in trouble?"

"You have no idea." I handed him the phone.

We paused outside my door and both stared at it. Staying in the hallway suddenly gained instant appeal. Going into my apartment meant my haywire plan would unfold.

"We really going to do this?" Ben's mouth turned down.

"Is it 80s night on Friday?" I asked.

He answered with a blank stare.

"Of course, we're going to do this. What other choice do we have?"

"Exactly how strong is this guy in his natural form?" His voice wavered.

"Pretty strong. Don't worry. I called for backup." Texted, actually, but I couldn't say, "Texted for backup," with a straight face.

"Who'd you contact?"

If he'd checked his phone, he'd know.

The door to the building opened and citrus and sunshine flowed down the hallway in a giant, overwhelming wave.

Ben turned back to me, and rolled his eyes. High school girls would've sold their best friend to pull off the look.

"What?" I hissed at him before greeting Tristan

with a big smile. "Hi."

"Hi." He leaned down and pecked me on the cheek. "Nice outfit. Are we going to stare at your door, or are we going in?"

I unlocked the door using the spare key from under the mat, and pushed open the door. "You go ahead. We'll be in shortly."

Tristan nodded, cast Ben a wary look and then sauntered into my place.

"What's his deal?" Ben turned to me, mouth twisted down. "We've met before. He's been to my place for karaoke."

"He's an Alpha. They don't tend to give their backs to people. Makes coordinating a get-together a bit awkward."

"But he backed down to me?" Ben looked confused.

"Hah! No. His inner leopard must've decided it was more important to enter my place first and scope it out, or deemed you as a non-threat. Or both."

"Bloody cats."

"I've seen you use a beer bottle as a microphone. So has Tristan. Don't judge."

The building's front door opened again and this time a stream of rosemary and sugar flooded my senses.

Ben groaned.

"Let's do this," Wick said as he approached. He enfolded me in his arms, and planted a kiss on my lips. His gaze rested on the knot holding my towel in place. He licked his lips.

"Go on in. Tristan's already here," I said. "Ben and I need to have a quick chat."

Wick nodded, slapped my butt and then strutted

into my apartment.

Ben waited until Wick's footsteps faded away before he reached forward and closed my apartment's door, shutting us out. He turned to me. "Are you kidding me?" he asked.

"What?"

"They're more likely to kill each other than hurt the *big bad Demon*." Ben's hands flew to his hips.

"You're such a diva."

"No. You are. Why didn't you at least get them to bring their packs, or prides, or groupies, or whatever."

"Have you seen my apartment? No way they'd all fit."

"More would be better than none, and we could've done the summoning elsewhere."

"And risk Bola enthralling innocent bystanders? No way. The pack and pridemates would probably end up as liabilities, too. You've texted the elders so they'll hopefully have their hit man on the way, in case we can't contain the situation. We have the strongest Werewolf and Wereleopard in the GVRD sitting in my living room—"

"Probably growling and hissing at each other."

I ignored him. "And you're standing here bitching about the calibre of backup?"

"If you tell me beggars can't be choosers, I'll—"

"You'll what? Fling a really nasty curse at me and knock me out? Oh wait!" I snapped my fingers. "You've already done that."

Ben huffed, and rocked back on his heels. "You're never going to let that go are you?"

"Nope."

"You were going to kill one of my denmates."

"For the greater good," I said.

"What if it had been Patty or Matt?" he paused. "Or me?"

His question stumped me. My neurons stopped firing, and I stared at his face. Could I have done it? My heart hollowed out, leaving my chest empty and barren. I released a long breath. "I'm not sure I could've done it," I said.

Ben's shoulders sagged, and he stepped in to give me a big hug. His warm witchy scent surrounded me. Then he stiffened, and pulled away. His lips compressed into a straight line. His look of concern melted my smile away.

"What now?" I groaned.

"Your boyfriends aren't going to beat me up, are they?" he asked. "I forgot how sensitive all your noses are."

"For giving me a hug? You're my friend."

"I know that, but do they?" He glanced at the door, and a shudder vibrated through his body.

I reached out and grabbed his stiff hand. Giving it a squeeze, I leaned in. "I don't have a lot of friends, Ben. If they try to harm one hair on your body, I'll not only dump them, but I will make them pay."

Ben smiled back at me. "Yeah?"

"Yeah."

He nodded. "Okay, let's do this!"

When we stepped into the living room holding hands like schoolyard kids, both men stiffened. Wick's nose flared, and Tristan's eyes narrowed.

Tristan recovered first.

"There's no reason to fear me, Witch. I'm not going to hurt you," he said. "Although, if anything ever attacks Andy again in her home, I hope you'll come better prepared."

Tristan referred to the time a horde of Kappa-possessed norms swarmed my home. Ben had showed up with his denmates looking like children from *The Goonies*. Complete with water guns.

Ben sniffed. "Those guns were full of hexes and curses. We'd have taken down those humans."

Tristan nodded. "Uh-huh."

Everyone turned to Wick, whose shoulder muscles hunched with tension. He took a deep breath and closed his eyes. "If you ever cause her harm, Witch…"

Now probably wouldn't be a good time to tell Wick about the beach.

"I don't make a habit of hurting my friends," Ben said, his nervous glance told me he thought along the same lines.

My heart swelled like a mamma bear that he'd managed to speak a half-truth and not give away a lie. Technically, he'd hurt me pretty bad only a couple hours ago. I squeezed his hand and let go.

"Where are your denmates?" Wick asked.

"They're too inexperienced to help," Ben said.

"Liabilities," I muttered. Ben cast me a bitchy face. I turned and shrugged at him.

"Where's your salt?" Ben asked. I pointed to the kitchen and within minutes, Ben drew a summoning circle with salt in my living room. While he worked, I changed into some shorts and a tank top. I planned to shift, but Bola might be a tad apprehensive if he showed up at a summons to find me naked. I wanted to catch him off-guard, not cue him in to my plans right away.

After I emerged from the bedroom, Wick and Tristan went in to shift. They left the bedroom door open and planned to wait until Bola arrived and I broke the circle.

"Blitz attack," they'd both said, and then glared at each other for having the same idea. Fucking Alphas. I hoped they weren't in there playing fisticuffs as a warm up. An attack of any kind wouldn't work if they knocked each other unconscious before Bola showed up.

Ben withdrew the ceremonial knife he had sheathed and attached to his belt. A six-inch blade winked in the artificial lights as the sun set outside. Without a word, Ben ran the knife across his palm, and walked around the summoning circle. The smell of blood overwhelmed my nose, drowning out the addictive Alpha scents.

Ben finished and stood beside me. He whispered the incantation under his breath. He probably did it for my benefit, or maybe he had to put more effort into the summoning because of the moon phase. *"Hekate. Si placet, ancora nobis ad orbis terrarium. Gratias tibi ago."*

Ben took a deep breath and turned to me. "You sure?"

My heart hammered in my chest. Was I really about to do this? Purposely call forth my beast to fight a powerful Demon? My partially-shifted fingernails dug into my sweaty palms and drew blood.

"Andy?" Ben asked again.

I shook my head. "Nope. Let's do this anyway."

Ben nodded and continued. *"Hekate. Si placet, advoco Daemonium Glasya Labolas ad nobis. Gratias tibi ago."*

A tremor streaked through my body as the air in the room stirred like a miniature tornado. The portal snapped into place, and the air grew heavy as a giant figure materialized in the center of the circle.

His stench hit me first. Steel and blood, tainted almond and waves of rotten grass. Sweat trickled down between my breasts. I clenched and unclenched my fists, but I refused to flee despite the terror racking my body.

Bola turned to face us, naked and terrifying, and started laughing.

Chapter Twenty-Eight

"Rage, rage against the dying of the light."
                                    ~*Dylan Thomas*

The room crackled with cold energy and a foreboding sense of danger. Did Bola suspect what we planned? Could he sense the Alphas in the other room?

"Did you wish to make a deal, Carus?" he asked.

Guess not. "Yes. What payment do you want to vacate Christopher's body and return to the demonic realm?" I inched closer to the circle.

Bola cackled. The room filled with the smell of stale grass. "Break the circle, my dear, and your wish is my command. Though you might not live to enjoy your…success."

I had no wish to draw this conversation out. The longer I waited to make a move, the harder that move would be to make. I couldn't risk losing my nerve. Not now. Sweat continued to drip down my spine. It pooled on my lower back above the waistband of my shorts. My muscles tightened. I lifted my chin and met his overconfident gaze.

"Gladly," I said and stepped over the line.

Bola's eyes widened. The air popped as the circle's power imploded. Pain lanced across my skin as if blade-sharpened hail pelted against it. A huge wall of pure energy slammed into me. I flew across the room, twisting in the air. With a face-first landing, I groaned and turned to face Bola.

The Demon cranked his salivating dog head back, balled his giant fists and roared. Spittle flung from his mouth, spraying the floor. It reeked of iron and decaying grass.

The deep vibrations of Bola's call woke the beast within me. Normally nestled into my core, she rose with a burning fury. My skin lit on fire, stretched and tore open, the shift so sudden and brutal, I swallowed vomit and writhed on the floor. With my beast face smushed against my filthy rug, I took a millisecond to let the shift settle before I lurched to my feet. Sensory cues flooded my nose and ears, overwhelming and unwanted. Fire and strength coursed through my veins. The beast prodded my brain.

Destroy, she growled.

I swiveled and faced Bola again as the Ualida. A ball of rage bubbled up from my gut and a deep roar of my own ripped from my throat.

"Impressive," Bola said.

We leapt for each other at the same time and collided over the destroyed summoning circle. Salt and blood coated our scaly hides as we rolled and grappled, straining to strangle, struggling to defend. Acid burned my throat and hollowed my stomach. The room filled with sounds of grunting and thrashing, but nothing else, just the hum of silence, of waiting. Where were Tristan and Wick? Were they waiting for the right opportunity to strike?

"Give up," Bola growled at me. He clutched my throat and shook.

"You first, asshole." My beast voice low and

gravelly. Inhaling deeply, my lungs filled with air until they burned. Fire ruptured from my throat, and hit Bola in the face.

He chuckled, and wiped his dog face with a taloned hand. "I'm from hell. Fire has no effect on me."

I knocked his other arm away and shoved him back. We sprang to our feet and circled one another, hands wide, and talons out. The tang of steel and iron flooded the air, so heavy the metal coated my tongue. Bola swiped at my head. I ducked. We circled some more.

"You can't beat me," Bola said.

"Who are you trying to convince?" I asked.

He lunged, tackling me low. The impact of his body sent us flying back, slamming hard against my kitchen's tiled floor. He landed on top with a grunt. His large canine jaws gaped open and thick saliva dripped onto my face, stinging the skin it contacted. Rotten grass filled my nose. I wrapped my tail around one of his legs. Bola's head snapped forward and time slowed. I watched in horror as his stench-ridden teeth came closer and closer to my face.

I wrenched my tail with all my strength and pushed off the ground, flinging Bola back. By the time I staggered to my feet, Bola was on me again. I kicked out. He stumbled backward a few steps. My heart thudded against my rib cage, and my limbs shook with the adrenaline racing through my blood.

Wick and Tristan sprinted from the bedroom in their animal forms. Wick rammed into Bola, blindsiding him, while Tristan, faster and more agile, snaked around and leapt to attack from the other side. The Weres ripped at the Demon's skin with their teeth.

Their claws dug into flesh and dark, rank blood flowed onto the floor.

A wave of their Alpha power rolled through the room like a tsunami. It slammed into my body. I staggered as my mountain lion and wolf rose from within to join the Ualida.

Ben poked his head out from around the corner and mumbled. White light blasted from his hand and cracked into Bola's exposed chest. The Demon stepped back with a howl. Both Weres clung to him as he dropped to a knee. Skin torn, dark red blood poured from the wounds, and the air shook with his rage.

Ben blasted him again, and Bola grunted. His hand shot out to support his weight. His body convulsed as the Weres clung to him, raking their claws and teeth against his thick hide.

Bola's body shook. His head lifted. When his cold eyes met mine, he smiled.

Wait, what?

I leaned forward. Those dead orbs glinted with laughter. He was laughing!

Fuck!

Without warning, he surged up and flung the Weres off his body with such force they flew through the air and slammed against the opposite walls. The apartment shook; the whole building trembled. Ben stepped forward and blasted him again with blue fire. Bola dropped his head and laughed. Then he swiped his arm out, smacking Ben across the hall. He hit the wall and crumpled to the floor in a bloody heap.

I reached out for Ben.

Bola growled a warning.

I stopped and turned to him.

"Pitiful," Bola sneered. "Bringing your boy toys to the fight. Do they know I've had you? That I've sunk myself deep inside your body as you howled with desire?"

My blood burned as it raced through my body to my fast beating heart. The beast surged forward in my mind, demanding control. She snarled and raked her claws against my brain. Maybe I should give her control, maybe she'd take Bola without my fighting inferiority holding her back. She could show me what this form could really do.

I swallowed and focused on Bola. "Howled in rage," I corrected.

Bola smirked, and his weight shifted forward.

Before the Demon could launch his body at me, Tristan careened into Bola's side and latched onto his arm with sharp teeth and claws. Tristan's hiss filled the room and burnt cinnamon rolled off him in waves. Guess he heard Bola's taunt.

The Demon's eyes met mine again and another sickening smile spread across his awful dog face.

No!

The glint in Bola's gaze telegraphed his intent. In sickening slow motion, I watched as Bola twisted his arm around somehow and grabbed Tristan by the nape. He slammed him into the floor and stomped on Tristan's neck. A sick snap broke the deadened silence in the room.

I stopped breathing. A broken neck didn't mean death. Not to a Were. Not to an old Were like Tristan. He wasn't dead. He couldn't be. Sweat trickled down my face. My heartbeat raced, yet my limbs hung heavy and useless as weakness consumed my body.

Bola chuckled and left his foot on Tristan's neck, pinning him to the floor.

I stepped forward, claws out, teeth barred, but Wick flew out of nowhere and barreled into Bola's side. The Demon laughed again, and I watched in horror as he repeated the exact same move with Wick.

Snap. Crunch.

No!

My heart sank in my chest, and I sagged to my knees. My beast roared, but defeat plagued my heart. I shouldn't have asked for their help. If they didn't survive. If they got hurt…

Wick twitched under Bola's foot. He lived! Did Tristan? A sudden coldness spread through my chest. *Please Feradea, let Tristan be alive. I'll do anything.*

I didn't dare move forward. Bola could easily end the lives of Wick and Tristan. He wouldn't require much provocation. That he hadn't killed them meant he wanted something. From me.

"What will it be, Carus? The lives of two for the lives of many?" Bola asked.

I shook my head. The world spun slowly before me. I couldn't make that choice; I couldn't live, and let them die. My heart beat in my throat. If I chose to fight Bola instead of bargain with him, he'd kill Tristan and Wick. And could I best him on my own? I wasn't exactly winning before the Weres and Witch joined the fight. I gasped for air. Bola wanted me to sacrifice Tristan and Wick or the humans in the Lower Mainland. My heart convulsed. My arms hung limp at my sides. I didn't want to live in a world where Tristan and Wick didn't exist.

But I couldn't sacrifice innocent people to save

them, either.

A high pitched whine came from Tristan's throat. Bola's foot clamped down harder.

Save yourself, Tristan said. *Save the others.*

I...I can't, I replied, and meant it.

I've lived long enough, Tristan said. *Do it.*

Andy, Wick said.

Bola roared and drowned out whatever Wick planned to say. But it didn't matter. I knew his sentiments would echo Tristan's. I knew what he'd want me to do.

But I couldn't do it.

I took a step forward. "What about one life for the lives of many?"

Bola's head snapped up, and his weight eased off Tristan's neck. His chest swelled. "Your life?"

I licked my dry lips and nodded. My chest dropped as an emptiness blanketed my heart. "In exchange for you returning to the demonic realm immediately, and your word to never harm these men again, ever." I made a large swooping gesture with my arm so he knew it included Wick, Tristan and Ben. Scratch that, I was dealing with a Demon. I better spell it out for him. "And by these men, I'm referring to Wick, Tristan and Ben."

No! Tristan and Wick bellowed in my head. Ben gurgled.

Andy, no, Wick said.

Don't do it Andy. We're not worth it, Tristan said.

"You will belong to me," Bola said.

I nodded. *I'll find a way out of it,* I told the men, though I didn't believe my own words. At least they'd live, even if I couldn't be with them. Images of the horrific things Bola had done to me in a host body flittered across my mind. I squeezed my eyes shut and pushed the bloody and painful images away. My limbs trembled, and I bit back a sob as it threatened to race up my throat. What awful things did Bola plan for me? Did it matter? The weight in my chest sank lower, leaving my heart with a dull ache.

Bola flicked his nail across his wrist and dark blood oozed out. "I, Glasya Labolas, do so swear to leave the realm of Earth and release my possession of the Witch known as Christopher. I also swear to do no harm from now to eternity to the three men in this room, named Wick, Tristan and Ben, in exchange for the sole ownership of Andrea McNeilly's body, mind and soul by her own sworn word for the rest of her existence."

Every single one of his words cut at my very being like shards of glass, but I ignored the pain. I had to. I couldn't stand by and watch Wick and Tristan die. Not when I had the chance to stop it.

I bent down and retrieved Ben's ceremonial knife from a pool of his blood. I glanced at his pale face and noted his shallow breathing. God, I hoped he was okay. I wiped the blade on my leg and held it up to my palm.

Something compelled me to look up and meet the anguished expression on Wick's face. He strained against Bola's hold, thrashing around as if sheer force of will would set him free to stop me. Then I turned to Tristan. He'd gone limp, but his feline gaze trained on me, taking everything in.

Goodbye, I told them both.

Chapter Twenty-Nine

"Smells detonate softly in our memory like poignant land mines hidden under the weedy mass of years."
~*Diane Ackerman*

The knife bit into the sensitive flesh, and the smell of the forest erupted. Instantly, my mind transported back to the night of my fourteenth birthday; the night when I'd walked into the forest, sweat soaked flannel pajamas, hair plastered to my head. The night I met my original three feras. The night my world changed.

Why this memory? Why now?

Because we are you, you are us, we are one, my feras wailed in my head.

The memory played out. Twigs and dry branches littered the forest floor. They dug into my naked, unseasoned soles. The dense branches of fir trees brushed my skin, sending tingles up my arms while pine needles sprinkled into my hair, like glitter. The loamy scent of deep rooted earth plugged my nose, making it impossible to smell anything else; my connection to the forest undeniable and overwhelming. I stumbled into a clearing, flailing face first onto the forest floor.

How did I get here? What was I doing before? Did it matter? A surge of warmth spread through my body. Something moved in the trees before me. Something I wanted. Something I loved.

On my hands and knees, I looked up to watch a lone mountain lion weave around the trees to stand in front of me. A sense of safety consumed me. Of being home. At rest. For the first time since pubescence. Gone was the uneasy feeling of something not quite right. Gone were the headaches behind my eyes that made my skull feel like splitting.

All that existed were the two amber eyes studying me, beckoning me to reach forward and touch her. One touch. My hand extended, and then something out of the corner of my eye made me hesitate. My arm faltered and dropped to my side. A wolf, gray and regal, loped into the clearing to sit beside the mountain lion. A small hawk-like bird swooped in to rest on the mountain lion's back. The animals stared intently. Waiting.

I reached forward again, this time overwhelmed with an adrenaline rush and a feeling of anticipation and excitement. The feras leaned in.

"Andrea." A deep voice startled me.

The vision of my feras melted away like a disappearing mirage.

Wick. Tristan. Ben. Bola.

What the heck? They were dying in my living room, and I was skipping through the forest frolicking with my feras and finding myself.

I leapt to my feet and whirled around. Sid stood behind me in the clearing, thankfully clothed.

He opened his mouth to speak, but I didn't give him a chance to spew seductive words at me. I lunged forward, grabbed his shirt, and like a true Canadian, pulled it over his head in a classic hockey move before feeding him my right fist. Repeatedly.

"Why am I here? Send me back, you fucked up perv!"

Sid grunted and twisted out of my hold and away from my strikes. "Crazy wench! Relax! You're not really here right now, either. You're frozen in your living room, slitting your palm to give yourself to Bola."

I hesitated. Had to give Sid an "A" for his summarizing skills.

"I can't let you do that."

"So what's happening right now? Have you possessed my body and locked me in this memory?" My scalp prickled like a deranged Martha Stewart wannabe stabbed my head repeatedly with sewing needles. "My friends are dying."

"No, they're not. Time is frozen in the mortal realm," Sid said. "You and your gaggle of lover-boys have retreated into your minds, to your safe places. They're alive and will stay that way for the time being." He paused. "What a surprise to learn your safe place is the sacred moment you bonded to your first feras. Touching."

"Fuck you." The idea of Sid in my happy place…Warning bells didn't go off in my head; my entire entanglement of dendrites screamed a cacophony.

Sid held his hands up. The supplicant gesture somehow genuine.

With a deep breath, my heart beat slowed down. The boys were safe. For now. Sid was up to something. *Pay attention, McNeilly.*

I narrowed my eyes at Sid. "What's going to happen now?"

"Now?" Sid asked. He took a step closer.

"Yes, now."

Sid took another step, now only a couple feet away from me. "You will owe me for this intervention."

"Isn't it too late?" I asked.

"What do you mean?"

"I've voluntarily drawn blood."

"It's not a deal until you utter the words to bind the agreement."

"Oh. Okay." I wrung my hands together and looked at my feet. "Can I put limitations on the payment?"

"No."

"Will it involve rape or sexual intercourse or ownership in any way?"

Sid sighed. "Those would be limitations. Wouldn't my ownership be more favourable than Bola's?"

I let my death stare speak for me. How much worse would servitude to Sid be compared to Bola? I didn't know what Sid would do or what he was capable of, but I knew the answer for Bola. A shiver racked my body. *Better the Demon I know, than the Demon I don't?* To hell with that. I'd take unknown Sid over the atrocious and sadistic Bola any day.

Sid watched my face a moment longer before speaking. "No, little one, I will not ask for sex or ownership of your mind, body or soul."

"Can I have your word?"

Sid slit his palm with his talon without hesitation. "By my word, I, Sidragasum, swear not to ask for sex or ownership as the favour Andrea McNeilly owes me for my aid." He winked at me. "Your turn."

What other options did I have? Slowly, I nodded.

"Say it."

My fingers tingled with sharp prickly pain as I shifted a nail into a talon and repeated Sid's actions. "I, Andrea McNeilly, will owe you, Sidragasum, for your intervention and help to successfully return Bola to the demonic realm, before he kills my friends or enslaves me."

Sid smiled and silence fell over the forest, or at least, the imaginary forest of my safe place.

"Do I have to play twenty questions before you tell me how we get back? Does it involve me clicking my heels three times?"

"A *Wizard of Oz* reference? Really?"

"For a Demon, you're incredibly judgemental."

"You should talk." He took a step closer. Now only a foot of space separated us, and I didn't like it one bit. "I need your blood," he said.

My blood turned to ice, and I shivered. "Is this my payment?"

Sid's eyes narrowed and then he shook his head. "No. I need your blood to return us to the mortal realm."

"Bullshit."

"I do."

"You didn't need it to bring me here. How'd you do it, anyway? I had no idea you wielded that kind of power." *Keep him talking. Keep him distracted.* If he wanted my blood, all he had to do was insist. He had a favour he could claim. I owed him.

Sid's gaze cut away.

"Sid?"

When he didn't answer, I crossed my arms. If I had been frozen in the real world along with everyone else, I could afford the time to wait for an answer.

The sounds of the forest grew louder as Sid shuffled his feet and hesitated. "I didn't bring you here."

Nausea gnawed at my guts as a feeling of apprehension slid over me. "Then who did?"

"I did," a woman's unfamiliar voice answered.

I spun around and froze.

Feradea.

Chapter Thirty

"I wanted to have an all-female band that took over the world."
~Courtney Love

Piercing obsidian eyes under dark sculpted brows assessed me as I stood frozen, regarding the deity for all Shifters. Feradea, the goddess of beasts and the hunt. She had strong cheekbones and a straight nose, like Cher in her younger years. Thick orange hair surrounded her head like a lion's mane, highlighted with lighter yellows and fiery reds.

A fringed triangle bra made of soft leather barely covered her ample breasts, and she wore a matching fringed thong and metallic arm bands. The outfit looked more like something from a politically incorrect lingerie catalogue than the attire of a goddess. But damn, she had a great body.

Atop her unruly mane sat a crown, or maybe she called it a headdress. Five roe deer skulls with blackened antlers adorned the piece, with the largest in the center. Embedded underneath each skull, sat polished brownish-red stones, probably cornelian, surrounded by sculpted oak leaves. Jagged teeth strung on a coarse thread hung around her neck; a large canine sat in the center and plunged into her cleavage.

She wore a quiver across her back, but clutched the

bow in one hand. With a knife strapped to her waist, and another at her thigh, stories of her fierce brutality resurfaced. Legends and myths told of her swift accuracy with her weapons of choice: the bow, the dagger, and her hands.

A white stag, larger than a bull, with shining translucent horns walked up to stand beside the goddess, and she reached out to rest her hand on its haunches.

She smelled of the forest.

Internally, my body warred with conflicting emotions. My throat grew thick as my heart beat heavy in my chest. This goddess watched over all Shifters and was responsible for bestowing my considerable "gifts." She'd also stood by while norms slaughtered the majority of Shifters during the first few years of the Purge. A hard goddess to like. A hard goddess to hate.

She oversaw all beasts, all Shifters, but she also looked after the men and women who hunted them. My mind and body reeled with how to respond to her presence.

"Should I bow?" I asked. My tone made it clear the answer in this case should be no. Seconds passed, and despite Sid's reassuring words, my mind kept drifting to the image of Tristan and Wick under Bola's feet and Ben slumped against the living room wall.

Feradea tilted her head. "We came to help, and you respond with attitude? With sarcasm? Should we leave and let Bola destroy your lovers and friend? Or perhaps allow you to sell your soul to the sadistic Demon so you can live out an eternity in hell? By all means, we could leave."

Well, damn. When she put it like that…

I bowed.

The goddess snorted. "Mortals," she said, as if it provided all the explanation in the world.

I straightened and ignored the warmth spreading across my cheeks. This was no time to be intimidated by a deity. Wick and Tristan may sit frozen under the control of Bola, and Ben lay in a pool of his own blood. The only reason I wasn't jumping up and down like a five year old needing to pee was I knew Bola was also frozen, and the men were in no imminent danger. Not until something happened here.

Focus, McNeilly.

"What should I call you?" I asked.

"I have been called many names. The Greeks called me Artemis; the Romans, Diana; the Egyptians, Pakhet; the Celtic, Arduinna; The Navajo, Hastseoltoi; the Semites, Aspalis; the Thracians, Bendis; the Finnish, Mielikki; the Hindus, Banka-Mundi; the Inuit, Pinga; the Slavic, Devana. I could go on. Shall I? I think not. Some have wrongly called me the Great Mother. There is only one mother, Gaia, and she is the reason all Shifters are bound. But I digress." She squinted at me. "Does this answer your question?"

"Unless I'm supposed to conclude, 'hey you,' is the best course of action, no, not at all."

"You may call me Feradea. My name matters not. It is my essence that is worshipped, not the label. I am of the hunt, of the forest and of all wild things."

Before she continued on another monologue, I asked, "How come no one figured you were all one and the same?"

"Well, they did. The ancient Greeks and Romans caught on. Damn them. I'd grown complacent. But generally, I revealed myself in different forms, and slightly different roles. You wouldn't recognize me in my Chinese guise."

I raised an eyebrow, but she didn't elaborate. "So what I'm seeing now is one of many disguises?"

"No child. What you see now is the truth."

After working for the government for fifteen years, I had a new understanding of the word truth. I bet she used that line with all her worshippers.

Her fiery mane shone under the moonlight.

"Homer did refer to you as a lion among women," I said.

The goddess's lip twisted up into a half-smile. "Homer! Now, he was a man." Her expression flattened when she refocused on me. "I'm surprised you know of his words."

My hands flew to my hips. "I read. It's a hobby." Or so Tristan had informed me on our first date. Tristan… Enough of this chit-chat. We needed to get back and kick some Bola ass.

"Fera," Sid said. I'd forgotten about him. His tone came out higher pitched and my head snapped to him. Why did he sound so weird?

"You," Feradea said. "Are not allowed to call me that." Her tone turned cold, and her lips compressed. "I'm only working with you out of necessity, Satan's spawn. Never forget that."

Sid nodded and stepped back.

Weirder and weirder. Call me a genius, but I sensed history between these two, and it didn't end amicably.

"Can we go now?" I asked, squeezing my eyes against the broken and bloody images of Tristan and

Wick. My mouth dried out. "Do we hold hands and sing 'Kumbaya'?"

Feradea's eyes narrowed. "No, child. We hold hands and return to the mortal realm." She reached out and clasped my hand without hesitation. We both turned to Sid. He held his arms out to each of us with his palms open. He looked entirely too content. When my hand slipped into his, his skin tingled against mine, sending shocks up my arm.

I gasped, and my arm instinctively retracted. Or tried to.

Sid tightened his hold on my hand and met my wide eyes. "Sure you don't want to rethink that restriction?"

"Ugh," I said. "Get over yourself."

Feradea chuckled, and Sid's darkened gaze focused on her. "I don't know why you're laughing," he said to her. "You enjoyed my attentions."

Feradea shook her head, her fluffy orange mane padding against her cheeks. "And like all lovers in my past, I bored of you quickly. I'm glad to find another woman is impervious to your charms. Are you done with your seduction attempts? May we go now?"

Sid grumbled and clasped her hand.

Feradea smirked, and the world folded away.

Chapter Thirty-One

"Go to Heaven for the climate, Hell for the company."
~*Mark Twain*

My eyelids scraped against dry lenses. The blur in my vision cleared to reveal the expectant look on Bola's face. Leaning forward, arms spread wide and talons extended to rip into flesh, he looked ready to snatch me up as soon as I closed the deal.

Wick and Tristan sprawled in frozen positions, in a struggle to get out from under Bola's taloned feet and stop me from agreeing to Bola's deal.

Snap! The air crackled as movement, sound and time resumed.

Bola straightened, and his eyes widened. With tense muscles, he dropped his arms to his side.

Tristan and Wick both sagged and somehow frowned at the same time. The wheels in their heads visibly running on overdrive to figure out what had happened. They were alive, and they'd heal, if given time. A quick glance over at Ben and his shallow moving chest, told me he lived as well. Thank Feradea!

"Sid." Bola's voice slithered and captured my attention. "I should've known you'd interfere."

The "good" Demon's presence vibrated to my left.

The air crackled again and another body appeared on my right. She radiated an inferno of heat and smelled of a pine forest under a fresh winter's snow.

Bola's head snapped in her direction. "Feradea!"

Feradea's lip twitched up, but she shuttered her face from showing any further emotion. She stepped forward. "Bola. I'd say it was a pleasure, except, well, it's not."

She extended her arm, palm forward, fingers splayed. Bola gasped, dropping to his knees. He clutched his head and moaned.

"You have reaped enough havoc with my child," she said.

Her child? More like grandchild to the power of infinity, but who was I to correct her with semantics?

I cracked my knuckles. Time for some Bola asskicking.

"Sid." Feradea's command stopped me in my tracks.

Sid leapt forward, grabbed Bola and dragged him away from Wick and Tristan. Sid had to clasp both his arms around Bola to hold him tight. Despite Sid's powerful seven foot frame, Bola in Demon form was considerably larger and more powerful.

"Shifter, make a circle, and make it quick," Feradea ordered. "The dog fights me even now."

I watched as Bola writhed in Sid's arms. Could Sid hold him? Why did Sid need to hold him if Feradea could do her awesome brain pain thing? The goddess's voice had somehow stopped me from jumping in and delivering much-deserved cheap shots. When would I get a turn? Bola needed to feel my knee driven hard into his groin. Again and again.

A red flame vibrated beside me. I turned to find Feradea looking at me expectantly. She'd asked the

Shifter to make a circle. The Shifter…

"Oh! You were talking to me." I stumbled forward and scrambled to pick up the box of salt. I ran around Sid and Bola like an excited puppy and poured the salt in a circle. No time to waste. I wanted the men safe from Bola more than I wanted revenge. My hand throbbed as I cut it again for the blood offering and sprinted another lap around the struggling Demons.

"That okay?" I asked as I completed the circle.

"That's perfect," Feradea mumbled. She held her hands out again and uttered some gibberish in a language that sounded clipped and archaic, as old as time.

Bola head butted Sid in the face and broke free of his hold. He threw himself against the circle and bellowed. Blue sparks flew up as the circle formed an invisible wall and kept Bola contained.

"Too late, Demon scum," Feradea said. "It is done."

The Demons both howled as a portal opened. The air whipped against their bodies and lashed at their skin. The dark power of the demonic realm snaked out and ripped at their forms, piece by piece until they dematerialized into nothing and winked out. The gaping vortex snapped shut, and the stormy air in the room settled.

Chapter Thirty-Two

"If confusion is the first step to knowledge, I must be a genius."

~Larry Leissner

As the dust settled to the floor, a collapsed form appeared in the circle. Emaciated and huddled in the fetal position, Christopher's breathing was shallow, but visible. He would be okay. Wick and Tristan lay sprawled in their animal forms outside the circle beside him, also alive.

Feradea stood beside me and contemplated whatever a deity contemplated, while I tried to process recent events. Sid took one for the team. That looked excruciating. Feradea must've needed his help to subdue Bola long enough for her to work whatever magic mojo she did to send them to hell.

Wick and Tristan's chests rose and fell as their healing bodies cracked and snapped, slowly shifting back to their human forms. Their proximity to the vortex must've knocked them out. Or maybe the pain from their injuries. My breath caught, and I squeezed my eyes shut. A shudder crawled up my spine.

I'd almost lost them.

My feras howled a sorrowful tune in my brain, in complete harmony to the stabbing pain in my heart.

Pull yourself together, woman! There's time to sink

into self-pity later. You're alive. Your men are alive. Your fr—Ben!

I turned to the Witch to find him slumped against the wall. His wounds had sealed up, and he looked like he slept, in a deep, restful, slumber. Mr. Sleeping-Fucking-Beauty. Was he dead? I reached forward to check for a pulse when Feradea's words stopped me.

"I healed your Witch for you." Feradea broke her silent contemplation. "Free of charge. He's in a restorative sleep and should not be disturbed."

"Thanks," I mumbled. The urge to go the men ran like fire in my veins, but the presence of the deity froze me in place. She wasn't to be ignored. Survival kicked in. Somehow my brain inherently *knew* ignoring her to rush to mortal men would be a mistake. For everyone. "Do I owe you for Bola?"

"No child. Renenutet and Sobek do. But they consider their debt to you paid and asked me to convey that to you."

"Message received." The ancient Egyptian gods had owed me a favour for helping them reunite. Guess I used my favour after all. Guess I'd never know about my family. I pressed my hands to my temples and tried to massage out the sudden ache in my skull. My heart spasmed as if giving up from the whirlwind of emotions and shrunk inside my chest cavity.

An eerie quiet settled over my apartment as we stood and observed the blood drying and caking onto the rug.

"So," I said, breaking the silence. "Do you know where my birth family is?"

A sly smile spread on the goddess's lips. "Yes, but that is your journey."

Huh? Well, it was worth a shot. Feradea stood in a relaxed stance as she studied my place. May as well pick her brain for as much information as possible. Starting with Sid. I owed him, and that meant I needed dirt. "Any chance you'll tell me what's between you and Sid?"

Feradea pursed her lips and glanced up at the ceiling, as if checking some deity clock. She must've decided she had some time to spare because she didn't smite me where I stood for my impertinence.

"Sidragasum has always wanted what he can't have."

"Huh," I said. Not exactly a witty response, but she didn't look open to elaboration. "Will you answer another question?"

She checked her Divine Time again. "You may ask. I will decide whether I answer."

"Why did you choose me?"

"What do you mean?"

"The Shifters call me 'The Chosen.' I assumed that meant you chose me to be the Carus."

Feradea laughed, a deep resonating chuckled that somehow delighted and pissed me off at the same time. "You are not chosen."

"Come again?"

Her mouth twitched as if she held back a laughing attack. "The Carus is nothing more than the resurgence of characteristics from your Shifter genes spontaneously reconfiguring themselves in a chance combination where previously dormant genes in your parents became expressed." She paused and fiddled with her bow string. "I believe biologists call it atavism."

Good thing my hobby involved reading scientific magazines. "I'm a genetic throwback?"

She snapped her fingers. "Precisely."

I rubbed the back of my neck. Not sure how to react to that. Was Feradea messing with me? Avoiding the truth without lying or being fully truthful? A foot away, the goddess stood in my living room with arms folded and eyes twinkling.

In the past, my alleged "special" status helped carry me through some dark moments. Now? Now I was a freak of nature. "So there's no prophecy, or divine path I must follow? No grand task to complete on behalf of all Shifters?"

Feradea started laughing again; a deep husky sound somewhere between a growl and a purr.

I was going to *kill* O'Donnell. Okay, not really, but I might throttle him a little. *I'm an idiot!* It didn't help that my patron goddess giggle-snorted at my question.

Feradea wiped a tear from her eye, and straightened a little. "Depends on your point of view, young one. Some Shifter extremists believe if the Carus lives long enough to reproduce with another Shifter, his or her offspring will be like my...like you, with full capabilities. So your 'grand task' is technically procreation with a Shifter extremist." She shrugged. "Although their theory has some genetic validity, the Carus has never lived long enough to test it. You all end up going crazy and being put down."

I ignored her final remark. "So these extremists think I'm a broodmare."

She waited before nodding. "That is an accurate analogy."

"Why did you just hesitate?"

Feradea scoffed. "You try speaking every language on the planet, old and new, and see if you jump on every reference."

"Point taken." I paused, and she blinked at me. Well, now or never. I might never have an opportunity to grill her for answers ever again. "What about the animal magnetism?"

Feradea's eyebrows punched together.

"I've always attracted men, especially norms, but it seems like it's been on hyper-drive lately."

Feradea chuckled. "That's not animal magnetism. It has nothing to do with your animals, and everything to do with your beast. The mundane have always been attracted to the divine, and that's what the Ualida represents. Where the norms are mildly drawn and manipulated by you, they'd swarm to me like flies to a slaughter."

"But what about the supes? It's not just the norms that've been attracted to me lately."

Feradea shrugged. "Supes feel a slight pull, too, but not anymore than they'd notice a pretty girl."

My lips scrunched up as I digested her words. I knew why Tristan and Wick wanted me. I'd already established Clint had no real interest aside from pissing me off, but Feradea's explanation didn't fit Sid and Bola's fascination with me.

"You look pensive, young one. Did I not answer your questions adequately?" A trench burrowed between her perfectly-shaped brows, and her model-worthy shoulders stiffened.

Ah fuck. Is she going to smite me?

"No, Feradea," I said quickly, glancing at the healing men. "You answered them perfectly, thank you.

I guess I'm still trying to figure out why Sid and Bola want me."

"Ah…" She tapped her chin, and the tension flowed from her body. "You're essentially a divine mortal tied to this plane of existence. With that anchor, comes great power and intriguing possibilities."

That didn't sound good. "What *kind* of possibilities?"

"The kind that tempts even the divine. Be careful, my child. I have a feeling Sid will make his intentions known soon enough."

Without a farewell or grand gesture, Feradea disappeared. One moment she stood there, looking down at me with condescension; and the next, the space where she cocked a hip was empty. Just like that. Just like Booth.

Huh.

I didn't even have a chance to mentally freak out about shooting the shit with a deity. As soon as her presence left my apartment, the need to go to Tristan and Wick wiped out any thoughts of the goddess. An invisible weight settled on my shoulders. Tristan and Wick lay bloody and broken on my floor. Alive, but damaged.

I sat down in front of my Weres and cradled my head in my hands. I caused this.

My fault.

Tristan groaned and rolled over on the floor, his arm draped over his face. Dried blood caked his skin while bones cracked and crunched to snap into place. I winced with every sound, every reminder I couldn't help or make it easier. Wick grunted as his broken and bloody body continued to heal as well. The gaping wounds from Bola's sharp talons, the ones exposing the tissue, fat and bones, had long since sealed, but the internal injuries, the ones not visible to the naked eye, would take longer. Their bodies made enough sound it could be the nature channel playing in the background, or the holiday channel with the eternally burning log in the fireplace. *Snap! Pop!*

Tristan recuperated first, confirming my guess his age probably doubled Wick's. He flopped over, and crawled to where I sat cross legged.

Without words, he reached out and ran his fingers down my cheek over and over again. His sapphire gaze bore into my soul. His intensity mesmerized me.

"Don't you ever do that again," he finally said. His voice cracked.

"Save you?" I asked. Attitude might've ejected from my mouth, but guilt racked my insides, twisting it into a knot. Tristan and Wick had been hurt because of me. Tristan almost died because of me.

"Risk yourself," he said. "You can't do that again. Promise me."

I shook my head. "Only if you make the same promise."

He grunted and pulled me into the warmth of his body. Cradled and stroked, a calming peacefulness flowed through my veins. Why did he comfort me? He had his neck broken and almost died, not me.

I twisted my head around to take in his expression. His eyes closed, he rested his head on my shoulder, inhaling deeply to take in my scent. He looked at peace, too. Maybe this was his comfort. I held him close, and melted into his warmth.

We stayed like that for what seemed like a blissful

eternity, our hearts beating in unison, our feline energies entwining.

The moment with Tristan shattered when Wick grunted and stood to his feet.

I tensed. How would this play out? Another fight when they'd just recovered wouldn't be good for either of them.

Tristan released me, and pulled back to stand up. He reached down and offered me his hand. When I took it, he hoisted me to my feet.

Then, Tristan took a step back.

Wick lunged in to envelope me in a bear hug. My breath wheezed out. Yes, Wick's hold threatened to crack a rib or two, but…

Tristan had stepped back to allow Wick this moment.

Almost as if… Almost as if they'd silently agreed to a momentary truce. Emotionally heal first, fight for the girl later.

The control over their animals amazed me, but then, they'd had a long time to practice.

"I thought I'd lost you," Wick mumbled into the sensitive skin of my neck. He ran his nose against the pulsing beat of my carotid artery. "Don't you dare do something like that again. Ever."

I rolled my eyes. A complete waste of sass since Wick couldn't see it.

Tristan cleared his throat and chucked Wick his clothes. "Better get dressed," Tristan said. "Your phone's been ringing non-stop."

Wick pulled away to catch his clothes.

Only then did my ears register the sound of Wick's cell—the theme song to a shark movie blasted out of the little device, the ringtone reserved for Lucien.

Wick's expression hardened, and his grasp on my arm tightened. "I don't need to answer it." He turned to me. "We're being summoned."

Chapter Thirty-Three

"Life is hard. After all, it kills you."
~*Katharine Hepburn*

I knelt in front of Lucien, and wished this night over. I'd already reached my daily quota for dealing with douche nozzles. With ragged breath and straining heart, I couldn't take much more "excitement." Running over to Lucien's mansion to answer his summons didn't rank high on my list of priorities. Hell, if I had a choice, I'd have a date with my pajamas, a hot drink, and my pillow-top mattress instead.

Lucien sprawled like an Italian model on an haute couture shoot. All snooty faced and indifferent. He appeared completely nonplussed by my making it to his place in record time with Wick. Allan stood beside us with a cold mask and blank eyes. Did we pull him away from his private BDSM chamber? If I listened closely, would I hear the dying screams of his latest victim? The silence in the room droned on, filled only with the buzzing of the lights and the night-time sounds of summer insects.

My skin rankled as I continued to kneel on the floor beside Wick, waiting for *His Majesty* to grant us the privilege of hearing his voice.

After we had carried Ben and Christopher next door to be doted on by their denmates, Tristan left to check on his pride. It cost Tristan to leave me with Wick, his discomfort shown by his grimace and pinched eyebrows, but he kissed me gently on my cheek, and asked me to call when it was over. I'd simply nodded and tried to ignore the pain caused in my chest as the physical distance between us grew. I wanted to stay cocooned in his warmth and bask in his scent.

"I'm not impressed," Lucien said.

What the heck is he talking about? I asked Wick.

No idea, he replied.

"Why, you might ask?" Lucien leaned forward. "I'll tell you why. Because of your incompetence in dealing with Bola in a timely fashion, you've made me look inept in front of the entire Vampire community. There's buzz within NAVA that Vancouver is ripe for the picking, that I'm weak." The wood of his throne-like chair creaked as he clutched the armrest and squeezed. "You might dislike me as a ruler, but I'm Mary fucking Poppins compared to the alternative."

Whoa. Lucien swore. Not a good sign. My palms began to sweat. Lucien spouting cuss words didn't happen often. Normally, I held the "Potty Mouth" crown in this company.

Lucien slammed his hand down. "Now I'll have to deal with even more attempts on my seat, thanks to you two."

We kept our heads bent in supplication.

"Well?"

Well what?

"Do you have anything to say for yourselves? Any defense you would like to offer before I decide your punishment?"

Punishment? I glanced up. When my gaze met the dead, cold stare of Lucien's, I looked away. Intense. This supe not only pulled my strings, but Wick's as well. "I'm sorry," I mumbled.

"What was that, Andrea? If you're going to say something, you should speak up."

"I'm sorry," I said, louder. "I tried my best. I'd like to point out the threat was neutralized tonight."

"Eventually," Lucian spat.

"Bola is an Earl of Hell," I continued. "Not exactly a lowly minion. He wasn't an easy target to take down. Please take that into consideration."

Should I expel this jerk now and get it over with?

Wick tensed beside me as if he'd heard my thoughts.

No. Lucien hadn't passed judgement on Wick yet. I might free myself from the Vampire Master, but Wick couldn't. If I dispelled Lucien as the blood-sucking fera he truly was, his punishment for Wick would be extreme. Besides, with Allan and Wick under his control, I had no guarantee I'd make it out of this room alive, bond-free or otherwise. Unless I went beast. But then I'd have to hurt Wick.

The throne creaked as Lucien scooted to the edge of the seat and peered down at us. "How about you, my pet? Any defense?"

"No, master," Wick said. "I failed you."

Lucien jerked his thumb in Wick's direction. "At least this one knows how to be obedient. Sometimes."

Was he talking to me or Allan?

"Well, I have decided how you will both make recompense." Lucien snapped his fingers, and the door at the other end of the room swung open to emit Clint and someone else. The human servant moved to the side to allow the guest to walk forward, and I gasped. I recognized his tall frame and familiar face all too well.

Obviously, Lucien hadn't received the memo regarding my daily limit for asshats.

"Sid!" My mouth involuntarily curled up into a scowl. How'd he recuperate so quickly from Feradea's banishment?

Wick froze beside me, gaze calculating.

I wanted to rid myself of this guy for the foreseeable future. Hell, I planned to avoid him at all costs. I owed him a debt, and I didn't want to pay up.

Could Ben wave a magic wand and block the Demon for me? I'd have to ask him later.

Sid made a little bow with his chin. He walked to stand beside Lucien's chair with Allan. Clint joined them. My skin itched to run. My chances of escaping alive if I rebelled went from difficult to improbable.

Lucien laced his hands together and rested his elbows on his chair. "I do so love to…what's the saying? Kill two birds with one stone? As punishment to the two of you and as my payment to Sid, Andrea, you will give your blood to Sid willingly. Wick, you will ensure she does. You're my insurance. I have a feeling she won't fight you."

"But I owe Sid, not you," I stammered.

"Actually, we both owe Sid." Lucien's dark tone explained just how much he liked this concept. "You were taking too long to resolve the issue, and I sought alternative solutions. I found this Demon's price very reasonable. Stand."

Lucien's compulsion wove around me. I staggered to my feet. I folded my arms tightly around my stomach. *This couldn't be happening.*

"My payment is to provide access to you. Sid had concerns about tracking you down to collect your debt. For some reason, he thought you'd avoid him or find some Witch to block him. I provided a solution. Your payment to him, Andrea dearest, will be your voluntary blood donation."

"I don't understand." I turned to Sid. "You could've asked for blood as payment when we were in my forest. You *did* ask for it, but not as payment."

Sid's mouth twisted up.

I connected the dots like tic-tac-toe, and my head heated as if I'd physically blow my top like a choo-choo train.

"You bastard! You tried to get my blood for free and an additional payment."

Sid shrugged.

"You're such an asshole."

"Demon," he reminded me, again.

He was right. What the hell would he have asked for if I'd fallen for his gambit? A shudder ran through my body like a wave. It didn't really matter, did it? Sid had requested my blood as payment now. I owed him. Breaking Lucien's bond or going feral wouldn't save me from this fate, only delay it. To refuse payment of a Demon debt meant forfeiting my soul to Sid for eternity…if he caught me.

The odds weren't in my favour.

Lucien smirked when my attention slid back to him. I wrung my hands together. Sure, Lucien was a complete jerk, and he looked out for himself above all others, but he wouldn't give up one of his minions. He'd certainly never allow someone else to mark them.

Would he?

"Lucien," I started.

"What do you people say nowadays? It's a done deal," he said.

My insides flipped like a pancake. I glanced at the Master Vampire. The corner of his lips quirked up, and he had that smarmy expression he often got when he knew he'd get his way. He planned to go through with this.

I gaped at him. My heart pumped against my ribcage so hard the echo of it rang in my ears. *This is totally happening.*

"But that makes no sense," I stammered. "When Sid requested my blood as payment for Kappa information, you told me not to because of our connection. Why now?"

"Sid has already made an oath not to reach me through the blood bond or use your connection with me in any way," Lucien explained. "I'm very grateful you didn't give him your blood earlier." He eyed the Demon with pressed lips. "He would've had us both by a blood link, and we'd still owe him favours. At least you did something right, Andrea."

"The sunrise is near." Sid smiled and rubbed his hands together. "It's time."

"Wick," Lucien snapped his fingers. "Hold Andy, and don't let her escape."

Wick grunted and lurched to the side, his hand enclosed around my arm, and I tried to snatch it back.

When Wick pushed me forward, I locked my knees and slammed my weight back. To hell with this.

"Andy, either you let Wick hold you down, or I will eviscerate him. Really, I shouldn't have to repeat this threat. You should've learned by now I will not think twice about using my pet dog against you. Would you be the cause of his pain?"

No, I wouldn't. And the sick bastard knew it. He didn't even need to put a command through our blood bond, but he did anyway. The compulsion weaved around my willpower and squeezed tight. Even my beast settled, though she grumbled a bit. Wick's other hand came around to grasp my free arm, now limp and void of tension.

"Please, master. Don't make me do this," Wick said.

Lucien smirked. "This is punishment for you both. For your incompetence. A Vampire Master should never have to take matters into his own hands. You failed me. Consider yourselves lucky I'm not taking your lives instead."

"She will hate me, Lucien. Forever. She will never forgive me for this," Wick said. A weird buzzing sensation consumed my brain as I processed his words. Pieces to the puzzle snapped into place. He was right. Even though Wick had little control over his actions, I'd barely recovered from the first time he held me down, but to have him used against me more than once. It seemed as if…

"I want her to choose Tristan," Lucien said.

Wick recoiled behind me; the grip on my arms slackened. "Why?"

"Because," I whispered, realizing the truth too late, "he believes he can control the Wereleopard pack through me if I'm bonded to the pride leader," I said, the jigsaw pieces falling into place too late. My head pounded as red consumed my vision.

Lucien smiled, and his lack of denial confirmed my accusation. Silence stretched across the room and weighed the air down with suppressive force. My lungs constricted. Breathing became difficult. I fed my body oxygen in short, successive gasps. No. I'd never allow him to control Tristan through me. I'd already endured that pain with Wick. A cold wave travelled through my body, leaving me numb and washed out. No more. Lucien would never use someone I cared about every again. Not if I could help it.

"Enough of this," Lucien said. "Sid, my debt is paid." He waved at Wick and I with a flourishing sweep of his arm.

Sid nodded and stepped forward. "Yes, Lucien, your debt is paid."

I shook my head at Sid. "Let me pay my debt another way."

Sid tsked. "You must give me your blood freely."

My muscles tensed as he approached and cradled my head with both his hands. They zapped my skin as soon as they made contact, sending tides of tingling sensations down my body.

Wick's fingers dug into my upper arms.

"Say it," Sid said. "Give me permission."

I opened and closed my mouth, but I couldn't make myself say the words. Sid gave my head a little shake.

Lucien cleared his throat. "Say it, kitten. Do I need to remind you of the consequences?"

I squeezed my eyes shut. If I refused, Lucien would harm Wick, and I'd still owe the Demon, not just my blood, but my soul.

I'm so sorry, Andy, Wick said.

My wolf howled in my head, shaking my skull. My

falcon screeched and flapped her wings. My mountain lion...she paced. She wanted out, she wanted to turn feral and destroy everyone and everything. She wanted me to release the beast.

From the rage blistering in my core where my beast paced and bellowed for me to let her out, I *knew* she hated everyone in this room, including Wick. I could do it. I could release her and try to best a powerful Demon, two Vampires, a Werewolf Alpha and an un-killable human servant. If I survived, I'd be done with this. At least until Sid tracked me down. Then I'd be in a bigger mess.

I couldn't do it.

Even if I broke free and kept enough control to not hurt Wick, I'd still owe the Demon and Lucien would still punish Wick for my disobedience and defiance. Despite hating the situation, despite hating what I was about to say, about to do, I wouldn't fight it.

I couldn't cause Wick harm. I couldn't hurt him. I...I loved him.

Sid's dark, calculating gaze met mine when I finally looked up and squared my shoulders. If my beast couldn't best Bola, it was unlikely she could take Satan's assistant anyway.

Ice flowed through my veins as I made my decision. "I give you permission to take my blood as my payment for the debt I owe you."

Sid's white teeth flashed. One of his hands snaked down to my wrist, and he ran a sharp talon against it. A sharp sting radiated out from the cut on my skin. He pulled my arm to his head and ducked down to clamp his Demon-hot mouth over the wound.

My vision blurred as he drew blood from my body.

He only drank one pull, but my body's reaction continued after he lifted his head away from my sensitive skin. The tingling sensations from the gash morphed into a throbbing need.

My core burnt with an internal inferno, building and building until the heat became unbearable. Then, something inside broke, shattering and splintering the pleasure into infinitesimal shards radiating from my groin out to my fingertips and toes. Lightning danced the mamba in my vision, and I sagged in Wick's hold, breathless and sated.

After the last waves of pleasure rolled away, a layer of grime settled over my soul.

That rancid piece of Demon street meat just gave me an orgasm. Fire blazed through my veins. My fists clenched. I wanted to rip off Sid's arm and beat him with the wet end.

Burnt cinnamon rolled of Wick in waves, and his hands clenched painfully around my arms.

Sid straightened and wiped his mouth. He reached down and gripped my face with one hand, placing his thumb between my eyebrows. "*In aeternum mea es tu. Mea es tu.*"

I didn't speak Latin, but the meaning of his words coiled around my heart and sank in. *You are mine forever.* I closed my eyes and took a number of deep breaths before I stood and shook off Wick's hands.

Sid reached out to…I'm not sure what he planned to do. I batted his hands away.

"Don't be so shy, little one," Sid said. "I have that effect on women."

"I hate you."

Sid nodded. "I have *that* effect on women, too."

Chapter Thirty-Four

"Mathematics, rightly viewed, possesses not only truth, but supreme beauty—a beauty cold and austere, without the gorgeous trappings of painting or music."
~Bertrand Russell

Wick pulled up to my building, and I wanted nothing more than to teleport into my apartment to skip the conversation that would come next. Wick shoved the gearshift into park and turned to me. "Andy."

I shook my head, threw open the door and hopped out. Maybe I could just run away from this. The sound of Wick's door slamming after mine told me my wish fell on deaf deity ears.

"Andy," Wick called out to me. "We need to talk. Please, don't walk away from me."

I spun around, halfway up the walkway. Wick stood on the sidewalk, his mouth turned down, and his gaze fierce.

"There's nothing to talk about," I said.

"Of course there is."

I shook my head again.

"We need to talk about what I did. About what you did."

"About what I did? I did nothing! Nothing except play the victim, again! And now I have to live with it."

Wick took a step forward. "We can work through it

together. We can—wait, what are you doing?"

Vaguely aware Wick closed the distance between us, I shut my eyes and drew my attention inward. My animals snarled in my head, and my beast stretched and tested the bindings that held her. There, in my chest, two more links throbbed with pain. Sid's mark coiled around my heart, with barbs digging in. One word, one thought from him and it would probably constrict.

The other, more subtle, flowed in my blood, but stayed concentrated near my liver, as if the organ desperately tried to filter out Lucien's taint. I focused on his mark and gathered it up.

I dispel you. I poured all my rage and hate and disgust into the command. Nothing happened. I tightened my hold.

Lucien, I dispel you, I repeated with more force. Something ripped inside me. The instant it worked, my body convulsed. I dropped to the cemented path and clutched my abdomen. Searing pain lanced out from my core and diffused through my veins and arteries. Pain streaked through my body, and I twisted on the ground, unable to deal with it, yet unable to make the agony go away. Then, slowly, the pain abated. My skin throbbed, raw against the cold cement.

A shadow started to form beside me, but before Lucien could appear, if he'd appear, I added another command, just in case. *Dematerialize.*

"Andy!" Wick knelt beside me. "Andy, what's happening?"

"Getting rid of Lucien." I gritted my teeth.

I picked myself off the ground and straightened. Wick tried to help with a hand on my elbow, but I shook him off.

Lucien would retaliate. He'd have to save his precious pride. My gaze met the melted chocolate of Wick's, and my heart stopped beating. As long as Lucien believed I held feelings for Wick, he'd use Wick against me, repeatedly, to torment me, and lure me back to his lair.

I might have to kill Lucien. Heck, I wanted to kill Lucien, to see his stolen blood pool on his expensive Italian tiles before he shriveled into dust. But he didn't stay undead this long for nothing. I needed time to plan. Taking out the Master Vampire of a large city had other implications as well. The change in power would create a ripple effect through the entire supernatural community. I had to remove the one thing Lucien would use to control me. Not just for my sake, but for Wick's.

"I can't be with you," I said.

Wick stepped back. His gaze narrowed. "You don't mean that."

I wiped off the blood trickling down my chin with my sleeve and then shook my head. I did mean it. "As long as you're under Lucien's control, he'll keep using us against one another. It cuts too deep. I can't do it. I can't let him use us like that."

He leaned forward and then hesitated. "We're mates."

His words vibrated through my entire body. My wolf howled. "Maybe, Wick. But I can't keep hurting like this. I can't keep fearing I'll destroy you, or vice versa. It's not right. We have to…we have to let each other go."

Before Wick could say anything more, before I lost my courage, I reached within and called the wolf. Still new to dispelling, I didn't know if I could do two in one night, but I planned to try.

I dispel you.

My wolf howled again. Deep and full of sorrow, its resonance rocked my core. My heart stopped. Then it started again, pumping furiously. The wolf, enmeshed into my very being, ripped from my essence, tearing muscle and cartilage. I staggered and dropped to my hands and knees again. Blood poured from my nose. Sharp stabbing pains shredded my brain and darted down my spine. As if ripped in two, a ghost wolf separated from my body to stand beside me.

I looked up into her large, colourless eyes. They studied me, deep and soulful. I wanted to run my hands down her thick, gray fur, bury my face into her side. But I couldn't. If I did that, I'd never find the strength to do what I had to do next. "De…" A sob racked my body. "Dematerialize."

She pawed the ground and disappeared. My heart sank into my stomach. A hollow pit developed in my mind where my wolf used to curl her warm, reassuring presence. We'd been together for a long time. I took a shuddered breath before I collected myself and stumbled to my feet.

Wick's gaze met mine. He staggered.

The pain in his chocolate brown eyes speared me where I stood, and all thoughts or things I planned to say flew from my mind.

Did I just make a colossal mistake?

My eyes prickled. No! I squeezed my eyelids shut to stem the tears threatening to fall and thought of Tristan. The image of his wide, bright smile evened out my heartbeat and lifted the sinking weight in my stomach.

Wick was a great man. He didn't deserve my indecisiveness, nor being strung along. I knew why we couldn't be together. And if he took a moment to be honest with himself, so did he. It didn't make losing him any easier.

Then it hit me. The smell after a lighting strike; the heady mix of deep rooted soil, veining up to meet the hard impact of the energy bolt, the aftermath of thunder. Thick heavy storm clouds with raindrops dampening and clinging to the air, the scent of heartbreak.

I opened my mouth, then closed it. What could I say?

Wick turned and walked away.

Epilogue

"It's easy to fall in love. The hard part is finding someone to catch you."
~Bertrand Russell

Curled up on the ledge of my bay window, I watched the runners in the rain and nursed my third cup of coffee. After dispelling Lucien's blood bond and my wolf, my apartment had turned into a temple of silence. No phone calls, no e-mail, no television, nothing. As if a moratorium had been placed over my home.

Wick had looked broken as he slunk to his shiny black SUV with his head hung low and drooping shoulders. Not the first time he'd left my place hurt and denied, but this time, finality hung in the air. God, part of me wanted to call him back and let him wipe the bad memories from my mind, and my soul. The other part of me knew I wouldn't and couldn't. I'd made the right decision.

Right?

I wish I could see Lucien's face. He wouldn't have foreseen this move from me. He'd been so sure of his mark, so sure of his hold on me. Now punishing Wick wouldn't benefit Lucien, since I also expelled my wolf and any claim on the Werewolf Alpha.

I rubbed my neck. What do I do now? No longer blood-bound to the Master Vampire, I couldn't fulfill my role as an ambassador. Nor could I go back to the SRD—Booth no longer sat in her office rooting for me. Tucker sure wouldn't reinstate my agent status, even if I could stomach working for him.

Lucien would seek retribution for ditching his bond.

I drummed my fingers along my now cold coffee mug. I'd cross the Lucien bridge when I got there. He'd take his time plotting his revenge.

The doorbell rang.

I stared out the window, seeing and not seeing at the same time. A painful tightness clamped around my throat, and my lungs constricted, making it difficult to breathe. I couldn't see who stood outside, ringing the doorbell, but I didn't need to. I wanted to open the door to find out what Wick had to say, what he hadn't said already, but I also wanted to hide. There wasn't a cave deep or dark enough to bury the feelings currently overwhelming my heart. I was bonded to a Demon who scared the bejeezus out of me.

The doorbell rang again, this time more insistent, as if the person ringing it tried to send me a message by Morse Code.

I stumbled from my perch by the bay windows and shuffled to the kitchen. I put my cold, half empty coffee mug beside the others on the counter by the sink and looked down at my outfit. Two-day-old sweats. Gross. I probably smelled, but I didn't care. Whatever. Let Wick see me at my worst, and maybe then he'd leave me alone.

When I flung the door open, my mouth dropped open in surprise.

Tristan smiled. His eyes twinkled before they

travelled up and down my body, but the wide, panty-melting grin faltered when he took in my face. I didn't need anyone to tell me I looked as terrible as I felt.

He held his hand out.

I glanced down to see a bouquet of red roses, their scent twirled up to my nose, mixing with Tristan's intoxicating scent. My gaze riveted to his face.

His smile returned, but this time, tender, more sincere. "May I come in?"

I grabbed the flowers and tossed them to the side. They bounced against my plush throw rug, and their scent floated up to my nose. But I didn't care. My fingers dug into Tristan's shirt as I pulled him into my apartment and sagged into him. My face smushed into his soft blue sweater, and the ache inside my heart welled up.

I sobbed.

My body shook, and the tears kept coming. Tristan just held me, rubbing my back and murmuring nonsense into my ear. He picked me up and cradled me in his arms like a child before he kicked the door closed behind him.

I should protest. I should demand that he put me down. I wasn't a child. No one should see me like this.

Citrus and sunshine with honeysuckle on a warm summer's day. His scent continued to cocoon and protect me. I said nothing and let him carry me while I clung to his sweater and cried. Tristan sat on the couch and pulled me into his lap, my face snug against his neck. His beautiful scent flowed into my body with each ragged breath, and my muscles started to relax.

His strong hands ran along my side, over and over again, until I could breathe. "Lucien used Wick against me, again."

Tristan's body tensed, but he said nothing to fill the silence, he kept rubbing.

"He made Wick hold me so Sid could take my blood. As payment for his debt to the Demon. My payment was to voluntarily give my blood. Now that sadistic Demon has it, and I have no idea what he can do with it."

Tristan bowed his head. His arm under my legs curled up, pulling me tighter against his chest.

"I dispelled my wolf. I ended it with Wick."

Tristan's hand faltered. He inhaled deeply and then continued to stroke me, sending calming Alpha waves through my body. We sat in silence. Me, drinking in Tristan's soothing scent; Tristan, thinking whatever Tristan thought.

"Well, that explains the text," he said, finally.

"What text?" I asked.

"It doesn't matter."

"Yes, it does. Tell me."

Tristan sighed, his shoulders sagging a little. "I got a text from Wick, saying 'congratulations.' "

I stiffened and pushed away. "So you came running over here to collect your prize?"

"No," he said. "I came running over here to make sure you were okay."

He tried to pull me close again.

I pushed against his chest. "Just because I've chosen not to be with Wick, doesn't mean I've chosen you," I lashed out. The smell of my lie filled the room.

Tristan used the back of his knuckles to brush away the last of the tears from my face. "This has nothing to do with me. Or our relationship. This has everything to do with you, though. You are hurting as I thought you might be, and I wanted to ease your pain. I want to be here for you. Will you let me?"

More tears welled up, but I blinked them back. My head became suddenly light. I nodded.

Tristan clutched me to his body and stood with me in his arms in one smooth move. He carried me to the bedroom. In a move that defied human strength, he held me close as he pulled the bedding aside with a free hand. My head sank into my soft pillow.

I didn't protest when Tristan slowly removed my clothes. He took his time and infinite care with each article of clothing as if afraid I'd shatter. There was no seduction in his movements, though, no attempts to take advantage of my weakened emotional state. Only gentleness existed in his moves. He left my panties and bra on and then stood to remove his own clothes, leaving his black boxer briefs in place. He crawled into the bed beside me, gathered me in his arms and whispered into my ear, "It will be okay, Andy."

If only I could believe that.

The warmth of his body pressed against mine. Eventually, his breathing evened out, and his arms slackened. I twisted around to snuggle into his side. Still cradled in the protective cocoon of Tristan, my eyelids drooped. I could no longer fight the heavy lids or the sleep that beckoned, yet I tried anyway. Tristan's face looked so serene in the night. Such hard angles and chiseled features, yet the smoothness of his porcelain skin gave him an angelic appearance. I hoped to dream of him tonight.

Yet I knew I wouldn't.

Karma was a bitch. I'd dream of Demons.

J. C. McKenzie

A word about the author...

Born and raised on the Haida Gwaii, off the West Coast of Canada, J. C. McKenzie grew up in a pristine wilderness that inspired her to dream. She writes Urban Fantasy and Paranormal Romance. You can visit her website at
www.jcmckenzie.ca

Thank you for purchasing
this publication of The Wild Rose Press, Inc.

If you enjoyed the story, we would appreciate your
letting others know by leaving a review.

For other wonderful stories,
please visit our on-line bookstore at
www.thewildrosepress.com.

For questions or more information
contact us at
info@thewildrosepress.com.

The Wild Rose Press, Inc.
www.thewildrosepress.com

Stay current with The Wild Rose Press, Inc.

Like us on Facebook

https://www.facebook.com/TheWildRosePress

And Follow us on Twitter
https://twitter.com/WildRosePress